Death ......

Simon Maltman

To Christin,

Hope you enjoy it!

All the best,

Simon

Copyright © Simon Maltman 2024.

The right of Simon Maltman to be identified as the author of this work has been asserted by him in accordance with the Copyright, Designs and Patents Act, 1988.

First published in 2024 by Sharpe Books.

DEATH NOTICE

Prologue: So Much for The Ten-Year Plan

I ran. I didn't just run; I ran like all hell. It was 1992, almost eight years ago, to the day. It was late at night in Victoria Park, East Belfast. One of my MI5 handlers had arranged a meet with me along with another asset called Tom Cooper. We'd hugged our coats close as a frost formed on the ground around us. Even the river to our left had begun to freeze over in patches above the dirty green water. There was no moon that night, dim illumination was given to us from one solitary streetlight. I'd been reluctant to go to the meet at all, already hearing whispers from above about Cooper's loyalties. That's why he came. He wanted to get out right away. As far as I knew, nobody was on to me yet.

It had only been a few minutes when a crack echoed through the empty city park. As I turned, the back of my handler's head was blown away. He fell in a bloodied mess. Cooper and I went for our weapons. Two men with guns raised were coming down the grassy bank on our left. Smoke rose from the first one's barrel. I ran for cover behind the old toilet block, but Cooper chose to crouch and plunge off a round first. There was a boom from his revolver and the birds in the trees and undergrowth all began to go nuts. His bullet took out the first guy, sinking into his chest. He was down. I peered around the side of the worn paintwork of the toilet wall, a foul smell emanating from inside. I couldn't get a clear shot.

"Tom, hurry!" I shouted.

As the second man came closer, now yards away, I recognised him as someone from my own IRA section. John Evans. Evans raised his Glock as Cooper sprinted towards me and shot him in the back. Cooper's eyes stared through me, watery and fearful, then he stumbled to the ground and was still.

Rage coursed through me as I stepped out from the shelter of the wall, my Colt in hand. I fired at Evans, but he raced behind a large sycamore tree. I fired again, the bullet splintering branches and settling somewhere in the huge trunk. Two shots came back at me. I hid back around the wall.

"I see you, Walker!" Evans shouted. "You're dead now, mate."

There was no option to run. He knew it was me.

I'd never get far, especially not now they'd taken out my handler. I peered around the corner. Took in the scene. The other three were surely dead. I couldn't see Evans. Then another pot-shot came my way. I hid back around, bouncing on my heels.

Think.

"Is that you, Evans?" I called. "What the hell? I thought you were Special Branch."

"That's a pile of dung, Walker. You're a dirty tout."

"We're on the same side. I was spying on these two. Sullivan sent me."

There was a moment of silence.

"Sure he did," Evans called back. "Like I wouldn't have known."

"It's a different section. Above your level, Evans. Frigsake. We're on the same team. They're not going to thank you if you pop me. You'll get one in each knee at the very least. It's been on the go a while now. *Operation Tonto*. Ask them. Bloody ask them! Cops'll be here in a minute. The Army Council won't like it if we get lifted either."

Quiet.

He was thinking about it.

There was only one way out of this for me. The only way I had a chance to not be blown, was if nobody knew I was here. If I was taken back, I'd be brought in front of the ISU. They were the most feared within the IRA. Also know as The Nutting Squad, they were the organisation's Internal Affairs. If they didn't like your answers, you'd be left by the side of the road with two in the back of the head. That would be after being blindfolded, hog-tied and beaten and burned for days on end. That wasn't for me.

The birds had settled down somewhat but were still flapping about in sporadic flocks.

"Throw out your gun," he said. His voice was unsure.

Good.

"Oh yeah, and then you drill me when I come out," I shouted back.

"I won't. If it's like you say, you come with me, and we'll sort

DEATH NOTICE

it. If it's not like you say, I'll kill you later."

I inched my head around the wall and saw him come out from the undergrowth, his gun pointed towards me. Sirens started somewhere close. Maybe just a mile away.

"Throw it out," he said again, walking slowly towards me.

I rotated the Colt in my right hand and held it by the barrel. My trigger finger still inside the metal ring. I dangled the gun out in front of me. Evans was now no more than twenty feet away.

"Okay, I'll do it. I'm telling you the truth, don't shoot," I said evenly.

He came closer. The sirens grew louder. The birds began to flap a little more again.

"Throw it down," he commanded, his gun steady, but his stance now wide and exposed.

"Okay."

I made like I was going to chuck it, instead swivelling the gun in my hand and firing quickly, plunging off two rounds. They both hit centre mass. He went down and his gun spilled away. I jogged across and looked down at him. Blood streamed from the wounds in his chest. His face was ashen. Evans looked down at his wounds, then up at me. Blood seeped from his open mouth.

"I spent a lot of time watching *The Lone Ranger*, practicing with my potato gun," I said. "Sorry, mate."

Then I shot him in the head.

Part 1: Trigger Inside

Eight years later. 2000.

Chapter 1

The killer exhaled. The breath caught in his throat. He took in another huge lungful of air, before expelling it all. He got up off his knees with a groan and looked down at his work. The girl was dead. It had taken a little longer than expected this time, but that was okay. He wiped his hands on his trousers and nodded once, pleased with his efforts.

The killer swivelled his head, looked around the room. Now for the mundane part. The tidying up, the disposal.

He looked down at her again.

Most important of all, her death mask contained a smile.

She died laughing.

DEATH NOTICE

Chapter 2

I walked out of the cinema and lit up a smoke. Brandon followed suit, but he lit up a joint.

"You want to wait until it's a bit more discreet?" I asked.

Brandon shrugged. "Nah. So, what do ya think, Mick?"

"Aye, it was good," I said.

"My head's melted."

Brandon took a long drag as we headed out of *The Deuce,* the district that was still the seediest in the city. New York was very cold that night and snow was threatening again. The Hornet was parked a few streets away and we trudged off, our minds spinning from *Memento*.

"It was very stylish, like," I said. "Very cool idea."

"Yeah, man. I never seen a movie all filmed backwards like that. It feels like I'm already stoned." He raised his joint and took a smooth drag.

"Brandon, you were already stoned when we went in," I said.

He shrugged again. "Just a little."

"Funny to see your man from *Neighbours* in a big Hollywood movie," I said.

"Who? The main guy? What's Neighbours?"

I raised an eyebrow. "You never saw *Neighbours*? It's a crappy Australian soap. Like *Dynasty* or something, but worse."

"Oh."

We took a few turns, the street growing quieter as we got further away from the hustle of the main *Deuce*. I threw down the cigarette and lit up another. It was bloody freezing. I hugged my coat to me. Soon we'd be in my nice warm car, on the way to our nice warm apartment.

"Tell you what," Brandon said, pulling his black beanie hat down over his ears. When he wore it, I always thought his babyface looked even younger than its twenty-something years. The New York chill had meant a temporary replacement of his usual baseball cap.

"That movie was a load better than that made-for-TV one we

watched the other night," he said. "What you call it?"

"What's that? The old one with your man who's in *Fraiser* now?"

"Yeah, that one. Man, that was bad. There was that funny bit where he's following that woman with his tongue out and she turns around and... well... she didn't look so great." Brandon made a face.

I grinned. "Body of *Baywatch*, face of *Crimewatch*?" I said.

"What?"

"1690," I said with a wink, enjoying Brandon looking even more confused.

"Sixteen from the back, ninety from the front."

Brandon rolled his eyes.

"Sorry, I'm just being a dick," I said, "Let's get out of this bloody cold.

It'd been over six months since I'd first met Brandon. He had robbed me, got me in bother with a local gang, which then drew an IRA hit squad onto our tails. Yeah, it's a long story. But what I gained was a friendship I never saw coming. He was like a nephew or something to me now. We'd rented an apartment in the city, no real plans on what our futures would hold. For now, we were glad of some down time, funded by the FBI and MI5. Amy, the third side of our little triangular surrogate family, had rented an apartment nearby. Amy had helped me when I was on the run, working for the FBI. She'd left them soon after all the chaos was over. That girl took a bullet for me, literally. But she hadn't been around much recently, needed by her *blood* family. Her mother had serious heart troubles back home in Ohio. I hadn't seen Amy in several weeks and I missed her. I knew Brandon did too.

We stopped for some food, then turned up an alley beside a rundown hotel, now only five or six minutes' walk from where I'd parked the Hornet. Brandon had finished his fries, but I was keeping my kebab for home. The alley was empty, save for a plume of grey smoke exiting from a pipe on the wall by a few dumpsters. Then a tall, thin figure appeared at the far end of the alley, walking towards us. His hands were deep inside his zipped-up coat, the brown hood pulled down, in part concealing his face.

DEATH NOTICE

"Keep an eye out for this guy," I said in a low voice, stepping a pace ahead of Brandon.

Brandon's eyes narrowed and he gave me a little nod, "Okay, cool."

When he was about three metres away from us, I could see the man had wild eyes and sallow, flaky skin. He made like he was going to move away to pass us, then suddenly stepped towards us, pulling a large kitchen knife from his pocket.

"Gimme your fucking money," he grunted, brandishing the knife in the air.

"Take it easy," I said, taking a step back and putting a protective hand on Brandon's chest. I was saying it as much to him. I'd been doing some training with Brandon the last few months. A little gym work, a little boxing. But I didn't want him rushing into a guy with a knife to try out his new skills. You do that without thinking and you're going to get cut. I don't care who you are.

"C'mon, hurry up," the man said in a gravelly voice. His bloodshot eyes darted all around.

I looked at Brandon with a questioning glance. He met my stare and gave the briefest of nods. I set my tin-foiled kebab gently down on top of a dustbin.

I turned back to the guy with the knife. "Okay man, no problem, I've just got to unzip my jacket, okay?" I raised my hands in a passive gesture.

"Do it," he said, pointing the knife at me.

I slowly pulled the zip down, holding the man's stare. "Just take it easy, you can have it." The zip made it to the bottom. I pulled it free from the catch.

"Okay..." I said slowly. "... Now!"

I pulled my left sleeve with my right hand, pulling the jacket half off and whipping it across the man's face. Brandon took a step around us to the side. I then took the jacket off fully and wrapped it around the man's knife arm. Brandon must have already been pulling back his swing, because straight away he smashed a hard right hook into the man's jaw. Then another one. The man's dazed head swung back and forth like a junkshop jack-in-the-box. I eased my grip around the coat before kicking the guy hard in the chest, letting go as I did so. He tumbled away, falling awkwardly against a dumpster before crumpling to the dirty concrete. The knife came away in my jacket and fell to the ground with a thud.

"You alright?" I asked Brandon.

"Fine," he said, cradling his right hand with his left.

"Feels different without mitts, doesn't it?" I said, with a half-smile.

"True enough," he said.

We both turned to the man. He was breathing hard, but just about conscious, slumped on the ground. I skipped a few steps and kicked the knife away to the wall on the other side. I checked my jacket was okay and put it back on and zipped it up. I blew on my hands as we walked up to the guy. The adrenalin was pumping, but I was still bloody foundered.

"Don't go robbing anybody else," I said.

He looked at me, frowning. Blood ran down one cheek from a small cut there. He nodded.

I carefully picked my kebab up from the bin lid. "Do you know how hard it is to get a kebab in this city? If it's cold- I'm coming back."

I felt kind of sorry for the guy.

"Go find a hostel or something, man. It's freezing," Brandon said.

We walked on up the alley. I decided I wasn't waiting any longer and unwrapped my dinner.

DEATH NOTICE

Chapter 3

The drive home was less eventful. Brandon had gotten into the Hornet out of the cold, while I finished my kebab. Last thing I wanted was kebab sauce on the upholstery. We were both glad to get back to the warm safety our new home. First thing I did was to get a bag of frozen peas for Brandon's knuckles. He flicked on the lamps and put his feet up on the sofa and switched on the telly. I grabbed us both a bottle of beer and checked the phone for messages. Nothing. I joined him in the living room and placed my own feet up on the coffee table with a contented sigh.

Our apartment was small but served us well. Just outside The Village, it was fully furnished with a kitchen/living room, two little bedrooms and a bathroom. What else did you need? There was even a reserved parking space outside for my baby. After the events of six months ago, our possessions had been shipped to us, but neither of us actually owned a lot to ship. Most of it still lay unpacked in boxes in the communal storage locker. The apartment didn't have much of a homely feel, but neither of us cared. It was almost like living in a pretty decent hotel. We'd made it a little messy and it had somewhat of a student feel. I felt a little bad about living like a student in my forties, but I didn't care enough to change anything. We'd been given a decent enough sum of money to keep us going, but one day soon we'd have to both think about getting a job. For now, we'd be okay. We'd killed some bad guys for Queen and President, and they owed us. I didn't feel too bad about taking their cash.

"How's the hand?" I asked, lighting up a smoke.

Brandon lifted the bag of peas off his now mahogany looking knuckles and made a grimace. "Not bad."

"Keep it on for a while. They won't be so sore in the morning."

He nodded and typed away one handed on his new cell phone. A Nokia 5190.

"You did well earlier, Brandon," I said, "Good reflexes."

"Thanks, Mick." He paused his typing and lit up a pre-rolled number.

I grabbed the remote from the seat beside him, flicked through the channels, settling on the world news. Tiger Woods had become number one in golf, Eminem was topping the charts, and Brad Pitt and Jennifer Aniston had got together. Where was the proper news? I turned it off, got up heavily and selected a CD from the pile, and switched on our little stereo system. Joni Mitchell's *Blue*. Perfect for this time of night.

I settled back down and lit another cigarette. I looked across to Brandon, huddled on the other sofa. He was alternating between typing and lifting his beer for a few swigs. He looked up.

"Amy's coming to the city tomorrow," he said.

"She is?"

He smirked. I'd probably sounded a little too eager.

"It's a hell of a drive," I added.

"Yeah." He returned to one-handed typing. "… 'Bout ten hours."

"She's not flying then?"

"Nah, she's watching her pennies. She's already flown back and forth twice this month."

"Oh, aye. Those consultancy jobs."

After leaving the FBI, Amy had begun to take on some security consultancy work before her mother got sick. She'd been a good daughter and that didn't surprise me any. Pity though that it put a wrench in her new work. I still felt guilty that what happened to us had ultimately led to her quitting the FBI.

"What else did she say?"

"Just a sec."

I breathed out. Brandon looked up and caught my eye. "Do you know you could get one of these too, Mick?"

I laughed, "What would I want with one of those things. I've got a phone." I gestured to the landline on the table.

Brandon set his cell down. He took the peas off his hand and stretched out his fingers. "She wants to meet us for dinner tomorrow night," he said. "She's leaving early in the morning, but has a few things on in the afternoon."

"Great, be nice to see her."

"Hard to tell with texting, but something else seems up. She wants to ask us something."

"Oh?" I frowned and taking a long pull on my ciggy. "Hope she's okay."

Brandon shrugged, "I guess we'll find out tomorrow." He took a slug of his beer, then carefully placed the peas back onto his hand with a wince.

"So, what do you want to do during the day? Any plans?"

Brandon shrugged.

"'Life is a long preparation for something that never happens,'" I said, quoting Yeats.

Brandon rolled his eyes.

"You up to some training in the morning then, mate?" I asked.

"Sure, I'm always ready to whoop you a little bit."

I smiled.

Chapter 4

Brandon doubled over with a groan.

"I'm sorry buddy, I didn't think it was that hard," I said.

He straightened up and caught his breath. "Damn, Mick."

"Well, you did say you were going to 'whoop me,'" I said, patting his back and grinning.

"Dirty Irish scum," he said.

I laughed, "C'mon Brandon, let's do a little on the heavy bag."

We'd been sparring for a while in the gym nearby; a little place, with some rough characters and rough edges in its décor, but it had decent equipment. It was named after its owner, a man called Hawk. Apparently he was some huge tough guy from Boston, but I'd never met him. I lowered the ropes for Brandon, and we got out of the ring. We filled our water bottles from the fountain at the side and took long sips. A ripped guy in a grey vest, over at the mats and weights, paused his lift and gave me a wink.

"You should go easy on the kid. A sucker punch won't teach him anything."

It was in good humour.

"That wasn't a sucker punch, but true enough. Let me know if you want to spar with me sometime, and I'll teach *you* a couple of things."

He gave a low chuckle, did two reps with his stacked dumbbells and said, "Sure, anytime... I'm always ready to learn something new."

"That's the spirit," I said, leading Brandon towards the annexed weight machines in the back, "'Some day you will be old enough to start reading fairy tales again,'" I said, leaving him with some confusion at my C.S Lewis quote.

"You're a pretty weird guy, Mick," Brandon said, laying down on the seat as I selected a good starting weight for him.

"Yeah, I know."

After various texts throughout the day went back and forth from Brandon's phone, we arranged to meet Amy at 7pm in *Tom's*. It was great little restaurant close to our apartment. Nice but not too pricey. It had become a regular spot for us all before Amy's mum had taken sick. We hadn't seen Amy for a few weeks, and I was surprised at the little flutter of nerves in my stomach. They had Guinness on draft and that helped settle me a little. Brandon chose a bottle of Bud.

Just after half past, Amy walked in. She had on a white blouse, black trousers and a fitted black leather jacket. Her face was a little harassed and she appeared tired, but as always, she also looked incredible.

"Hi guys," she said with a warm smile.

"Amy, come get a seat, you must be wrecked." I got up and pulling out a chair.

"Hi Aimes," said Brandon.

We both gave her a hug. Her perfume smelled like a rose garden.

Amy swept the hair from her face and sat down. I sat back down beside her.

"Wow. Well don't you two look smart?" she said.

I pouted. Brandon looked a little embarrassed. We were both only wearing casual shirts and jeans, but maybe that said more about our usual attire.

Amy let out a big sigh. She smiled and leaned over the table and took one of each of our hands. "I missed you guys."

"We did too," Brandon said.

"So, I bet you're starved," I said. "You eaten anything today?"

"Not really... let's take a look." She picked up the laminated menu.

We chatted about what we would have and asked Amy about her day.

"So, you're staying at your place for the night?" I asked.

"Yeah, I'll be having a couple of these first, though." She held aloft her gin.

"What about you mum, how's she doing?" I asked, lighting up a smoke, careful to blow it away from her as the end caught.

She puffed out her cheeks. "Alright, I guess. I mean... the surgery went well. The main surgery. But then she's got the follow up one in two days. She'll especially need me for another few weeks after that one."

I nodded.

"Tough going," Brandon offered.

Amy nodded.

"That kind of links in with what I wanted to talk with you both about," she said, her forehead gaining a couple of temporary worry lines.

"Shoot," I said.

Just then a waiter appeared with our mains. He set down medium-well-done steaks with fries in front of Brandon and me, and a salmon dish in front of Amy. We thanked him and all began to tuck in. The smell of the steaming steak and red wine sauce was too much. I immediately began to cut off a few slices, as did Brandon. Amy twiddled her fork around some vegetables.

"So, about what you were saying… You know we'll help you any way we can, Amy."

She gave a half smile. "Thank you, Walker,"

"Walker? We're not back to that are we?" I said jokingly.

She looked flustered, "I'm sorry… *Mick*, I'm all over the place."

"I'm only messin', Amy" I said, feeling bad, but also worried that our friendship had slipped backwards. Cards on the table, in the future, I wanted more than just friendship.

"Just name it," Brandon said eagerly, between chews.

"You guys are the best," she said. "Okay…" She forked up a piece of salmon soaked in parsley sauce, chewed, then pushed her plate an inch or so away. "There is something I wondered if you could help with, but just say no if you can't… please."

I nodded.

"My Auntie… I think I've mentioned her to you. Auntie Rose. She lives in North Carolina with my cousin Lisa. My Uncle passed away a few years ago and now it's just the two of them. Thing is, my cousin's gone missing."

She looked up at us.

"Shit," Brandon said.

"I'm sorry to hear that." I put my knife and fork down. "How old is she?"

DEATH NOTICE

"She's seventeen. Still lives at home."

"No other family?" I asked.

She shook her head. "My cousin, Lisa. I haven't seen her all that much recently, but we've always been close, you know? And she's a great kid. She's almost never in trouble. B-plus student, good to my auntie, nice group of friends."

"So, what happened exactly?" I asked.

Amy told us how the girl had been at a friend's house studying. It was less than a block from her home in the small town of Six Mile where she lived with Amy's aunt. She'd left just before 9pm to walk home. Lisa never made it home. She hadn't been seen since. Nothing. This was three days ago. Her Auntie was frantic, and nobody has heard a thing from her. She didn't own a cell phone and didn't drive.

The family were okay for money. The auntie worked part time and there was a pension from the uncle, but they weren't exactly wealthy either. The local police didn't want to know. They had said she's nearly an adult anyway and was probably just crashing at some friend's house. Maybe partying too much. Thing is, Amy said Lisa didn't drink, far as the auntie knew. And wouldn't touch drugs. She even taught little kids at Sunday school.

"So why aren't the cops more interested?" I asked. "Has she done anything like this before?"

Amy leaned in close again, her face screwing up like she had just tasted something in her meal she didn't like. "It was a one-time thing. After my uncle died, she went a little wild. She did some secret drinking and stayed away without telling my auntie."

"How long for?" I asked.

"One night," Amy said shaking her head, "One night and that damn sheriff has her written off as a drunken teen runaway. They hadn't shown much interest that time either. Now they think it's just the same thing again."

I nodded and took a sip of my drink. Amy's eyes stared at me, full of anger and frustration. And a lot of worry.

"You're sure it couldn't be that? Things getting on top of her again?" Brandon said carefully.

"No... I don't. I mean, I don't know for sure... But she's a different person now. She found who she was again. Found herself and grew. Grew into this lovely and sweet seventeen-year-old."

"And the cops won't do anything at all?" I asked.

"No, nothing. I've even tested my sway with my old contacts, but zilch. It's an electoral state for law enforcement. The sheriff has a lot of power. He's been no help to us with this, but he's very popular with the masses."

"What can we do?" I asked, leaning in and patting her hand for just a moment.

"Whatever you need," Brandon said.

Amy looked like she might cry, then visibly controlled herself. She gave the briefest of smiles and blew us a little kiss across the table. "Will you help me look for her?"

"Of course we will," I said.

DEATH NOTICE

Chapter 5

A weight visibly lifted from Amy after that was settled. She asked for help and got the response she had hoped for. It was something. A step in the right direction. She started eating again, took some of her drink and then began to talk more easily and fluidly about her cousin. About what she thought needed to be done and what we could do to help.

"Thing is, I'm not going to be able to leave my mom for some time. At least two weeks, I would think. That's too long to wait to start looking. Way too long. I can't leave her, but I can't leave my auntie with this by herself either. She's all alone."

Amy's Auntie was beside herself with worry, and after no dice with the cops, had asked Amy if she should hire a private detective. That was when Amy had the idea instead of talking to us. She knew that I had a certain kind of expertise and that she could trust and rely on us both. In these kinds of things, time was everything.

I had no idea what I was getting into, but so far it didn't sound that hopeful. I was already frightened for Amy. Of what the outcome might be. But I would do whatever I could to help. It was about a seven-hour drive from New York to the little town according to Amy. We said we were happy to leave early in the morning. If we didn't stop too often, we could be there in the early evening. She said she'd see if her auntie wanted to meet us tomorrow night and apologised that she couldn't be there in person. Her mother couldn't be left any longer. Amy had a hell of a lot on her plate, and I wished I could have only done more. She insisted on paying for a motel there for us, for as long as we stayed. With the look she gave me, I knew there wasn't any point in arguing.

We had a few more drinks and a pot of coffee after dinner. Everything was set. We walked Amy to her door at about half nine. She was doing okay but was exhausted. Me and Brandon headed home and packed a bag each. We got the general essentials and then I packed the weapons. They could prove essential too. Best to be prepared. I got out the Colt, a Glock for Brandon, and a few boxes of ammo. I laid it all out on the living room table. I put on the news, brewed a fresh pot of coffee and set about cleaning them. Brandon had a couple of joints, I had a few ciggies, and we got ourselves ready. When the clock ticked past midnight, we sunk a last beer each and headed to bed.

DEATH NOTICE

Chapter 6

The Hornet was ripping along at a nice clip. She was handling well on a full tank of gas. We'd had plenty of coffee before we locked up and left. Prince was pumping away on the stereo. This time I was introducing Brandon to *Sign of The Times*. He was digging it. We had set off at eight thirty, a little later than I'd planned. By midday we were both starved and I pulled off at services some place near Philadelphia. After my experiences there last year, I had no plans for a return visit.

We wanted to keep to our schedule, so had allocated ourselves a half hour for burgers, fries, Coke and coffee. The diner was like any other I'd seen along the freeway. Lots of Formica, lots of grease, hassled looking waitresses. But the food was pretty decent.

"Good grub," I said.

"Yep," Brandon said, unleashing the ketchup bottle, splattering a healthy dose over the remainder of his still steaming fries.

"Terrible music, though," I gestured to the speaker above us.

"Not great."

"Who is it?"

"*Destiny's Child*, I think," Brandon said.

I gave a disinterested shrug. I picked up a chip and dipped it in my own little puddle of red sauce. "So, you feeling okay about all this?" I asked.

"Yeah... I mean... Amy needs us."

I nodded. "I just mean, are you doing okay? Kinda reminds me of some of our road trips last time."

Brandon smiled, then took a hit from his glass of Coke, "It wasn't all bad... some of the time."

"Yeah, well maybe the better bits were when hired assassins weren't trying to kill us."

"True enough. Those parts sucked," he said.

"What's your gut on this Brandon? What do you think's happened to Amy's cousin?"

His eyes bulged for a moment. He blew out his cheeks and shrugged. "I don't know what to think. What about you?"

I shook my head. "I don't like it. I don't have a great feeling. From what we know so far, it's not all that hopeful. And it's already been... what... four days now?"

"Yeah."

We each took a fresh bite of our burgers. I stared out of the window at the parking lot.

"What you thinking?" he asked.

"Aww, nothin'. I don't know. I'm just a bit worried I suppose."

Brandon nodded thoughtfully, bit his lip.

I tilted my head back. "What?"

His lip curled slightly. "You're worried about how you'll feel if you have to bring Amy bad news."

I tilted my head and smiled widely. "You're quite the intuitive little sod, aren't you?"

Brandon smiled, before picking up a fry, shaking off some sauce and throwing in into his mouth.

The next stretch of the trip was harder going. We passed signs for Washington, and much later, ones for Chicago. The Hornet sped along. I spun some Neil Young and Tom Petty CDs, heartened to see they were both growing on Brandon. His musical education was progressing well. I held the wheel lightly, one-handed, and took in the scenery as it flashed by. Maybe one day I'd get to visit these places. For now, I took some pleasure in touring across this massive country, seeing signs for places I'd only ever seen in movies and on TV. We stopped again for coffee late afternoon, then fired on towards North Carolina.

Six Mile was through forestland between Raleigh and Durham. We made a few wrong turns somewhere near to Petersburg and eventually rolled into the small town at about seven. A little wooden sign with pictures of happy residents told us we had made it. We cruised by a large housing development, then past a school and some kind of leisure centre. There were plenty of mature trees planted all around or left behind from when the town had grown into what it was now.

Brandon had been firing texts back and forth to Amy throughout the day and she had now given Brandon Auntie Rose's phone

DEATH NOTICE

number for Brandon to keep in touch with her directly. We agreed to aim to go to her place for about eight after we checked into the motel and had a quick bite. We were tired and hungry again. It's amazing what sitting in a car all day can do for your appetite. We had a map from the motel to her house that Amy had drawn for us, but finding the motel itself proved to be a problem. After circling the town centre and the outer ring a few times, I still couldn't find a sign. I pulled over in a layby near to a small shopping mall for us to regroup.

"Let's get out and stretch our legs for a second," I said. "Maybe have a wee smoke."

Brandon nodded keenly and we flung open the doors. I got out with a sigh, stretching out my aching limbs. It was already quite dark. Behind us was a forested area. On the road only a few cars came and went. It was cold enough, but nothing like New York had been. There was a cool breeze, but no rain and mercifully no ice. I lit up a cigarette, Brandon extracted a blunt from his pocket.

"We'll have these, then circle around that outer ring again and see if we can find a sign for it. Does that sound okay?"

"Yeah, Mick. Cool." Brandon arched his back.

We smoked in silence for a moment, then we both clocked a cop car pass by on the other side of the road. It made a turn back towards us.

"Five-0," Brandon said before taking a long drag.

I nodded and sighed. "Best put that out, Brandon."

He looked at the Hornet's beautiful bonnet, like he was going to stub it out on my paintwork.

"Don't even think about it," I said.

The car headed straight towards us, a few hundred metres away now.

"Just chuck it, mate. Quickly," I said.

Brandon looked at the half smoked spliff mournfully, before tossing it over the fence into the undergrowth beyond. He flapped a hand, cutting through the remnants of a cloud of dope smoke. The cop car pulled up right in front of the Hornet, a Sheriff's Department insignia etched on the bonnet. I carried on smoking, staring off absently towards the front seats. There were two cops inside. One looked quite bulky, buzz cut, maybe late forties. The one who'd been driving looked younger by a good ten years. They were both white men, dressed in tan uniforms, the younger guy also sported a black Sheriff's Department baseball cap. The bigger guy pushed his door open with a wheeze. He stood upright, eyed us both with cold blue irises. He unclipped the buckle on his sidearm and began marching towards us. His partner was a beat behind, hurrying to keep up with his buddy.

"Evening, officers," I said coolly, continuing to smoke, blowing a plume out above my head.

"Hands where I can see them," the first one said to us, an easy aggression in his voice.

Brandon raised his hands up a little. I held my cigarette up and wiggled the fingers on my other with a little wave. "You can see them here, just fine," I said. "Unless there's something the matter with your eyesight. What's this about?"

I scolded myself internally for starting right away with the cheek. But I'd been stopped by too many bully-boy cops in my lifetime for doing nothing. I had my pan knocked in by many for having the wrong accent. Yeah, maybe sometimes I had been up to something, but not every time I'd been picked up.

"I'll ask the questions," he said sourly. "And no more of your lip, or I'll wipe the smirk off your mouth." The second guy looked a little uncomfortable and shifted from one foot to the other.

"No need to be that way, officer," Brandon said evenly.

He turned towards Brandon, a vein starting to throb in the side of his beefy neck. "I'll decide what way I need to *be*, boy."

"Boy?" I said, taking a step forwards.

The cop's eyes widened. He pulled out his weapon. "Stay where you are," he commanded. He raised the gun and aimed at my chest.

"Hey… come on, man," Brandon said with a pacifying gesture.

"What the hell?" I said, raising my hands and standing still.

The younger cop put a hand on the end of the revolver, his eyes steady, with a calm resilience I hadn't noticed thus far.

"Easy Lester," he said quietly to his superior.

Lester gritted his teeth, then let his gun hang down at his side.

DEATH NOTICE

"Gentlemen," the younger man began. "Please tell us your business here in Six Mile. And I'd like to see your licence and registration," he said, looking at me. He spoke firmly and there was something else in his eyes that told me it would be better for everyone if I just did as he said.

"Sure," I said. I gestured towards the Hornet. "Okay if I get them out of the car?"

"Certainly," he said.

"And macho man over there, he's not going to shoot me for it?"

Lester took a step forward, his eyes kindling. The younger man put up an arm to gently stop him.

"No, *sir*. Officer Lester and I just want to ask you a few questions."

"Well okay, then," I said, raising my hands again dramatically, before opening the driver's door and ducking inside for the paperwork. "Me and Brandon here are staying in a motel for a few nights. Or we're meant to be. We pulled over when we couldn't find it."

"Maybe we can help you with that," the younger man said, as I eased back out from the car, with the paperwork.

I stepped across and handed it to him before giving Lester an exaggerated smile. I noticed the ID on the younger man's uniform said he was called Officer Samuels. He read over my documents carefully. I looked up at Lester and he scowled at me, then turned the scowl on Brandon.

"I saw you throwing what you were smoking over that fence. Smells like marijuana around here. Can you explain that?"

Brandon shrugged and his eyes grew wide, a blank expression on his face. "I don't know nothing about that. I had a twig in my hand. Just threw that over there."

Lester made an irritated guffawing noise, "Sounds like bullshit to me."

"Don't know what to tell you," Brandon said. "I never touch the stuff."

Lester turned his angry, ruddy face back to me.

"Don't look at me officer. I'm too old for that nonsense. I'm just high on life," I said.

His mouth formed an angry 'o' shape before the walkie talkie attached to his shirt crackled into life. I heard a muffled voice say, "This is base, come in please. We got a possible nine-three-four-zero at Hillside Road. Please respond."

Lester plucked it off his shirt, walking away, kicking dirt as he answered, "This is Lester. What's up Jim?"

Samuels folded my licence and paperwork into a little pile and handed it back to me. "Everything's in order here, sir. You take care now. You're free to leave."

With that he tipped his cap, nodded to both of us and returned to the car. Lester finished his conversation with the buzzing voice from the other end of the line. He gave me one last glare for good measure, then heaved himself into the cop car and they sped away with a 'blip, blip,' from the siren and the lights flashing.

"What was that about?" Brandon said.

I shrugged. "Dunno, but I guess we're left to find our own way to the bloody motel."

DEATH NOTICE

Chapter 7

We discovered a sign for the motel after driving for another ten minutes. We'd missed it the first time around. Another five minutes later and we were checking into our room. There was a little office and five motel rooms. All one-storey. There was a neon sign that had seen better days, a small gravel parking area and a vending machine. That was about it. No restaurant on site, but that was fairly common anyway. The vending machine would have to suffice for now.

Our motel room was dead on. Nothing much, but fine for what it was. The furnishings were old but clean enough. There was a decent sized living area come kitchen/diner, two small bedrooms and a little shower room. It was all that we needed, and I'd never been accustomed to much more.

"We got time for a coffee?" Brandon asked.

I checked my watch. "Best not. Will you send her a wee message and say we're on the way."

"Okay cool. Quick smoke?"

"Sure, why not?"

Brandon sent Auntie Rose a text and we had our smoke. We dumped our bags in our rooms, grabbed some snacks from the machine, and headed back out in the Hornet. Amy's directions were spot on, as I knew they would be. We arrived in fifteen minutes. Rose lived in a smart little house in a nice street on the edge of town. It was red brick with a wooden veneer on the front and a little roofed porch. I'd changed out of my Neil Young T-shirt into a half decent lumberjack shirt and Brandon had put on a clean black tee. Coats were needed too. After the sun had gone down, the temperature had dropped with it. We finished another smoke in the car, crumpled the butts into my overflowing ashtray and then headed up the steps.

I rapped the front door. A moment later I heard footsteps and the outside light clicked on.

"Michael? Brandon?"

"Hello, Mrs Kendrix. I'm sorry we're a little late," I said.

"Not at all, not at all, please come through," she said. "And please, call me Auntie Rose. Everybody does."

Auntie Rose had a kindly face. It was also handsome, strong and filled with stress. In perhaps her mid-sixties, I imagined that her expression was usually less strained. There were also a lot of laughter lines around her eyes.

"This way, fellas. Come on through," she said, leading us into a neat and tidy living room, filled with ornaments, family pictures and old but well-maintained furniture. There was a pleasant smell of lavender in the air.

She stopped and we all stood together in the centre of the room. She looked at us both intently, her eyes sparkling.

"Thank you both so much for coming... for trying to help us," she said, her warm, deep voice cracking just a little.

"We're happy to help," Brandon said.

"Anything we can do for you and Amy." I offered her my hand.

She tutted and gave a little smile. "Please." She opened her arms out for a hug.

I gave her a little squeeze and then she reached over and did the same with Brandon. His cheeks reddened just a drop.

"Now, boys... coffee? Or would you like something a little stronger?"

We looked at each other.

"Coffee would be great, thank you," I said.

"Yeah, please," Brandon said.

She disappeared from the room. We sat down listening to the sound of a kettle boiling and the clink of cups being set out. I stood and walked around the room. I stopped at the sideboard, littered with photographs, framed college certificates and assorted ornaments of animals and angels. I picked up a picture of Rose, taken maybe just a few years earlier, in a smart dress in front of an oak tree and some kind of school. On one arm was a man of about her age and on the other a pretty teenage girl.

"That's Lisa."

I turned as Rose came into the room, carrying a tray with a French press full of dark coffee, cups and a plate of cookies. "And my late husband."

DEATH NOTICE

I nodded and took a seat on the sofa next to Brandon. Rose set the tray on a coffee table and sat down on a low chair on the other side. She began to pour the coffee. It smelled great. Rose indicated for us to help ourselves to cream and sugar and sat back and crossed her hands on her lap.

"So," she said, now looking a little unsure of what to do next.

"Just take your time," I said. "Start from the beginning."

Brandon nodded and offered her an encouraging smile.

She took a breath.

"Okay. Up until that night, everything was normal. Things were fine. More than fine. Lisa had been doing great in her studies, her friends were nice, we were happy here at home." She paused and glanced across to the photograph I had set back in place. "We had *adjusted* to life without my husband. It had been rocky for a time, but now we were looking forward to our futures... I was looking forward to Lisa's future." Her eyes welled up and she reached for a tissue to dab at her eyes. Tears began to flow. She looked embarrassed. "I'm sorry," she said, dabbing at her eyes harshly. Brandon looked uncomfortable. I felt the same.

"Please. Don't worry. You've been through a lot... There's no need to apologise, just take your time." This wasn't really my forte. Cracking heads; yes. Comforting strangers in pain? Not so much. I just did the best I could.

"Thank you... you're both very kind." She composed herself.

Brandon gave her a brief smile and took a sip of the coffee. "Great coffee. Just what we needed, thanks."

"Good," she said and smiled warmly, "My husband always said, 'Why drink dishwater? We're not savages.'"

"A wise man," I said.

"Alright, I'm okay now." Rose adjusted her position, took a sip of coffee and continued. "Lisa had gone to a friend's house to study. Zara. They had been working at her mom's place from after dinner time. About seven. Lisa left her house at nine. But she didn't come home. I was frightened, but I hoped there was a simple enough explanation. Even so, I rang the police in the early hours. They didn't want to know." Her eyes flickered with anger. "And they still don't want to know. That pompous, self-serving sheriff couldn't give one solitary shit." She looked momentarily embarrassed. "I'm sorry."

"Don't be. He sounds like an asshole," I said.

She smiled.

"The next morning, I rang everyone I could think of and nothing. Still nothing now."

She paused and lifted her coffee cup, blowing over the top of it, tears again in her eyes. I nodded thoughtfully. Speaking to her hadn't made me feel much more hopeful. It was very strange. From what we knew, she didn't sound like the kind of girl who would just voluntarily disappear into thin air. But what had happened to her on that short walk back home in a quiet neighbourhood? We were going to have our work cut out, that was for sure.

"Mrs Kendrix, sorry... Auntie Rose," Brandon started cautiously, "Amy said there was one time that Lisa had gone missing before."

Rose's eyes grew dark. I wasn't sure what her reaction was going to be. She set down her cup and let out a long sigh.

"Yes," she said, nodding wearily. "But that was some time ago. We were both crushed by my husband's sudden death. Lisa and Bill were very close. He was a wonderful father. She went a little off the rails, as you might expect." Rose raised her hands in a shrugging gesture. It was just one night, and she was so very sorry. When she saw what it had done to me, I know in my heart, she would never do it again."

There was a heavy silence and then we continued with some further questions.

"Was Lisa in a... romantic relationship at the minute?" I asked, feeling even more uncomfortable.

She gave a tut and looked out of the window. "There was a *boyfriend* for a while. It ended a few weeks ago thankfully. Not a great match in my opinion. Not a nice boy. I was glad when she ended it with him."

"Lisa ended it?" Brandon asked.

"Yes. And she wouldn't have gone back to him. He has been spoken to by the police already. Some of the little that they *have* done."

Rose looked very tired now and it was getting late. I got out my notebook and took down the names, addresses and phone numbers of those people who were close to Lisa: school friends, her ex-boyfriend, teachers, neighbours.

As she saw us to the door I turned and put a hand on her shoulder. "We'll do everything we can."

But I already knew that wouldn't be enough.

Chapter 8

The killer knew it was time to move the body. He finished his coffee, washed his cup and placed it in the rack on the neat kitchen counter. He picked up the fresh painting overalls, dressed in them over his clothes and stretched on a new pair of latex gloves. He walked along the hallway and opened the door to the cellar with a loud creak. He pulled the cord and made his way down the old wooden staircase. He was greeted by the sight of his neatly stacked paint tins, boxes of Christmas decorations and assorted tools. There was also a new putrid smell, adding to the mustiness. It was always this way after a few days. He walked past it all to the back of the room. On the concrete floor was a crumpled tarpaulin. He pulled it back. The gruesome smile was still fixed in place, although the cheeks were hollowed now and the face a sickly grey.

"Good evening. It's time we went for a little drive."

DEATH NOTICE

Chapter 9

"How'd you sleep, Mick?" Brandon asked, yawning at my bedroom door. He was dressed in a vest and boxers, his hair ruffled. I was still in bed, puffing on my first cigarette of the day.
"Awful, thanks. How 'bout you?"
"Not bad, really. Want some coffee?"
"Is the Pope Catholic?"

We breakfasted at the little kitchen bench. Well, we had coffee. I put on the telly and watched some news. Alec Guinness had just died, which made me feel a little sad. I remembered well, going to see the first *Star Wars* with my dad. It was a year after I'd joined the IRA. He couldn't have been prouder than if I'd joined the Rebel Alliance. I flicked to another news channel. The weather was due to pick up, which made me feel pretty good. Back home, a fresh batch of political prisoners had been released under The Good Friday Agreement. I had mixed feelings about that one.

After our coffees, we found our way to a place called 'Burt's Diner' in town. It was the same as most others, though the only difference was that it appeared to exclusively play music from the 1950's. Chuck Berry, Little Richard, Buddy Holly. I was cool with that.
"How's yours?" Brandon asked, tucking into his pancakes, bacon and eggs.
"It's good," I said. I'd opted for the extra healthy bacon, sausage, fried egg and hashbrowns. It was no Ulster Fry, but it did the trick.
"So, it's Saturday, isn't it? Hopefully we have a fair chance of catching people at home. No college and that. I say we start with Lisa's best friend. What do you reckon?"
"Want me to text her number?" Brandon asked, lifting out the sheet with all the contact details.
"Nah, that might be weird. We'll just call and see if she's in."
"Yeah, two strange men calling for a teenage girl unexpectedly. That'd be just fine."

"You speak for yourself. Strange? And you're a *man* now, are ya?"

"Yeah. A man with boyish good looks. You're just an old fella."

"Eat up, Tonto," I said.

Brandon took a slug of his coffee, a smile playing on his lips. "That some kind of racial slur?"

"You're so sensitive. You're my sidekick, that's all. Did you not know that's how this works?"

"Maybe I'm Holmes and you're *my* Watson."

"Ok, *Holmesboy*, let's get going."

We found Zara's house easy enough, just a few streets away from Auntie Rose on a street called Mori Parade. We parked up outside and finished our post-breakfast smokes. Zara's house looked nice. Well-kept with a light-blue trim over the wood. There was no car in the driveway.

"If she's in, do you reckon she'll talk to us?" Brandon asked. "She might tell us to get lost."

"She might. But I'm counting on her wanting to help find her friend. Besides, in the words of Yeats, 'There are no strangers here, only friends you haven't met yet.'"

Brandon rolled his eyes. I patted him on the arm, and we got out.

"Hello? Are you looking for my mom?" The girl who answered the door looked around seventeen, slight, with pale skin and red hair.

"No. I'm called Mick, and this is Brandon. We're looking to speak with Zara."

Her intelligent eyes narrowed for a moment and then she tilted her head. "You the guys Auntie Rose told me about?"

"Yeah, I guess we are," Brandon said, adjusting his cap.

"We just want to ask you a few things about Lisa, see if we can help," I said, trying to look as unthreatening as possible.

Zara glanced back at the house and the inner porch door. "My parents aren't home," she said.

"That's okay," I said, "We can just chat out here if it's better. It's a nice morning."

DEATH NOTICE

It *was* a nice morning. Any overnight frost had been melted away by the high sun in the almost cloudless sky.

"I guess that would be okay," she said, biting her lip. She reached in her back pocket and took out a packet of Marlboros. "I was going to come out for a cigarette anyway," she said.

"Parents don't know you smoke?" Brandon asked.

She offered a wry smile. "No, not really."

"We won't tell them," I said, giving a half smile.

Zara took us over to a pair of benches underneath a cherry blossom tree towards the side of her house. She sat across from us, lighting up her cigarette.

"So, you're Irish?" she said, fixing her eyes on me.

"Guilty as charged," I said, lighting up and offering the pack to Brandon. He took one a little reluctantly. I'd already told him he couldn't be smoking joints in front of the witnesses, even if they were only "light one skinners," as he put it.

"You must be really worried about Lisa. Not nice to not know where she is," I said.

Her face fell. She nodded.

"Rose tells us that Lisa with you until about nine that night and she never came home."

She nodded again, looking at the ground. "Yeah," she said in a quiet voice. "I just don't understand it."

"Anything off about Lisa that night?" Brandon asked, "Anything weird you can remember?"

Zara puffed on her thick Marlboro Red and shook her head, waving the cloud of smoke away from her shoulder length hair. "Nothing. We did our homework, we chatted, listened to music. She was just fine."

"What were you working on?" I asked.

Zara looked confused.

"What was the homework?" I clarified.

"Oh, I don't know... em... just an English assignment we had due, I think."

"Okay," I gave a brief nod.

Zara fidgeted with her cigarette, passing it through her fingers.

"You any idea where she might be? Any idea at all?" Brandon asked.

Zara pursed her lips. "I wish I did." She shook her head. Her eyes moistened and she blinked the tears away.

"I know this is difficult," I started gently. "But is there anyone you can think of who might have wanted to hurt Lisa?"

"No... God no... everybody loves Lisa. I just don't understand it."

"No creepy men hanging about? Anyone with a grudge? How about her ex?" I tried.

She shook her head. "No, she's been finished with BB for a while now."

"What's he like?" Brandon asked.

"BB? He's alright, I guess... well, I mean I never really liked him all that much."

"Why not?" I asked.

"Nothing much... just he's a bit of an asshole. A jock. Not really Lisa's usual type if you ask me."

We asked a few more questions, but Zara began to clam up and said her parents would be back home soon and she had things to do before they did. We thanked her, got back in my orange beauty and sped away towards the town.

"What you think?" I asked, as we each lit up.

"I don't know. Not much there really."

"You did good though, Brandon. We'll make a *Six Kill* out of you yet."

"What?"

"Me Spenser. You Six Kill."

"Lost me as usual, Mick." Brandon cracked the window and blew out dope smoke.

"Never mind. Just another crime-fighting duo. I'll tell you one thing, though. Zara wasn't telling us the whole story."

DEATH NOTICE

Chapter 10

I decided that BB should be our next stop. His house was in a richer part of town, notable for the wider roads, tree lined, with large spaced out detached homes and big cars. BB, or *Bobby Blacklock*, wasn't at home. His dad answered the door; a well-built white man with short receding hair, mid- to late-forties. I told him that we were investigating the disappearance without quite needing to say we were not *official* investigators. He appeared a little weary of us but did tell me that his son was playing basketball at the town park with his friends. I didn't hang about for him to ask any more probing questions about our credentials.

"Did he say west on East Moreland Drive?" I asked Brandon, while driving and struggling with a chocolate bar wrapper.

"What am I now, the navigator as well as the sidekick?" Brandon said.

"Yeah. Which way?"

"This left, then right, I think he said."

"I knew you'd be handy to have around for something."

"Yes massa."

I turned off the Therapy? CD that Brandon hadn't really been digging and concentrated on where I was going. I gave up on the chocolate too. American made sub-par chocolate anyway. It wasn't worth the hassle. We turned down Robert's Street, past a little Baptist church and a library, and were greeted by the view of a parkland and playing fields beyond.

"Bingo," I said.

I pulled up by the side of a bike-rack and kid's playpark as Brandon finished off a text.

"Amy?" I asked.

"Yep. Just filling her in on our progress."

"Not much to tell her. How's she doing?"

"Yeah, okay."

It was still warming up. Best weather I'd seen in weeks. I stripped off my shirt and put my jacket back on over my Bowie T-shirt and jeans. Brandon adjusted his cap and headed out just in his long-sleeve black Nike tee and black trackies. We headed through the iron gates, the path running along the side of the playpark towards the sporting area. I could smell flowers all around. No idea what kind. Church spires towered behind the park and the sun hung high above that. It was probably a nice place to grow up, for most people.

"You want me to wait while you have a wee go on the swings first?" I asked, lighting up a cigarette.

Brandon rolled his eyes and lit up a joint.

"Remember. Not when we're interviewing people," I said.

"I don't see us interviewing anyone right now."

He had me there.

The park was busy with hyperactive kids and hassled looking parents and grandparents. Further up was the sports field where teenagers were playing American Football at one end, and even some *proper* football at the other end. I wondered how The Glens were doing. I made a mental note to try and find the league table on Teletext later on. Last I'd checked, Glentoran were doing pretty well this season. My stomach gave a little flip as I pictured back home, the streets, the struggle, my family.

"Ya think that's them over there?" Brandon said, indicating one of two fenced in basketball courts up ahead. I squinted through the sun, returned to the moment. On that court were four tall white kids throwing hoops, drinking cans of Coke and smoking. On the other was a similar scene, but they were all black.

"Segregation is still working well."

"Looks like it," Brandon said.

We threw down our smokes and crushed them underfoot then headed towards the gate. I threw back the bolt and we went inside, shutting it behind us. Play stopped momentarily on both courts, and I felt all eyes on us.

"Did we just enter a western saloon?" I asked.

"There's quite the glare," Brandon whispered back. "Maybe they think you're Michael Jordan."

"Must be," I said.

"Or maybe John Goodman."

"Ouch."

The four white guys now stood in a semicircle facing us, a few metres away. All were tall and athletic, in a mix of vests and T-shirts despite the cold. The power of youth, I guess. They all gave me their best disinterested stare. None were very convincing.

"I'm looking for BB," I said.

The staring continued for a moment, then they looked between one another. The second biggest guy took a step forwards. He was maybe eighteen, bleached short hair, muscles and perhaps not much else.

"I'm BB. Who wants to know?"

I took another step and pasted on a half-smile. "I'm Mick, this is Brandon. We're friends of Lisa's family. We just want to ask a couple of questions. See if we can help the family."

He looked between me and Brandon, a smile playing on his lips. "So, you ain't cops?"

"No. Like I said, we're just helping out. We just want a few minutes of your time."

They all laughed suddenly at something that was apparently funny. It started with BB and appeared to be contagious. I must have already had the vaccine.

"Get the fuck outta here," shouted the largest of the group dismissively.

BB flapped his hand as if to dismiss us and turned his back.

I was readying my response when Brandon said evenly, "I'll play you for it."

"What?" said BB, turning around angrily.

"I'll *play-you-for-it*," Brandon enunciated slowly, as if speaking to a small child. "One on one. First to three hoops. I win, we ask you a few questions."

BB snickered, then turned around to his mates and they all snickered. He turned back, his eyes sparkling. "And what if I win?"

"Then I give you fifty bucks," I said.

He thought about it. "Your money. Let's go."

BB went over to his friends to get ready and fetch a coin. Brandon took off his cap and rolled up his sleeves. I gave him a questioning look. From what I'd seen, BB looked to be a seasoned player. He was also nearly twice as big as Brandon; height and muscles.

I gave Brandon some side eye.

"It's alright, Mick. I'm pretty good," Brandon said with a wink.

He looked confident. I liked that. Day after day that kid made me feel more and more like a proud father. "Okay," I said.

The three goons and myself formed a moon shape around the area below the net. I had no idea of the rules or what was happening exactly, but I assumed it involved getting the ball through the hoop. One of BB's friends told us we had lost the coin toss. Brandon just shrugged and took up position. BB did the same. The big guy put his fingers in his mouth and made a whistle. BB set off with the ball, pushing past Brandon, off like a hare, bouncing fluidly as he went. He took a shot and it whistled in through the net. He jogged back, giving one of his friends a high five. They all cheered. Dickheads.

They both took up positions again. This time Brandon feinted left, then swept around him like a whippet. BB caught up with him and Brandon passed him again, turned and shot, sinking the ball through the net.

"Good lad," I shouted.

BB looked pissed. His buddies shouted encouragement and sent a few glares in our direction.

The next play was a little longer. They took the ball off one another a few times, both breathing hard. Then Brandon plucked the ball in mid-air, sprinted off, bounced once and scored another.

This time I actually cheered.

"Fan-fucking-tastic," I said to him as he ran back to position, giving him a pat on the shoulder. "One more and that's us."

Now BB was really pissed. Brandon just kept his head down, eyes on the ball. BB set off, shoving Brandon out of the way and striding towards goal.

"Hey, come on," Brandon shouted.

BB shot and missed. Brandon bolted, caught the rebound and took aim. BB was running after him and stopped purposely late, piling into him and knocking Brandon down onto the hard ground.

"What the hell?" I shouted, advancing towards them. BB's three friends drew up alongside. I felt a rage in the pit of my stomach. Brandon got to his honkers and shook his head, a cut seeping through his tracks over the knee.

"I'm done with this shit," BB declared, kicking the ball away.

DEATH NOTICE

"How about you fight me for it then?" Brandon said in a low voice, picking himself up off the ground.

BB turned. "What the fuck?" he scoffed, breaking into a huge grin.

I turned to Brandon with another questioning look. "C'mon mate, let's leave it now."

"I got this," he said.

"You want to fight me?" BB called over the cackling of his friends.

"Yeah. Same deal," Brandon said. "What? You scared of a little black guy?"

BB puffed out his chest and immediately slipped into an over-zealous boxing stance. The rest of us moved in closer and Brandon eased into a low fighting position; knees bent, fists up, just liked I'd shown him.

They circled one another. Brandon bobbed a little on his heels.

"Fight!" shouted the big guy, like he'd played too much *Street Fighter*.

BB launched himself, looking to land the first blow. Brandon took a step away, ducked and avoided it. BB swung again. Brandon danced to the side and avoided that too. Then he swept in close and hit BB twice in the stomach. BB didn't have any defence and left his face exposed. Brandon pulled back, swung and smacked him hard in the kisser. BB went down. He looked up at the sky, stunned. He struggled for words, then looked to his buddies, "You... you gonna just stand there?"

The other three shut their mouths, hardened their faces and took a step towards me.

Brandon made a move to come across.

"It's alright Brand, you take a break," I said.

I wouldn't need him for this, and besides, I couldn't let him have all the fun.

"Fair's fair." I raised my hands in mock defence. "We don't have to do this unless you really want to."

I glanced over my shoulder and saw that a few park-goers had stopped to watch the altercation. The basketball game had stopped next door and the four of them stood watching at the fence, all with smiles at what had just happened.

I returned to look at the idiots in front of me. The big guy moved ahead of the pack, "Yeah we gotta do this," he said.

"Okay," I said and dropped into my own crouch.

We circled each other, the other two hanging back. He threw a few jabs nowhere close.

"I'll just stand right here if you like," I said and stood stock still.

His face reddened and he launched a right at me. I moved my head out of the way, then I popped him once with a fairly restrained left hook. He looked stunned. Then I hit him with a right and he went down and almost out. The other two approached me from each side.

"Really?" I said. "You sure?"

The first began to run at me. I bent down and swept my leg under his. He went up in the air like a slapstick clown and landed on his ass. The second guy stumbled around to try and glance me with a left. He was the smallest of the group. I pivoted and caught his hand with my left, then hit him once in the face with a hard right. I let go. He went down too.

Brandon came and stood beside me. We looked down at the four eejits on the ground. They'd been taught a lesson. I'd leave it at that. I shook my head and we walked away towards the gates and let ourselves out. The quartet next door gave us a little cheer and round of applause as we exited. I gave a mock bow. I admit that I quite enjoyed that. But not as much as showing up the cocky little bully-boys.

Brandon had a knowing little smile on his lips as we walked out and onto the pathway.

"Mate," I said, turning to him, "I gotta say, you were something else. Very bloody impressive."

His cheeks flushed. "Thanks, Mick."

"I mean it. Well done, bud."

I felt immensely proud of him. A year ago, he wouldn't have even spoken to those guys. I put my arm around him and gave his shoulder a little squeeze.

We walked on, feeling like 'the shizz' despite having learned exactly nothing about what we had come there for.

Then the cops arrived.

DEATH NOTICE

Chapter 11

Half an hour later and we were sitting in handcuffs in the town lockup. It was just a small substation. We had been placed in seats in the general admin area, beside other cops in Sheriff uniforms, on landline phones, making notes or drinking coffee. One was doing all three. Remarkable. It had been our friends Lester and Samuels who had picked us up. Samuels had been alright about it and Lester had been a dick. They were now in the corner of the office, in discussion with the desk sergeant.

"So, what's the play?" Brandon asked quietly.

"It's not ideal, this," I admitted. "They'll probably separate us. You say nothing. Only say you want a duty lawyer. That'll buy some time. I'll try and get us out of this."

"What about our phone calls?"

I thought about it. Who would we even call? I sure as hell didn't want to ring Amy. The first day trying to help her and her auntie and we get ourselves arrested for brawling.

"Just leave it for now. I'll try and figure something out."

"Okay, Mick."

Brandon was doing okay, though he did look a little worried. But we'd both been in much worse scrapes before.

Right about then, Lester came over and pulled me roughly to my feet.

"You're coming with me."

He tugged on my wrists. It burned, but I didn't let it show.

"See you in a wee bit, mate," I said to Brandon as I was led away.

He half-dragged, half-marched me to a little room at the end of the corridor. Lester pushed me down hard onto a cracked black plastic chair at the far side of a worn table beneath a window with bars on it. There was an overflowing ashtray on the table. The walls were originally painted white, though were yellowed from smoke. He stood and glared down at me, grinding his teeth. Samuels walked in, surveying us for a moment by the door.

"Officer Lester, will we have a seat?" he said in an even tone.

Lester came back around the table and plonked himself down.

"Can we get these cuffs off first?" I asked, balancing awkwardly with my hands tied behind my back.

"Sure."

Samuels came around with his key. Lester gave a snort.

Samuels sat back down beside Lester, and I massaged my wrists.

"So, what am I doing here?" I asked.

Lester nearly choked on the cigarette he had just lit up. "You don't know? How about for beating up a group of teenagers?"

"I didn't beat anybody up. If I had done that, they wouldn't have been walking... or talking for that matter."

"But you were seen fighting with four teenage boys and they have each sustained injuries," broke in Samuels.

I could have used one of Lester's cigarettes, but I didn't want to have to ask for one.

"I was set on by said teenagers, they swung on me first. I even warned them to walk away or I'd have to put them down. I had my back to the fence and had no other option. Simple self-defence. I don't pretend to know all the laws of your country, but any reasonable law gives the right of reasonable force in defending yourself."

Lester just grunted again, but Samuels kept his cool eyes fixed on me. "Witnesses say your friend Brandon started it all. He swung on one of the kids first."

"Not true," I said. "The kid BB knocked Brandon to the ground during a game of ball and then he threw the first punch. Yes, Brandon knocked him on his ass, but he had no choice. Same deal. Self-defence. Then the other three had a crack at me and I dropped them. After that we walked away. If we'd wanted to, we could have done a lot worse. All we did was leave. No crime against that."

"So, you battered a bunch of teenagers and that should just be fine?" said Lester, breathing hard while puffing on his ciggy. "You think this is how this is going to work?"

"We should have just stood there and let them hit us? Allow them to knock us down and give us a kicking? All we wanted to do was talk and then leave. There were at least four witnesses who

DEATH NOTICE

will tell you the same, I dare say. It was all out in the open, we've nothing to hide."

Lester sulked backwards in his chair. Samuels chewed on what I had said.

"What was your purpose in being there in the first place?" Samuels asked.

I looked away. I didn't really want to have to get into that, but I knew I had to. At least they hadn't seemed to know about Brandon challenging BB to a fight first.

"Look, a friend of mine asked us to come here. Her cousin is missing, and she asked us to come out and help look for her."

"And you came all the way from Scotland to do that I suppose?" said Lester, dripping with sarcasm.

"I've never been to Scotland. I'm Irish. And no, I came from where I live in New York. Amy's a friend and asked for our help. Wouldn't have had to if you lot were doing your jobs right. I didn't expect to get set on by four meatheads high on testosterone and whatever else. I'm a decent guy and I'll consider not pressing charges against these angry young men."

This time Lester gave a loud and mirthless guffaw. "Very good of you."

I gave him a wide-open smile of my own. "It is, isn't it?"

"Wait here," said Samuels. "We have some more enquiries to make."

"Don't reckon you two are giving me much choice," I said.

They both left.

Lester forgot his smokes so I grabbed one and lit up. Stealing cigarettes from cops was kind of my new thing.

I puffed away, anxious that they'd come back and take it off me. Five minutes later and there was still no sign, so I had another. I thought through our conversation. I reckoned I'd given it a good go. I'd argued our corner, and it was even mostly all true. I wondered if Brandon was being grilled right now. Hopefully he was holding out okay.

Forty minutes passed and then the door near flew off the hinges. A red-faced Lester strode in. He leaned over the table and got right

43

in my face. I reckon he also clocked the three new butts in the ashtray. The thermostat on his face passed boiling.

"I've got my eye on you. Do you understand me?"

I shrugged. "You have your eye on me. Okay, I got it. I'm not really interested in a romantic relationship right now."

His nostrils flared and he dug his paws into the table, his knuckles reddening.

"BB's parents happen to be a big deal in this town and they're friends of mine. You put one more step out of line and we'll throw the book at you. Get it?"

"Are you telling me that we're free to go?"

A vein pulsed in his wrinkled forehead. He lowered his voice. "You can go."

"Great," I said in a jolly voice and stood up. "Thanks for the hospitality."

I walked past him towards the door and then he put a hand on my shirt and pulled me around. Instinctively I swiped his hand away. He eyeballed me, came in close again. His breath was rancid.

"I want you out of this town, out of this whole county," he wheezed.

I held his stare.

"Well, that's not really up to you, now, is it? I'll see you around."

DEATH NOTICE

Chapter 12

The cops weren't offering us a lift, so we got a cab to go and pick up the Hornet. Once safely inside, we each breathed out heavy sighs of relief.

"Well, that was fun," Brandon said.

We talked it all through. It hadn't been ideal, and we had learned nothing new, but we had initiated what damage control we could.

"Lunch?" I asked.

"Yep."

It was after two now and we were both starved. There was a McDonald's on the edge of town we'd spotted the day before, so we hit up the drive-through. I wouldn't let Brandon eat it in the car, so we sat in the sun on a picnic bench outside. Brandon sent a few texts back and forth to Amy. We didn't mention the incident. She'd find out at some point and be pissed, but I preferred us to postpone that particular conversation. She arranged to ring us that evening after her Mum had turned in for the night.

Fed and watered, we visited a few more of Lisa's school friends. It was all a similar story. They didn't have anything new to tell us, but at least we didn't beat any more of them up. One did suggest we speak to Lisa's school counsellor, and another said that we should talk to Lisa's boss at her parttime job. Those errands could wait for another day. We'd had two days crammed with travelling hundreds of miles, knocking on doors, getting in a fight and being arrested. By dinner time we were beat. We headed towards home, picked up a sixpack each and some pasta to boil for supper.

By seven or so we were sitting on the sofas, curtains drawn, electric heater going, and on our third beers. I remembered to check teletext for the Glentoran result. Brandon teased me as I faffed about trying to find the page.

"Frigsake," I said, finally tracking down the result. Finding Irish League results from Teletext in America was like searching for the holy grail.

"What?"

"We were beat three to one against Cliftonville." I checked the league table. We'd dropped another place. "Bugger."

"Three to one? Is that it? Don't think I'd like a game where there's so little scoring."

I gave him a look and eased back against the old worn fabric. "It's a game of *skill*, young Brandon. Tactics. Most football matches you're lucky to see one or two goals."

"Forget that. Sounds boring as hell."

I sighed. "If teams have a good defence, then it's hard. Doesn't mean the games aren't good. What about *your* football? Stopping every few seconds to all line up again. Stop, start, stop, start. Soccer is known as 'the beautiful game' for a reason."

"It's not *my* football. I'm not that keen on it. Gimme basketball or baseball any day."

"Right, next time there's a match on the telly, watch it with me and see what you think."

"A Glentoran game?"

"No way. They'd never show it on TV over here. They hardly even show them back home. Irish League is small fry."

Brandon finished rolling a joint. He licked the paper while looking at me quizzically. "So why do you support them then?"

I sighed again and shook my head. "Because they're my team. They've always been my team. My family's team. That's what you do."

Brandon shrugged back. "I guess."

"Is there no team you're really into?"

Brandon took a drag, exhaled, and nestled himself in the corner of his sofa. "No, not really. Suppose there was nobody to take me to any games."

I nodded. I'd forgotten that his childhood had been pretty rough. I may have grown up in a war zone, but at least I'd had family. Now there was no war, but I also had no family. As Heaney once said, 'Childhood is, generally speaking, a preparation for disappointment.'

"Well, you name the sport, and we'll go some time."

"Deal."

Then Brandon sat up. "Oh, hey. I picked up a deck of cards the other day. Fancy a game?"

DEATH NOTICE

"Sure. What do you usually play? Poker? I know a few rule sets. Texas, seven card, Southern Cross."

"Nah, I've never played poker." He said got up and lifted the deck out of his backpack. "I only know one game. Continental." He sat back down, ripped the seal and began shuffling.

"Continental? Never heard of it."

"It's good. Pretty easy to get the hang of. Me and my gramma used to play."

"Okay, cool," I leaned forward over the little coffee table. I moved the beers and ashtray to make space as Brandon began dealing.

"Okay Mick, so you make three sets of trips in your hand. Each go you can pick a new card and throw one down. Once you make three trips in your hand, you throw them down face up, then you gotta make more trips out of what's showing. Get it?"

I made a face. "Hold on. Trips? You mean tricks?"

"No, trips. You got to match three of a kind. You start talking about *tricks* over here, that's something else." He grinned.

"Aye, well I know that. Anyway, deal them out. I'll pick it up."

We played for about an hour. We had another beer each and smoked our brains. Brandon kicked my ass despite his weed consumption. But it was fun. The time passed quickly. Then his phone started to vibrate and *cheep* at us. I think the tune it played was something by Mozart or Beethoven. We both stopped dead and Brandon scooped it up.

"It's Amy." He pressed the receive button.

"Hope she didn't hear about the cops," I whispered, pulling a face.

"Amy. How you doing?"

Brandon pumped up the volume button and held the phone between us.

"Brandon. Good to hear your voice. Are you guys okay?"

"Yeah, great. Mick's here beside me."

"Hi, Amy," I shouted towards it.

Brandon winced. "Hell, Mick. Not so loud.

Amy laughed at the other end. "Hi, Mick."

We told Amy about the day. I skipped over the incident with BB and the cops:

"BB? That's a long story, but we didn't get anything from him."

We went on to talk through the others we had visited, and she was keen to check that we were finding the motel okay and thanked us again for being there. Amy told us her mum was bedridden for now but doing well. She hoped to drive across to spend the day at some point over the next week. By then she might be able to leave her mum by herself again, visit her at the weekends, and keep daily contact by phone.

I heard her take a drink of something and her voice dropped a little.

"So, I wanted to ask, so far… I know it's early, but any thoughts? Be honest with me. What do you think's happened to Lisa?"

Brandon made a face. I raised my empty hands at him. He set the phone down carefully in front of us beside the cards and began building a new spliff. Clearly, he wanted me to answer that one.

"It's difficult, Amy," I began. "Like you say, it's early days." I was very careful to choose my words. I wished I hadn't had that last beer. It wasn't helping any. "Certainly, it seems very out of character for her to disappear like that. Everyone we've met so far speaks very highly of her."

I heard Amy breathing softly in and out, just listening. "Okay," she said in a knowing tone. "But, Mick, I'm a big girl. Level with me. You think she's in pretty bad trouble, right?"

Brandon's eyes bulged as he glanced over at me.

"Okay, look. There's really no way of knowing yet and I've no particular theory in mind… I really don't. But, I do think it's unlikely that she left on her own accord."

"Thanks for being honest with me."

"I'm just sorry that things aren't a bit brighter. But also, even if she has… been *taken* in some way… it doesn't mean..."

"I know, I know," she said in a quiet voice. "Guys, I'm sorry. I can hear my Mom's out of bed, I need to go. Thank you both again so much. Ring you tomorrow?"

"Yes… speak then. Hopefully we'll have learned a bit more," I said, uselessly.

DEATH NOTICE

"Take it easy, Ames," Brandon said, trying to sound upbeat.

"Bye."

She hung up.

We shared a look. "Jeez Louise," I said. "This is tough."

Brandon nodded. "Want some of this?" He raised up the fresh joint.

"Aye, I think I will."

Chapter 13

The next day was Sunday. We skipped church and went for a greasy breakfast. Afterwards we called to a few of Rose's neighbours. They didn't have anything much useful to tell us. Then we dropped by to see Rose too. She seemed pleased to see us and made us some coffee, while we filled her in what had been done so far. Again, we skipped over the icky bit with the fight. After we left, I parked the Hornet a little further down the road and we walked back and forth along the stretch that Lisa was meant to have trekked that night she went missing.

There was nothing much to take note of. Most of the houses looked well kept. Some were concealed by hedges, others built quite close to the street, with little driveways. It felt like an area you would feel safe in. It was too early for streetlights to be on, but I noted there were ample amounts of them dotted around. There was nothing else around other than houses. No shop, no park, nothing.

"So, what now, big chief?" Brandon asked, finishing off a discreet little one-skinner.

"Now we knock on some more doors."

We did just that. We called to about a dozen houses. Nine of them answered. Most who did only spoke for a second or two to tell us they had seen and heard nothing that night. Others just slammed the door on us. Two of them had said they had been visited by the Sheriff's Department. At least the police had tried something. But nobody had anything useful to tell us.

Dejected, we walked up to the door of 2 Cain Street. We walked along the path, by the neat flowerbeds, up to the front steps. The windowsills were ordained with pretty flower boxes and there was a stitched sign on the door with some bible verses written on it.

I gave the door a loud rap and waited for a few moments.

"Will we knock again?" Brandon asked, looking keen to call it a day soon.

"The postman only knocks twice," I said.

"What?"

DEATH NOTICE

"Nothing."

Just then the door was pulled back and a large, stout black lady of perhaps eighty looked out at us.

"Hello?" she asked, a little uncertain, but in a rich, crisp voice.

"Hello, sorry to bother you," I said. "We're looking into the missing girl. You may have heard about her. Lisa Kendrix?"

"Yes, uh-huh." She looked over her large, purple-tinted glasses at each of us.

"We just wanted to know if you heard or saw anything the night she went missing?"

"Well... Yes... Are you from the Sheriff's office?"

"No... We're private. We've been instructed by her mother. Rose Kendrix." I said.

She tutted loudly and frowned. I thought she was about to ask us to leave.

"I'm sorry. It's just that I've left them several messages and they are yet to return my calls."

"Oh," Brandon said. "So did you see something?"

"Why, yes," she said, giving us a little smile. "Please come through, won't you?"

We thanked her and said we'd be glad to.

She told us her name was Anna Ross, as she led us through a tidy but cluttered hallway, on into a snug living room, cosy with old timey sofas and pine furniture. We declined the offered refreshments and were invited to sit on a small sofa with a blanket on it stitched with chickens and other assorted farm animals. Anna Ross took the other sofa, wincing in pain as she bent her knees to sit down.

"Again, Mrs Ross, we apologise for disturbing you."

"Not at all, not at all," she said waving it away. "And it's actually Ms Ross; I never married. But please call me Anna."

Brandon smiled and nodded.

"Thank you, Anna," I said. "So... you said you had tried getting in touch with local law enforcement?" I could get used to this private detective lark.

"Yes, our inefficient, moronic Sheriff's Department," she said, raising an eyebrow and giving a little snort.

"We haven't had the best experience with them ourselves," I said, giving Brandon some side eye.

"I have left three messages for them over the last week and still no one has taken the trouble to get back to me."

"We're very glad to listen to you," Brandon said.

"Well, thank you, son. Such a nice young man," Anna said.

"Please, go ahead." I smiled and sat back a little.

"In the evenings, I like to sit and read. Over there, by the window," she said, waggling a finger. "I was doing so that night. Every now and then if there's a noise, I look outside, through the netting."

I could tell Brandon was supressing a smirk. Anna was clearly a bona fide neighbourhood curtain-twitcher. And that was exactly who we'd needed to find.

"And what did you see exactly, Anna?" I asked.

"Well, dear… it's more what I *heard*. At first anyways. I heard footsteps at the far end of the street. I set down my book and looked out and saw a girl making her way along the other side of the sidewalk there."

"And you're sure it was Lisa?" I asked.

"Well… I saw her picture in the local paper afterwards. I'm fairly certain, yes. And I saw something else."

Brandon leaned forward, as did I.

"I had gone back to my book, but a minute or so later I noticed lights streak across the blinds. I looked out again after a second or two. There was a van idling a little ways up. I heard a door shut and then it drove away."

"Did you see the driver?" I asked.

She shook her head.

"What about Lisa?" Brandon asked.

"I don't know for sure. But I saw no sign of her after that. If that even was her. I didn't think anything of it at the time."

"What colour was the van?" I asked.

"It was night, dear. I'm not sure. I think it was dark-coloured. Perhaps black."

"Did you see somebody actually get into it?"

"No, I didn't. I must have heard the door shut first. Yes, that's right. I saw the lights, heard the door shut and when I looked out it drove away." She shot us a sheepish smile. "Then I went back to my damn book."

"And the police don't know any of this?" I asked.

"No, they do not," she said crisply. "Despite my best efforts."

"Uh-huh," I said, rubbing my chin, looking at Brandon. He raised both eyebrows.

"What do you think?" asked Anna.

"I think that's a pretty crucial piece of evidence," I said.

"You think the man may have taken her?"

"It's possible," I said.

Her face crinkled and she looked over to Brandon, a question on her lined face.

"Might have happened that way," he said.

We finished up there a few minutes later and went out into the fresh air. It felt good. Then lighting up a smoke felt even better.

"Not good," I said as we ambled along further down the street.

Brandon shrugged, his face worried, "At least we found something out."

"True."

Spurred on by this, we called to a few more houses. Most of them offered nothing. But one gentleman in his sixties also remembered seeing the dark van driving up the street that night too.

We got back into the Hornet and I slotted in some Neil Young.

"Right, that's that, then. This time the cops aren't coming for us, we're about to go to them."

"What?" Brandon nearly choked on his joint.

"Yep. I want to get the feel for what they're doing exactly. And if they don't know about this van, so close to Lisa walking home, they need to."

"You think they're just a bit incompetent?" Brandon asked as the Hornet purred and we set off along the street.

"Either that, or they're hiding something," I said.

Chapter 14

I didn't want to bump into any of the cops we had encountered so far, so I decided we should head for the main county branch. It was about ten miles over in Blackwater. I didn't expect to see whoever was leading the investigation on a Sunday, if there *was* an investigation. But maybe I'd get an idea of the lay of the land and at least I could pass on what we had found out. Maybe that would make them take things more seriously.

It was early afternoon when we got to the town. Breakfast had kept us going, but we stopped for a takeout coffee and drank it in the car, sitting outside the copshop. It was situated just off the main road; a street substantially bigger than Six Mile, full of shops, bars and no less than three hardware stores. The head office of the County Sheriff's Department was a pretty big, red bricked affair, surrounded by a low fence and adorned with a couple of huge insignias. It was well maintained, with a neat patch of grass out front beside a car park with four or five panda cars parked there.

"You sure you want to do this?" Brandon asked, secreting his stash tin under his seat and dousing himself with a can of Axe deodorant. I knew it as *Lynx*.

"Yeah, why not?"

"Well, we haven't exactly been on good terms with them so far, Mick."

"That's their problem. And if they're doing a crap job of looking for Lisa, that's our problem. And we're going to make damn sure that it's also *their* problem to put right."

"Yeah, I guess. But between us lookin' into things on their patch and the stuff yesterday, they're gonna think we're just a couple of troublemakers. Just some guys trying to cause all kinds of chaos in their county."

I broke into a smile. "Ahh, but Brandon; 'The whole worl's in a state o' chassis.'"

Brandon rolled his eyes, "I guess I set you up for that," then he narrowed them again, "Sean O'Casey?" he asked.

DEATH NOTICE

I smiled wider. "Well, slap my ass and call me Betsy, the kid's been paying attention. Right, let's get going."

We marched up the concrete steps to the locked door. We had to give our names (well, our current names) into a receiver before getting buzzed in. There was a vague smell of damp and coffee as we passed through two huge old oak doors. Three cops in uniforms eyed as they exited past. We found ourselves in a narrow reception area with a long counter desk. Nobody was there. The door was ajar, leading to a larger office area. I shrugged and headed towards it.

"Mick... maybe we should wait..."

"Nah, frig it."

I pushed the door fully open and went inside, Brandon following close behind me.

Three people looked up as we came in. All were men and all looked vexed by our presence. A cop of about fifty, in civies, with glasses resting up on his forehead spoke first.

"You can't be in here. Go out and wait in the hall," he said irritably.

"Well now, you didn't say the magic word," I said, smiling out the side of my mouth.

The cop pulled his glasses off his head and scowled.

"Please," he said.

I knew that Brandon would be cringing behind me.

"Thank you," I said. "We're here to talk about Lisa Kendrix. We have some new information about her disappearance. We'll speak to the Sheriff himself if he's in."

We left the man with a fresh scowl on his face, rubbing a hand through his thin hair. We took a seat on a covered bench opposite the abandoned reception. Brandon shook his head and smirked.

"Mick, what's the matter with you?"

I shrugged back. "I'm just assertive," I said. "And I don't much like cops."

"You're blunt is what you are," he said.

"As Mr Yeats once said; 'Think like a wise man but communicate in the language of the people.'"

We waited for ten minutes before a severe looking woman with thick frames and blonde hair in a bun came to us. "Sorry for keeping you. The Sheriff will see you now."

"Oh… right," I said, a little taken aback. "Thanks."

We were led through the large communal area, all eyes on us, then on into a big office off to the left-hand side.

"He'll be with you in a few minutes," she said, starting to close the door behind her.

"Okay, thanks," I said.

Brandon gave me a look and we seated ourselves with our backs to the door in two sturdy, leather box chairs. There was a sprawling wooden desk in front of us with a phone, computer, piles of sheets and a family photo. The room stank of tobacco, and I thought maybe Bourbon too. There was a large window with horizontal slats looking out towards the town. On the walls were certificates, an old blackboard with faded chalk marks and framed photographs of the Sheriff shaking hands with people I didn't recognise. On the back wall was another large Sheriff insignia.

"How are you doing, folks?"

We turned in our seats as the Sheriff strode through the door behind us. He was in full regalia, complete with a side-arm and Stetson hat.

"Please, please don't get up," he bellowed, reaching down to shake hands with both of us.

"I'm Mick."

"Brandon."

"Trent Peterson. Pleased to meet you both," he said, pumping our hands.

He eased back up and whipped around to the other side of the desk, his long legs only needing a few paces. He was maybe close to sixty-five, but still tall and strong. He threw himself down in his chair and laid a hand on his bushy moustache.

"Can I offer you good folks something? Coffee?" He was white, but his charismatic voice sounded to me more like it belonged to a black southern Baptist preacher.

"No, we're good, thanks," I said.

Brandon waved away the offer.

DEATH NOTICE

"Fine, fine. So, what can I do you for?"

He leaned back in his chair, opened his drawer, pulled out a cigar and clipped the end off it.

"Sheriff, we're here to talk about Lisa Kendrix." I said.

"Ahh yes..." The sheriff struck a match. "The girl who's gone walkabout." His craggy face grew a few more lines as he *puff-puffed* to get the cigar going.

"We don't think she's gone *walkabout*," Brandon said dryly.

"Well, heck, what do you suppose happened? We have us a quiet couple of towns here. Good people going about their own business. We don't get much trouble."

"It doesn't seem like she'd be the kind to disappear like this," I said.

Sheriff Trent Peterson knocked ash off his cigar and placed a long-booted leg up on the desk. He eyed me with one twinkly eye. "And what exactly is your concern in this here thing, if I may ask son?"

"Lisa's cousin, Amy, is a good friend of ours. Amy and Mrs Kendrix asked us to come and help look for her."

"Uh-huh." He puffed for a moment. "Please, smoke if you'd like to," he said, gesturing to another ashtray.

He must have seen me fidgeting. I thumbed one out of the deck and another for Brandon. He kept his narrowed eyes on us. "I uh... hear you boys got in some trouble over in Six Mile."

I blew out some smoke. "You could say that. It wasn't anything we went looking for."

He waved a hand, dismissing it, "Oh, I don't care about that bullshit. I may have a nice quiet county to run, but it still takes some running. I got bigger things to worry about."

"Bigger things than Lisa going missing?" Brandon asked.

"Maybe even abducted?" I added.

"Aww, now. I didn't mean it like that," he said, forcing a smile and pointing a long finger towards Brandon. "Besides, seems to me this young lady will turn up in a day or two. I mean, heck, she's done this before."

"Just one time," Brandon said irritably. I put a hand on his leg.

"Sheriff, that was just a one-off thing. After her father died. A long time ago for someone so young. Everybody tells us she's a pleasant and quiet young girl, who wouldn't want to cause any more hurt on her mother. The whole thing seems strange to me. Just walking back home after studying. Doing homework with a friend, getting prepared for school the next day. Besides, we've learned a few things you don't know about yet."

There was a twitch in his face. He dropped the leg and leaned over the desk. "I'm listening", he said.

We told him about the neighbours we'd spoken to that morning. He listened carefully, puffing away on his cigar, chomping it between his yellowing teeth. When we'd finished speaking, he chewed that over too.

"Well alright then, fellas. We'll take another look at this thing, okay? We'll get a few men put to work on it. I'll speak to my deputies first thing tomorrow morning. Good enough?"

He stood up and it was clear the discussion was over.

"Real nice meeting you boys, you leave it to us now, okay?" he said and offered his hand again.

"We'll see," I said.

DEATH NOTICE

Chapter 15

"So, what did you think of John Wayne there?" Brandon asked after lighting up a spliff.

The Hornet pulled out of the street and towards the intersect.

"I think he was palming us off a little. I'm not sure he's going to do much."

"I'm sure he'll do nothing," Brandon said.

"Yeah, maybe." I popped a fresh cigarette in my mouth. "As my gran used to say, he's 'too sweet to be wholesome."

"Yep."

Amy phoned not long after we got back to the motel. We filled her in on everything for about a half hour and she told us she was definitely driving up the next day to spend a few hours with us. It was sending her crazy not being here, not feeling properly involved. I didn't try and argue. I knew she'd already be wrecked, emotionally and physically, from looking after her mum. A big drive back and forth looking for her missing cousin wouldn't be much of a breather. But I also knew well enough not to argue the point, and Brandon knew too.

Afterwards we ate a little dinner, watched some TV, then Brandon lifted up the deck and we fell into two hours of cards. We also got fairly drunk. We both needed to let off some steam. After playing a hand, well into the evening now, Brandon turned to me.

"So, Mick. What we got so far do you think? Anything?"

I looked up from my cards, relieved to abandon my inability to work out if I had three tricks or only two. I'd moved onto whiskey and things were starting to spin just a touch. I had got out a lovely bottle of Jameson and filled my tumbler with ice and just a splash of lemonade. Delicious. I set my cards face down and lit up a smoke, pushing my advancing drunkenness to one side.

"Well, bud, let's see. We know there was a dark van around the time that Lisa was walking home. If we take what Anna says as gospel, it sounds very much like she disappeared at that same time."

"Yup. But what about suspects? What do you think? Anybody sus we've met so far? I don't like the ex."

"I don't like him either, but do you *like him* for taking her?"

Brandon set his own cards down and took a sip of beer, "Well yeah... Maybe. Could have been him. Who knows what goes on in some meathead's brain when he gets dumped."

"True, I suppose. I have more of a red flag popping up over the cops, to be honest."

"Really?"

"Well, yeah. I don't like how they seemed so on our back as soon as we got here. Along with that, they haven't exactly been pushing themselves over Lisa. I can't decide if they're just plain incompetent or if they're hiding something. I could see that asshole Lester doing something like it. That guy is clearly unhinged."

"And the Sheriff?" Brandon asked, now rolling grass-filled papers skilfully between his fingertips.

"I don't know. Hard to know what he's really like. He was too busy being the all-American sheriff and fobbing us off at the same time. Could be anything behind that mask."

"You think it's a big act?"

I shrugged. "Probably, but who knows? We'll need to wait and see. Maybe not wait as such. We'll poke the bear again at some point soon, I'm certain of that. If we need to make nuisances of ourselves, we will. Maybe then we'll see if the mask moves any." A nice quote from Wilde slipped into my fuzzy mind, "'Man is least himself when he talks in his own person. Give him a mask and he will tell you the truth.'"

"Deep, man," Brandon said coyly, lighting up.

"I try."

"Maybe something will shake loose tomorrow."

"Yeah, I hope so," I said.

Brandon took a long drag before exhaling. "Did you any of this kind of detective type stuff when you were... you know... in the IRA?"

"It's okay, Brandon. IRA isn't a bad word. Actually, it's a synonym," I said slurring a little. "Or some sort of 'nym. But it's still not bad."

"Yeah, well, they did try and kill you. Me too."

"Aye, there is that. I suppose after last year I have an even more complicated view of my past than I did already. But to answer your question, young Brandon, yeah, I did a bit of this. Not detecting exactly, but similar skills. And sometimes…" I blew out my cheeks, "I had to weed out informers."

"You did? But…"

"I know. But you need to remember I was with them a long time before I became *a bloody tout* myself."

"You had good reasons to leave," Brandon said softly.

"Yeah, I did. But before that I believed in it like people believe God is up there on a cloud in the sky. It was everything to me."

"You did what you thought you needed to do."

"Cheers mate, that's true enough. Whatever I did is done and I know I can't change it. All I can try and do, is do better."

The ashes of the conversation hung heavily in the air. With anybody else the silence might have felt awkward, but not with Brandon. We had been through much together and had already discovered just about every side of one another in a very short space of time. With other friendships, that can take years. Decades even.

"It's getting pretty late, Mick. One more before bed?"

I lifted up the bottle of whiskey. "Here's another Oscar one for you, Brand; 'Everything in moderation, including moderation.'"

Chapter 16

My head was a little sore the next morning- nothing that some water and a few paracetamols wouldn't fix. We had a rather frugal breakfast. Plenty of coffee and little else. Then we hit the road to find Lisa's college.

"Right, lad," I said, rifling through my CD's as I drove. "Time to try you on a little Therapy? again."

Brandon groaned. "Which ones are they again?"

"Northern Irish rockers. Bit of metal, bit of punk."

"Terrific."

"Now, come on. I know guitar music isn't your main squeeze but give it a try."

"Do I have any choice?"

"No."

I made my selection and slipped it from the case, "Right, everybody likes the *Troublegum* album. Wrap this around your lug holes."

I cranked it up.

Brandon near jumped out of his seat as *Knives* kicked in with its meaty riffage and Andy Cairns's throaty, "My girlfriend says, I need help. My boyfriend says, I'd be better off dead."

Brandon made a guffaw. He didn't really dig the record, though admitted that *Screamager* was a good song. So, he was human after all.

"Looks like this is us here," I said, indicating and turning off towards the college along Civvy Street. It was a fine-looking place, all big trees, rich green grass and red bricks. We spoke with a receptionist who asked us to wait in a bright hallway with lots of art on the walls. To our surprise the headmistress agreed to see us right away. She appeared to have genuine concern for Lisa and agreed that it was out of character and deeply concerning that she had now been missing for most of a week. She was very open, but there wasn't much she was able to tell us that we didn't already know. We asked if we could also speak with Lisa's guidance counsellor; Angela Catherwood. Again, to our surprise, we were

DEATH NOTICE

almost immediately taken to see her. Angela Catherwood's office was on the top floor, along a corridor on the west wing, overlooking the playing fields.

Me and Brandon sat down on an empty row of plastic chairs in another echoey corridor. Our student guide told us that we'd be seen in a few minutes, before leaving us alone.

"I feel like we've been sent to the principal's office," I said.

"We've already been there."

"True."

"You didn't get in trouble in school, now did you, Mick?"

"Aye. Once or twice. I'm sure you were always a model student too."

Brandon raised his eyes. "You might be surprised."

"Well, I wasn't really that bad either. I do remember one time me and my mates getting scooped and sent to see the headmaster for a good beating with the hurley stick he kept under his desk."

"Those things hurt," Brandon said, giving me a look.

"Aye, I forgot about that," I gave him a wink. "Anyways, every week we'd been nicking this teacher's dusters at break time. Every time we had French class, we'd wait eagerly to see what the replacement was. The first few weeks there were just other dusters- but I guess there wasn't an endless supply. One week, he was reduced to using a cloth. We nicked that too. Then the next week was just a piece of kitchen roll. We snagged that. Finally, he was left using his sleeve. The day we went to pinch his jacket from his room, we got caught."

Brandon shook his head.

I regaled him with a few more schoolboy gems until the door opened.

"Sorry to keep you. Pleased to meet you both. I'm Angela."

The first thing to hit me was how young she looked. The second was that she was very attractive.

We all shook hands. She showed us into her bright and well-ordered office. As I sat down, I kept my eyes on her, barely believing that she was a member of staff. She had to be early twenties at most. Angela had quite the refined voice, an easy manner and a lovely smile. She had blonde hair tied back, a good figure, and was quite short.

"Can I get you guys a coffee? Water?" she asked after we took our seats.

"No, I'm grand, thanks." I turned to Brandon.

"No, I'm good." Brandon also looked a little smitten.

"So," she said, clasping her hands together, her long nails immaculate and painted scarlet. She frowned and her voice lowered, "The principal tells me you'd like to talk about Lisa?"

"Yes," I said, "We're friends of the family and have been asked to try and help find her."

She nodded and gave a little smile. "I understand. Anything I can do; I'd be more than happy to help. Lisa is..." she paused, looking like the words had caught in her throat, "...a really wonderful young lady."

"Can you think of any reason why Lisa would disappear?" I asked.

Angela looked over the top of my head and chewed on her lip. She opened her hands and shook her head, "I have no idea. Lisa is a great girl, good to her mother, a dedicated student. She works a part time job too and always manages her schoolwork well." She shook her head again, "She just seemed to be doing so well... She was happy."

"She's really made an impression on people," Brandon said. "Everybody keeps saying nice things about her."

Angela smiled warmly at Brandon, then her face cracked a little and a tear fell from one eye. She plucked a tissue from a box on her desk and carefully wiped her lower lid.

"I'm sorry," she said, a little flustered.

"Please," I said. "Don't worry. Take your time."

"Thank you." She looked out the window, took a deep breath and turned back to us.

"Angela, can you tell us anything about what you two talked about in here? I know that might be tricky," I said.

She nodded thoughtfully. "I understand. You're right, it is difficult. I'm her school counsellor and what we discuss is

DEATH NOTICE

confidential. However, that right to confidentiality could be broken if I had information that might help if she was in danger."

"Sure," I said.

"In a way it *is* easy, because I can honestly say that she told me nothing of concern. I said the same to the police."

"The police came to see you?" I asked.

"Yes. Well actually my... well, my *boyfriend* works for the Sheriff's Department. So, I haven't actually been interviewed officially by them as such." She shrugged, struggling for the words again, embarrassed by the word *boyfriend*. "It wasn't necessary because I don't know anything."

"I get it," I said. "We've actually met a few of the local police. Maybe we've seen him?"

"Oh." She looked a little embarrassed again. "Yes, he is called Officer Samuels."

"Yeah, we've met him," Brandon said.

"Nice fella," I said. "I'm not so keen on his partner."

She gave a wry smile. "Ah, yes." She laughed. "His bark is worse than his bite."

"I'm sure," I said.

The conversation wound up naturally after that and she showed us out.

"Woo," Brandon said in the car, with a cheeky grin.

"What?" I asked, not understanding the noise.

"C'mon, Mick, she was a fox."

I near choked on my cigarette. "A fox? Do people say that?"

"Uh, yeah. And c'mon. You know she is."

"Yeah. I mean, I suppose."

Brandon crossed his legs and took a pull on his joint. "Maybe you only got eyes for one lady."

I felt my jaw tighten.

We had never talked about any feelings I may or not have for Amy. I mostly tried to not think about it too much myself.

"Brandon, wise up."

He shook his head and blew smoke out the window. "Whatever, Mick."

"What did you think about what she said?" I asked, trying to change the subject without looking too irritated.

"About being with Samuels?" Brandon said.

"Well, yeah... everything. What did you make of her?"

He took another slow drag. His eyes were already beginning to dilate. "I guess she was okay. Seemed a nice person. What you think?"

"She seemed nice enough... I don't know."

"You think she was holding something back?"

I thought about that, took in a long drag myself and then expelled it. "Yeah, I think I do."

"You thought the same about Lisa's classmate. What you call her? Sara?"

"Zara."

"Yeah, her. Maybe you just have a problem trusting women, Mick."

"Aye, that must be it."

"And was Zara a *fox* too?" I asked.

"Shut up, Mick."

DEATH NOTICE

Chapter 17

Amy had texted to say she was looking good for arriving around three. We had some time to kill, so went into the town. I found a space in a car park off the main street easy enough and we had an explore around the centre. We called into Crawford Realtors which was where Lisa had a part-time job. The rather austere receptionist turned out to be quite helpful and said that we could speak with Mr Marcus Crawford in the late afternoon. That worked better for us because it meant Amy could come along too if she wanted. I understood that she felt disconnected with not being able to do much herself, so at least she could be there for that interview.

The town centre was well kept and busy, a nice little out of the way place. We found a shop that did some delicious sub sandwiches, ordered them with a couple of Cokes, and sat by a fountain outside the smart sandstone town hall. After the inevitable couple of smokes, we went on for another explore around the shops. We found a classy little second-hand bookshop. I merrily passed a good half hour inside, picked up a couple of thrillers and a collection of letters by Sean O'Casey that I'd never read. Even better, afterwards we found a very cool record shop called Bongo Fury. To my horror, Brandon picked up a few CDs that he said he would introduce to me during our travels. My poor Hornet's sound system might be sullied, but I kept an open mind. The prices were good, and I picked up five or six new CDs myself. I didn't currently own a turntable, but when I found a mint vinyl copy of Neil Young's *Harvest* going for a song, I snagged that too.

Sure enough, around three, Brandon's phone began playing its Sega-style classical music ringtone. We arranged to meet Amy in a carpark beside the bus station. As she walked across the asphalt towards us, I felt a flutter in my stomach. She was dressed in one of her no nonsense, stylish black trouser suits. Brandon waved and she waved back as we sped up towards one another. She was looking well and smiling. A step away, she pulled back her fist and hit me a hard punch on the arm.

"What the heck?" I asked, sore but smiling.

Amy was smiling too. But narrowed her eyes. "That was for your little scuffle the other day."

"Oh, you heard about that?" I rubbed my arm.

"Yeah, I did."

"It was all Brandon," I said with a wink.

Brandon made a pained expression before digging me on the other arm.

"Jesus, if youse keep punching me, I'm off. Racists."

Amy took us to a café she knew just a few streets away on Morrison Avenue. We asked her about her mum, and she filled us in. She asked about our progress, and we told her about that, little as it was. Despite the meagre pickings we had discovered, she was very grateful. She also pointed out that we had actually found out some new information and had pushed the cops into further action. I suppose that was true. Thankfully she wasn't really too pissed about the little altercation in the park.

Amy stirred the bottom of the glass of her latte, scooping up the last drops of coffee and mixing it with the remaining foam. She turned her wrist to look at her watch. "So, I really need to hit the road at least by nine. I'll make it home early morning if I do, then I'll grab a few hours of sleep. My Mom's neighbour is sleeping over tonight, and I can take over again mid-morning."

"Jaysus, girl, that's a lot," I said.

"Sure is," chipped in Brandon.

Amy picked up her spoon and licked some remnants of coffee. She shrugged. "Might as well stay for as long as I can. I've only just got here."

"I get it," I said.

"I'll come with you to see this realtor guy and then I'd like to spend a few hours with Auntie Rose."

"Sure, of course." I said, "Do you want us to come to her house too? We're happy to do whatever you want."

"Thanks, Mick." She gave me one of those genuinely warm smiles that only Amy could. "How about we all go see her, then I'll stay on, and you guys can get something to eat or something?"

DEATH NOTICE

"How about this," I said, necking the last of my own coffee before setting it down. "We'll leave you with Rose after a bit and then come meet you somewhere for a late dinner?"

She thought about it. "Yeah, that would be nice." She reached across the table and took each of our hands in her own.

Marcus Crawford was in his office talking to his receptionist when we arrived. He was tall and lean with pale skin and deep blue eyes. He was around my age, maybe forty-five. He was dressed in a good suit and nice shoes. Freshly polished by the look of them. He greeted us in a formal, but vaguely patronising way, the way some realtors can do. We passed on the offer of coffee and went into his office. The whole place was quite small, but his office was surprisingly large in relation. We took a seat on the leather furniture, opposite his glass-topped desk. The walls displayed a few certificates, a couple of noticeboards covered with house brochures and a few modern art pieces that were not to my taste. It was the kind of *art* that looked like a nursery child on a sugar high could knock off in three minutes.

"Terrible business about Lisa. Just awful," he said.

"It's very worrying," Amy said evenly. I could tell she was uncomfortable. She had carried out all sorts of interviews many times for the FBI. But not when it was to do with a member of her own family being in danger. I was kind of uncomfortable too. All week I'd been leading these things and now I didn't know how to position myself. I figured that I'd chip in when necessary and let Amy take the lead. Just like Brandon had done for me. Poor Brandon would probably be thinking the same and preparing to be practically mute for this one.

"And you're Amy's cousin?" Marcus said with sympathy, genuine or otherwise.

"Yes. And these are friends of mine. Mick and Brandon have come to help me find Lisa."

"Of course, of course. I only pray that you do. We're all praying for her you know, at Hardcastle Baptist… on Bridge Street?"

"Yeah, I know it," Amy said with the briefest of smiles.

"At Sunday service yesterday, the pastor led us in a special prayer for Lisa."

Amy's eyes narrowed, but she tried to force another smile, with little success, "Thank you, that's very kind. It's nice to know that people are doing all that they can."

He smiled widely, looking pleased with himself. Then he forced a solemn expression. "She will be remembered again at our prayer meeting on Tuesday night."

"Great," I said.

"Maybe some of your congregation could help give out some of the fliers? It might help with the search," Amy said. We're also trying to put some pressure on local government and law enforcement." Amy's voice was solid and her tone even, then it dropped just a notch, "Perhaps some of your congregation could help with those things too."

He got the message but pretended to ignore it. "Of course, of course, I'll talk with Pastor Simpson, and we will surely do anything we can. Be sure of that."

"Thank you, Mr Crawford." Amy said. "Okay, so could you tell me a little about what my cousin did for you?"

"Of course," he said, his smile a little forced. "Lisa was a great worker, super keen. She worked for us every Saturday morning… um… nine until about one. A little later if there was a lot on."

"What was her role exactly?" I asked.

"Oh, a little of everything. Lisa did some filing, answered the phones as Sheila doesn't work the weekends." He said nodded towards the door. "She also inputted some of our client information. Lisa was very good on the computer. Sorry, she *is* very good." He frowned, then picked up again. "Young people always seem to know what they're doing with computers," he said with a little chuckle.

Amy gave a taught smile. "Did you notice anything different about Lisa recently? Did she say anything to you that concerned you in any way?"

"To me? Oh no, nothing like that. I mean, I can't think of anything. Lisa just came in, went about her work, always with a smile, and went off again. Then I wouldn't see anything of her until the next week."

DEATH NOTICE

The conversation went on for another ten minutes or so, but frustratingly there was nothing new. We regrouped in a different coffee shop for some much-needed caffeine, particularly for Amy.

"He's a bit of a strange one," Amy said, starting in on her new latte.'

"God squad guys usually are," said Brandon.

"Yeah, but he's a little off, or is that just me?" Amy looked towards me.

"I guess he was a bit off. I don't know. Most people seem like pricks to me anyway," I said with a shrug. "I know what you mean, though He seemed maybe somewhat… nervous?"

"Yeah," Amy said thoughtfully. "Maybe that's to be expected. Us all landing in asking about his missing staff member. I don't know."

She breathed a long sigh, raised her arms and stretched them out. I tried to avoid looking at her body.

We talked some more about Crawford. I didn't know what else to say. He didn't seem like much to worry about to me, but I'd been wrong before. The trouble was, we still had so little to go on. I could tell it was all taking a toll on Amy. I also knew that there wasn't much else I could do or say to help that. There was too much on her plate, but it was her plate. We were all silent for a time, sipping our coffees. Perhaps I for one was taking my queue from Beckett. "Every word is like an unnecessary stain on silence."

Chapter 18

Auntie Rose plied us with yet more coffee, but none of us turned it down. The three of us sat in her living room while she buzzed about, following an emotional reunion with Amy. I felt a bit awkward being there and I could tell from Brandon's fidgeting and expression that he did too.

"I just want to thank you boys for all the hard work you're putting in," she said, easing back in her chair.

"It's our pleasure to try and help," I said. "Especially if you keep calling us *boys*."

She gave a little laugh and smiled.

"I can still pass as a boy," Brandon said. "Most people think you're my adopted dad."

She gave another little laugh.

"I would have raised him better," I said.

"We are both very grateful," Amy said, looking towards us.

"You know we want to do it," Brandon said simply.

Rose leaned forwards with a twinkle in her eye. She looked between Brandon and me. "I heard about the... the little thing in the park. With that good-for-nothing BB. Good for you."

A laugh started in my throat before another dig in the arm from Amy stopped it.

"Don't encourage them, Auntie," she said.

After a half hour, Brandon and I took our leave and left Amy and Auntie Rose to it. We headed back to the motel for some downtime. We sank a beer each, then had more coffee, some chocolate, a large bag of crisps. All the primary food groups.

"How do you think Amy's doing?" Brandon asked, sparking up a fresh joint during a commercial in an episode of *Friends*.

"Hard to say. She's holding up well I reckon, but you can see it weighing on her."

"True."

"She's hurting, like," I said. "And she'll be plum tuckered tomorrow."

DEATH NOTICE

"Plum tuckered?"

"Aye. Tired."

"Ah."

"God, another day and still there's no sign of Lisa. Not good."

"It's not, man," Brandon said. "What do you think happened to her? I mean…"

"I really don't know," I said, chomping on my ciggy.

"Do you think…?"

"Yeah, I think she's probably dead."

A little *bleep-bleep* sounded from Brandon's phone around six thirty. The text from Amy said she would meet us in a half hour at a spot called Ratz. We got ourselves tidied up again and headed out.

"Ratz?" I said when we were all seated together. "It's not the most inspiring name, is it?"

"It's a really nice restaurant," Amy said, looking indignant.

Sure enough, it was pretty fancy: classical music, heavy curtains, crisp tablecloths and sparkling cutlery.

"I'm sure it is, but Ratz?" I made a face.

"It's quirky," she said.

"Yeah, but I don't want to associate a nice meal out with vermin." I gave her a wink.

Amy shook her head.

"Some people just have no class Ames," Brandon said.

"I put a shirt on." I brushed a hand down my only mildly wrinkled black shirt.

"And I even left the cap at home." Brandon ran a hand over his cropped head.

"I'm out with two real gentlemen I guess," Amy said smiling, "I'm a lucky girl, and I mean that."

"You doing okay, Amy?" I asked, lowering my voice.

"Yeah, yeah I'm okay," she said, lifting the menu for a closer look.

A few minutes later and we had ordered and were sitting with our drinks.

We chatted about other things for a time, skating away from the pressing reason we were together.

"Did you hear about the last ibex?" Brandon said after supping on his bottle of Bud.

"Come again?" I said.

"The cat thing?" said Amy.

"Yeah. It was called a *Parny-something* Ibex," Brandon said. "Saw it on the TV earlier. It was the last of its kind and it died the other day. A tree fell on it."

"Is this the start of a joke or something?" I asked.

"No, for real. It was the last one in the whole damn world and a tree fell on it. Killed it stone dead. Now there's no more."

"Shit," said Amy.

"Shit indeed," I said. "Not the most glorious end to a species."

"Think I'd prefer an asteroid or something to wipe us all out. Like that movie," Brandon said.

"*Deep Impact*?" I asked.

"The other one."

I shrugged.

"More likely to be the Russians," Amy said.

"You were working for the FBI for too long, Amy," I said, then switched my gaze to Brandon. "And you... you're too young to be worrying about cataclysmic events."

"I'm closer in age to Amy than you are," he said.

I thought about that, doing the maths. "No, you're bloody not you wee eejit," I said.

"Yeah, but I made you think," Brandon said with a smirk.

Our food was soon served. Steaks for me and Brandon, a mushroom risotto for Amy. The conversation soon turned back to more serious matters.

"You sure you're okay going back tonight?" I asked between mouthfuls. "It's a big drive and it's pretty late."

"I guess," Amy said. "I don't really have much of a choice."

I nodded. "Hope you get a break soon."

"Doesn't look much that way," she said with a sigh. "With one thing or another. Well, that's not true. When my mom's asleep, I get to watch a little TV and do some sketching."

DEATH NOTICE

"Sketching?" Brandon asked.

"Yeah." Amy looked embarrassed. "I've tried getting back into some art."

"Cool," he said.

"I didn't know you could draw," I said.

"There's a lot you don't know."

"I bet. Do you paint too?"

Amy shrugged. "I used to do a bit of charcoal and chalk pastels. Not really painting. Mostly I like to sketch. It's… relaxing."

"I'd love to see some," I said.

Amy pulled a face, then changed the subject.

"I'm going to get in touch with somebody I used to work with tomorrow afternoon if I get the chance," she said.

"In the FBI?" I dipped a fat chargrilled piece of steak in my pepper sauce.

"Yeah. I knew a guy who has a good level of access. We worked on many things together. I guess we became pretty friendly. He's always been good at doing me a favour too."

"What are you going to get him to do?" Brandon asked.

"Run a check on the realtor first. Marcus Crawford. I don't know. I didn't really like the vibe I got off him. I mentioned that to Auntie Rose. She says she always found him pleasant enough, but once Lisa had said he made her a little uncomfortable."

"Really? How so?"

"He would throw about compliments sometimes. Say she was pretty or whatever. It was nothing more than that, but still. Anyone else I should run a check on while I'm at it?"

"That cop Lester maybe," I said.

"The cop? You think I should?"

"Couldn't hurt," I said, "He seemed to be on us from the start. I still don't like how the cops have dealt with all this. Maybe they're just bumbling hicks, but I can't be sure."

"Maybe check out the Sheriff too," Brandon said.

"Yeah, good call," Amy said. "Anyone else?"

"The boyfriend. BB or whatever his real name is," I said. "As you know he was somewhat *reluctant* to talk to us. And besides that, he's got reason to be involved in some way."

"I sure didn't like the creep," Brandon said.

Amy dabbed at her mouth with a linen napkin and looked up at the ceiling.

"Okay, I'll do that," Lisa said looking faraway. "Listen, guys, you know if this doesn't turn out well… I mean," she stumbled over her words. "Auntie Rose and me are both… realistic."

We nodded.

"You're doing great." I patted her hand. "You both are, really."

Amy forced a smile, then picked up her knife and fork and played with some stir-fried vegetables on her plate.

"Tomorrow, I want to go and speak with Amy's friend Zara again," I said. "And the school counsellor. Angela Catherwood. It felt like they were both holding back something."

"Damn," Amy said suddenly, setting her cutlery down with a clank. "I almost forgot to ask. Could you guys take Auntie Rose somewhere tomorrow?"

"Of course," I said.

"Where to Ames?" Brandon asked.

"I'm sorry. I meant to say earlier. My head is scrambled. A guy phoned while I was with Auntie Rose. He's from a missing persons' charity."

"Oh?"

"Yeah. He'd read about Lisa in the paper and offered his help. It totally slipped my mind." She shook her head, annoyed at herself.

I put up a hand. "Amy, you've a lot on. Don't be daft. Just tell us what you want, and we'll do it."

"Thanks. He's in Larnclair. That's a town about thirty miles west from here. Have you heard of it?"

"No, but we'll find it," I said.

"Can you pick up Auntie Rose around ten tomorrow?"

"Can do," Brandon said.

"No bother," I said." I think she likes us."

Amy smiled. "She does."

We had coffee after eating our meals, but skipped dessert. It was a quarter to nine and Amy needed to get back on the road. The streets were almost empty. It was chilly, but the rain and snow had

DEATH NOTICE

stayed away for the night. Brandon and I both chain-smoked as we walked Amy to her car, having made it all the way through dinner without sparking up. The car park was down a side street off the main shopping area surrounded by closed offices and a gym with its lights off. We hugged and wished Amy a safe journey back. I told her to stop for at least one coffee on route, take a break. I was worried about her. It was a long journey to start at night when you were already exhausted. We left her to get herself sorted and check her texts. We turned and walked back the way we had come. The Orange Beast was parked a street away on the other side of the town centre.

When we turned the corner, they were there waiting for us.

Three had scarves pulled up high over their faces and one wore a hockey mask.

Four big guys, all dressed in black.

Chapter 19

"I didn't make it to the last *Jason* movie," I said to the guy in the mask. "I heard it was a bit shite."

The man took a step forward, he seemed to be the leader. The second biggest stood beside him, both were slightly taller than me. The two flanking them were smaller: height and bulk. But they had baseball bats. I glanced at Brandon. He nodded and eased into a proprietary stance.

"Shut your mouth," Ski Mask rasped in a gravelly voice.

"That's not very nice," I said.

"You get once chance. Two choices. You leave town tonight or we make you leave. That simple enough for you?"

"Yeah, thanks for asking," I said. "I choose option three. We aren't going anywhere."

"Fine by us," he said, taking another step forward. There sounded to be a smile in his voice behind the mask.

"Four against two, including weapons. Not very sporting of you, but that's okay," I said undoing my top button.

"Four against three."

I turned as Amy lined up beside us.

"Thought you were gone," I said.

"Can't let you two have all the fun," she said and rolled her shoulders.

The two with the bats let out a cocky chuckle each. I was going to enjoy this.

"Last chance," snarled Ski Mask. "We'll teach you it's not safe to go walking around at night."

"In the words of Joyce," I said, "'You can die when the sun is shining.'"

The two on the wings advanced together, raising the bats as if they were about to try for a home run. I skipped forward two steps, crouched and leg-swept the closest one. He flew up in the air, bat still in hand. Before he landed, Brandon had moved in towards the second one. The guy swung the bat and Brandon dodged around it, shooting out a right hook, catching the guy in the face. He

DEATH NOTICE

dropped the bat and Brandon and him began exchanging blows. The second biggest guy pushed through the tangle as Amy advanced on him.

"I shouldn't really hit a..." he started to say as Amy fly kicked him in the face. While he was stunned, Amy moved in with a barrage of body shots.

Ski Mask squared up with me, boxing stance. He swung a right and caught my jaw. It hurt. That was okay, because I knew he'd leave himself open. I took it, ducked low and shot an uppercut into his chin. It was a good one. In fairness to him he pulled back and tried another punch. I dodged it and jabbed him a few times on the nose. It hurt my hand like all hell. I looked to see how the others were doing. The first guy was still on the deck, rubbing his head, blood on his hand as he inspected it. Brandon had taken a few punches but seemed to be getting the better of the guy. Amy seemed unscathed, still using her opponent like an old punchbag.

Ski Mask had recovered and tried putting me in a headlock. I slipped through and stomped my foot down his shin. He yelled and took a step back. Incapacitate your opponent in every way you can is a good rule to have. Next, I pulled back my arm to the full and launched a hard punch into his right wrist. He stumbled backwards, falling over the first guy and onto the dirty asphalt. Just then, Brandon threw an absolute corker and his one fell back against a stone wall before slumping down it. Amy had seemingly tired of giving the big lad a hiding and finished with a right foot to his balls. He doubled up and then went down.

Panting hard, we surveyed the scene. Four for four. All on the ground.

We regrouped, ready for any further attack. Amy looked fine. Brandon was okay, but bleeding from his nose and a cut on his cheek. My jaw was throbbing, and I could feel my hand already swelling up like The New Year Blimp. But we were alright.

The two smallest guys righted themselves, made it to their feet and started to run off. A moment later and Amy's guy staggered to his feet. He took a step and helped up Ski Mask. Brandon was off to one side, about three yards from them. He bent down and picked up one of the bats and held it at his side. Amy snatched up the other one.

The two wounded men looked at each other. I could only see their eyes. They told me everything.

"You better get the fuck out of here," Ski Mask said thickly.

Amy took a step forwards. They shuffled and then began backing away. Brandon moved towards them too, bat raised.

"Fuck you," one of them muttered. Then they both turned and hurried back along the sidewalk, their two comrades already lost to sight.

"Enjoy the rest of your night," I shouted after them. "You two okay?" I asked, turning to Amy and Brandon.

"Fine," Amy said.

"Not bad, you?" Brandon asked.

"Good. Yeah, I'm alright. Jesus. I wasn't expecting that."

"Nope," Brandon said.

"Well, I think I needed it," Amy said, smiling through her perspiring face. She bloody still looked beautiful.

"What the hell was all that?" Brandon said.

"I'm not sure," Amy said, pulling out her hair bobble and putting in a fresh ponytail.

"I know one thing. The guy with the ski mask… I knew his voice and the body fit too," I said.

"Who was it?" Amy said.

"Lester, the dick-head cop."

DEATH NOTICE

Chapter 20

I knew where I wanted to go the next morning. But first I'd needed a basin of ice. And coffee. Lots of it. We were in the Hornet by eight am. The night before, Amy had headed off after a short debrief. Physically she was fine. Me and Brandon not quite as good. I'd gone back to the motel and iced my swollen hand. My cheek was a little swollen too and I put some ice on that as well. Brandon had a cut on his cheek and a bloodied nose that I cleaned up for him. He also needed to ice his swollen knuckles on both hands. They were still nothing compared to my comical looking club-hand.

"No jerking off for a day or two," Brandon had said helpfully.

We'd watched some TV and chatted, too hyped up and sore to hit the hay early. We had the post-adrenaline rush need to unwind some. A documentary came on about Northern Ireland and the tentative peace agreement back home. I was happy to flick past it, but Brandon said to leave it on.

"Be good if I learned something. Maybe I'll understand a bit more about why we nearly got killed last year," he said.

The documentary was alright. It was a little Americanised, but then this was America. Brandon appeared captivated throughout. He smoked quietly, focused in on the voiceover, accompanying footage and stills explaining about the partition of Ireland, through The Troubles and up to the present.

"So how long was Ireland part of England?" Brandon asked.

"It was never part of England as such. It wasn't even a colony really. Well, they kind of invaded and took over hundreds of years ago, but there were always rebellions. Then later The Act of Union joined Ireland, England, Scotland and Wales into The United Kingdom."

"Pretty confusing."

"It truly is. And I'm from there."

"So why was only the north part still part of United Kingdom later on?" Brandon asked.

I exhaled, sighed and lit up a smoke. "Well now, that's the

question," I said. "Basically, there was a Protestant and Unionist small majority, so they fixed it that they would always be in control in the North. Some down South were happy enough to get any independence for Ireland, while some fought on. Then there was a civil war in the new Irish Free State. Those who wanted to push to get the north back. Brother fighting against brother."

"Wow, really?"

"Aye, even my different sets of grandparents were all on varying sides at different times. It's fair to say that Ireland and the Irish are in a constant state of flux."

"But you wanted a whole United Ireland?"

"Yeah, still do. Just, I don't think people should keep killing each other for it. You have to understand, when I was a kid in the sixties, Catholics didn't have jobs, and didn't have decent houses. Hell, most didn't even have a right to vote. Totally segregated."

"I hear ya," Brandon said with a look.

"It really was like that. That's why the civil rights guys took a lot of inspiration from the black movement over here."

Brandon looked thoughtful, then painfully raised up his beer and took a sip. "Apart from your taste in music, I guess it makes sense that we'd be buds," he said.

"And I'm thankful for that," I said.

By morning, all our minor injuries had faded somewhat. Popping a few paracetamols had taken the edge off. Brandon aided his with an herbal remedy too.

"Is there any point to this?" Brandon asked, sleepily looking out of the window.

"Might not be," I said, pulling up outside the Six Mile police station.

I lit up a ciggy, leaned back in my chair, and watched for the comings and goings. So far there weren't any.

"You don't even know if he's on today or what time he'd start."

"True. But it's worth getting up an hour early if we catch him."

"I suppose," Brandon said with another sigh. "It's not like he's going to admit anything anyways."

"Aye, but he'll know that *I* know."

DEATH NOTICE

"And what is that exactly?"

"Well, I'm not sure. But he was the one who led the posse to run us gunslingers out of town. And we haven't even slung our guns yet."

At five minutes to nine, our patience and curtailed sleep paid off. Lester arrived in an old brown Ford, pulling up in the parking lot.

"Told ya," I said, crushing out my fourth cigarette and getting out. I strode across to the open gates, just as he was getting out of his car. He had on his uniform, looking a little dishevelled. His right sleeve on his tan shirt was rolled up to the elbow. There was a bandage covering his wrist.

"Good morning," I shouted behind him.

He gave a start and swung around. His eyes widened when he saw me. Then he scowled.

"Good night?" I asked.

"What?"

"Did you have a good night?"

"Get lost."

We locked eyes, an understanding.

"Next time you'd best bring your hockey stick too," I said and turned on my heel.

"Well?" Brandon said as I got back in the car.

"Yeah." I smiled and lit up another. "Felt pretty fucking good."

We arrived at Auntie Rose's house in good time. She brought us inside for a quick coffee. I was glad. She made a good brew. Then we hit the road, Brandon in back, no smoking for either of us. I'd sprayed some deodorant about the car beforehand and left the windows down. It was a little cold, so I cranked up the heating to compensate. I had a middle of the road station on the radio, and we all chatted along quite happily. Rose was dressed particularly smartly in a cream blouse, skirt and decorative scarf. She had also applied a little more makeup than usual and was quite upbeat. I guessed that being able to do something more practical and having the offer of further help had caused the change in her. At her house, she had been concerned about our obvious injuries. We had told that her what had happened, but not of our suspicions of it being a crew led by Lester. She said it was probably BB's father and his beer buddies. I thought about that and supposed we both might have been right. I didn't think it was very likely to be anything directly to do with Lisa's disappearance but couldn't be certain.

"Do you know this place much?" Brandon asked from the backseat, as we sped along the freeway.

"Yes dear," Rose said turning. "My husband used to work there for a time. The commute was a bit of a chore. Sometimes we'd go there as a family on weekends too. Spring fairs, Thanksgiving, that type of thing."

"A nice place then?" I asked.

"It is. Not as nice as Six Mile, though I suppose I'm biased," she said.

An hour or so later and Rose had directed us capably to a row of offices on the edge of Larnclair. She pointed me to a carpark behind. There were various offices, a café, a bookmaker's and a corner shop. It seemed nice enough but had more of an inner city feel than anything in the other local towns I'd seen so far. Rose wiped her palms down her skirt and then asked for a moment to reapply some makeup. Then we made our way around to the front entrance. There was a small sign on the glass door and a smaller one beside the buzzer both inscribed with the abbreviation FAM and below it in finer print; FAMILY ADVICE FOR MISSING PERSONS.

"I guess we're here," Brandon said.

"Ready?" I asked, putting a hand on Rose's arm. She nodded.

We walked up the one floor to the FAM office. It was the middle level and took over the whole floor, though there wasn't all that much of it. There was a small reception area, a meeting room and an office. A chatty black lady of a about fifty greeted us on our arrival. She had thick curly hair, brown eyes and an easy smile. She left to make us some coffee as Dustin McKeith strode out of his office to introduce himself.

"Dustin McKeith, so very nice to meet you Mrs Kendrix," he said and offered his hand.

"Thank you so much for seeing us and for getting in touch,"

DEATH NOTICE

Rose said taking it.

"Not at all, not at all." He was about ten years older than I was, lean and tall. His pale face had a few streaks of raised blood vessels, but aside from that he looked healthy and trim. His pure black hair was parted to one side, no greys, either from lucky genes or a more synthetic method. He wore a navy suit, no tie and brown loafers. McKeith turned to me and Brandon. He offered his hand again.

"Pleased to meet you, Mr McKeith. I'm Mick, this is Brandon."

"Hi," Brandon said.

"I'm pleased to meet you both too," he said giving our hands a solid pump each in turn. "Please, please, won't you all come through." His voice was low, but somehow managed to be both authoritative and sympathetic at once.

He led us into his office comprising a desk in one corner, shelves, cabinets, two comfy sofas and a coffee table. The drinks and biscuits were brought in, and we took a seat.

"Have you two been in the wars?" McKeith asked, sitting down and smiling pleasantly.

"Yeah, something like that," I said.

"You should have seen the other guys," Brandon said.

Everyone gave a little chuckle, then went about adding sugar and cream as required, stirring the hot chestnut coloured coffee. McKeith asked Rose to start by giving an overview of the case from the beginning. I sat and listened carefully. I knew it all by heart, but still paid close attention. I also let my eyes scan the room. The walls were painted a dull yellow and the large windows made the room feel bright and cheery. They were bare except for three pieces of art that I guessed were only prints. I came to that conclusion because I recognised one of them. I didn't know who the artist was, but it looked to me like the same guy had painted all three. They were all portraits. All were quite stylised, verging on unfinished. The one I recognised was of an old man looking like he was dozing in his chair. The second might have been a self-portrait of a haughty looking face, looking side on, as if at a camera. The last one was of a girl crouching on the floor with her head resting on her knee. I liked them. There was something jagged and authentic about them within the strokes, something sketchy and brittle.

When Rose was finished, McKeith nodded solemnly and gave a half smile, "Thank you for sharing that with me, Rose... if I may call you that?"

"Of course, of course," she said, accepting a Kleenex and dabbing at her watery eyes.

"And please, all of you must call me Dustin. We don't stand on too much ceremony here. Perhaps I can now tell you a little about what we can do for people here at FAM?" he said.

"Please," Rose said.

McKeith let his eyes pass over each of us as he crossed his legs and cleared his throat.

"We are a small team, but a dedicated one. We are a charity first and foremost, here to help families in the community. People like you, Rose. Only two of us work full time and we have a number of part-timers and a team of willing volunteers."

He had slotted into a clearly well-rehearsed patter that he must have gone through many times before.

"We only receive very little government funding and mostly survive on charitable donations."

I wondered if this was the beginning of a sales pitch too.

"Of course, we never charge families for our services directly." He nodded a smile towards Auntie Rose. "Now, our role is varied, and each case is different. Really, we support families in whatever way that we can, in a person-focused way. For example, we can act as a liaison between families and law enforcement. That is often a great assistance in moving cases along. Some families look for a focus on publicity. From what you have told me, they might be two good starting points. Sometimes, we can even assist with physically searching for individuals."

Rose had been nodding along. "Fantastic, anything you can offer I would very much appreciate. Thank you, Dustin."

"How did you hear about Lisa?" I asked.

McKeith set down his coffee cup. "Oh, I saw it in the paper I think."

"Is that how you often find your *clients*?" I asked.

DEATH NOTICE

"Yes, we are still not all that well known. I would have been in touch sooner. I'm afraid it was a few days before I heard about Lisa. I was away at a retreat."

I nodded. A retreat? Maybe charitable work could pay pretty well: no tax, no shareholders.

"There does not appear to have been all that much coverage in the local press," McKeith continued. "That is something we could assist with right off the bat," he said.

"Please, yes anything, thank you," Rose said.

"Are you on the web too?" Brandon asked.

McKeith uncrossed his legs and gave a chuckle. "I'm afraid that wouldn't be my forte personally. I am quite the luddite. But we have staff who are very good at spreading the word that way." He made a note on his file paper.

"Have you been doing this a long time then, Dustin?" I asked. I found myself fidgeting. I was busting for a smoke.

"Yes, yes I have really. Several years now."

"What did you do before?" I asked.

"I was actually a dentist," he said, his pitch lowering a level. He smiled, but then it faded. His gaze moved to the window and he looked very far away for a moment. "I have personal experience of these situations," he said soberly, his eyes roaming back to hold my stare.

"I'm sorry to hear that," I said.

"Yes, I'm sorry," said Rose. "How did it… did you…?" Rose began.

He cleared his throat and leaned forwards, wringing his hands together. "It was my son," he said, his voice thickening. "My son went missing. I *was* able to find him… but…" He shook his head, opened his palms and then clasped them together again.

I nodded. Brandon offered a sympathetic smile and then cast his eyes back to the floor.

"I'm very sorry," Rose said.

"Thank you all," he said more composed. "So, you can see why I got into this line of work," he said. "It gives me much pleasure… much *satisfaction* to meet with families in your situation."

"Quite a change from what you did before?" I asked.

"Oh," he said and gave a little chuckle, with a twinkle in his eye, "Yes. That was difficult too sometimes. A different type of human suffering. I much rather the work I do now. So, if I may suggest us having another cup of coffee, perhaps a comfort break, and then we can begin devising an action plan. Sound alright?"

We were all in agreement. I was all for it. My comfort break would consist of some quick chain-smoking out front.

DEATH NOTICE

Chapter 21

During the drive home, Rose seemed drained but also in a strange way, energised too. She was very pleased with how the meeting had gone. There was now a concrete plan in place, and another person who could help who had done this kind of thing before. After we dropped her home, Brandon and I picked up some bread and meat and went back to the motel to make sandwiches.

"You want chicken and cheese, Mick?" Brandon asked, brandishing a butter-slathered knife.

"Aye, please," I said, easing onto the sofa and lighting up a cigarette. I was still behind on my nicotine levels. "Don't be hurting yourself now."

I turned in time to catch an eyeroll.

"Rose seemed happy with this morning," I said.

"Yeah, she did. What you make of him?"

Brandon shrugged. "Another middle-class white guy."

"Yeah, I guess. And another one I wasn't all that keen on."

"You didn't like him?"

"Oh, I don't know. I guess he was alright."

"You're suspicious of everyone. Anyone who's not Irish."

"Them too," I said. "I just thought he was a bit smarmy."

Brandon began carefully slicing the sandwiches into neat quarters. "You think he has an angle? He's just wanting to help, no?"

"Aye, but maybe help himself to some money too."

"Everyone wants to do that."

He had me there.

After our late lunch of sandwiches and full fat Coke, we went off in the Hornet to see if we could catch Zara after school.

"What's this?" asked Brandon, nodding to the speakers.

"It's The Gun Club," I said. "You approve?"

"Yeah, it's okay. Pretty funky."

"One of their last. The not so catchily named *Pastoral Hide and Seek*."

"Yeah, not too commercial that," he said, flicking some ash out the window.

"They were only really big in Holland or somewhere like that. Pity. A great band." I leaned back in my chair. "Ahh the eighties. They were good times. I was in my twenties, young and fresh faced." I raised an eyebrow.

"Were you ever young?" Brandon asked. "And I thought in the eighties you were surrounded by bombs and riots and BS all the time?"

"Yeah, there was that."

"So, when do I get to play one of my new CDs in this here automobile?"

"Patience, young Brandon, patience."

We lucked out and pulled up at Zara's house just as she was walking up the sidewalk towards home.

I cranked the window down.

"Hello again," she said, stopping alongside.

This time she invited us in, and we accepted a glass of lemonade each. We sat in what she called 'the den' off the kitchen. It was a very nice house, her parents had taste. She chatted easily enough and even gave her approval for our altercation with BB and co. Her eyes also lingered more than once on Brandon. When she went to get the jug of lemonade, I gave Brandon and wink and a smile, and he gave me a dig on the arm. When Zara returned, I stopped beating around the bush.

"Zara, I don't want to upset you, but I don't think you're telling us the whole story," I said.

Her face twitched and she set down her glass. "What?" She gave a curt little smile, "Of course I am."

I shook my head. "I'm sorry Zara, but you're not."

I could feel Brandon tense up beside me.

"All we want to do is find Lisa," I went on, "And I know that's what you want too. The thing is," I paused and took a sip of my drink, watching her. "If you don't tell us everything, we might miss something and maybe we won't help her in time." I kept my tone as even as I could.

DEATH NOTICE

Zara switched her legs over each other awkwardly. Her face had reddened, and her eyes were wide now. She cautiously put her drink to her lips and swallowed.

Zara gave me a long stare, her face looking pained. "It's nothing that could help," she said quietly.

"If you just tell us, then we can see about that."

"For Lisa," Brandon said in a soft voice.

Zara shook her head in annoyance and wiped away a teardrop. "People could get into trouble," she said urgently.

"We don't want that," I said. "But if they haven't done anything wrong, they've nothing to fear."

"It's not as simple as all that," she said.

"C'mon Zara," I said firmer. "Better telling us than the cops. Tell us."

"Okay," she said sighing, raising one hand, her young brow wrinkled.

"Lisa swore me to secrecy, but… I guess she really might be in trouble. God…"

"It's okay," Brandon said. "You're doing fine."

"On the night… the night she disappeared." She paused and blew out her cheeks. Her leg was jigging like mad. "She wasn't here the whole time. She left a couple of hours early. She was meeting someone."

"Like a *someone* she was having a relationship with?" I asked.

"Sort of. Nothing physical," she said quickly. "Lisa got picked up, then she was going to get dropped back to the street and walk home as if she had just come from here."

"So that nobody would know," I said.

Zara nodded.

"Who was it?" I asked.

She shook her head.

"C'mon now, Zara, who was it?"

She paused, hoked out her packet of cigarettes and fidgeted with the packet.

"We need a name," I pressed.

Zara took in a long breath, before expelling it.

"It was her school counsellor, Angela Catherwood."

Chapter 22

The killer paced about his living room.

He didn't like it.

He hadn't planned for this.

That Irish son-of-a-bitch and that black kid.

He made himself sit down and reached for the decanter; half filled with a rich brown substance. He poured himself two fingers of Scotch and threw it back. The burning felt good. He had another. He lay back in his usual seat and thought through all the angles.

He stayed like that for some time. The killer's mind flicked between the moving parts like acetates from an overhead projector.

He shook his head.

It wouldn't do. Everything else was fine, all was in his control. Except for them. He couldn't afford to have them snooping about. The police were nothing, the families were hopeless, and the media clueless. He hadn't finished building his house of cards. It wasn't time yet for it to fall, he still had much to do.

There was nothing else for it.

They would have to go.

Chapter 23

"Well, I wasn't expectin' that," Brandon said once we were back in the car.

"Me neither."

"What do you think?"

"Of lesbians? I'm all for it."

"You know what I mean."

I shrugged and turned off on the intersect at Jefferson Lane leading back towards the motel. "It's certainly some substantial new information. I don't know exactly what it means."

"Seems like just about everyone has been lying to us."

"Way of the world, young Brandon."

"Great."

"In the words of Beckett; 'You're on Earth. There's no cure for that.'"

Brandon slotted in the new Eminem CD he'd picked up. It was alright, I suppose. Not really my bag.

"I guess we'll need to speak again with the counsellor tomorrow. We need to know if Lisa was walking up the street at that time. Maybe she wasn't, maybe she was dropped closer to home. If she wasn't there then the whole theory about the van, and her disappearing around then, is shot."

"You think the counsellor's involved in her vanishing?" Brandon asked.

I blew out my cheeks. "I don't know. I mean, it's not great. She works for the school and Lisa's underage."

"Zara said they hadn't really done anything." He paused to take a long drag off a joint. "Bit creepy though."

"Yeah, it is that. And what if her boyfriend knew? Samuels?"

"Damn, yeah."

"Pretty good motive right there if he does."

I zapped us a couple of micro meals for dinner. We followed up with a beer and some coffee and waited for Amy to call. Brandon's phone did its thing about eight o'clock and he set it between us on the ash sprinkled coffee table.

"Hi, Amy," Brandon said.

"Hi, guys."

"Hi, Amy," I said.

"Well, how're you holding up?" I asked.

"Er... got a solid two hours' sleep, I think," Amy said.

Amy told us about her trip home, and we asked about her mum. We also talked about the fight last night and I filled her in on Lester and his bandaged arm.

"While we're talking about Lester, my guy has already started digging," she said. "He rang me back a little while ago and he's found some stuff on him."

"I'm sure Lester's a real peach," I said.

"Not so much," Amy said. "He's been disciplined a bunch of times. He ended up down there after stirring up too much heat in other counties."

"What kind of stuff?" Brandon asked.

"Em, hold on," Amy said, rustling a piece of paper. "Let's see, we have general insubordination... a good few of those, em... harassment of a fellow officer... excessive use of force... three of those. Oh yeah and he's been demoted twice."

"Like I said, a peach."

"Yep, a grade A asshole," Amy said. "I got a little on the Sheriff too. Let me see... he's fifty-nine, been sheriff there for fourteen years. He used to be a Statey. He had a few disciplinaries in the past too. Thing is he's pretty popular in the County. Elected time and time again. He's white, conservative, goes to church; all that jazz."

"Jobs for the boys," I said.

"Yeah. He doesn't have a record as such, but the FBI have investigated him a few times."

"Oh?" I said.

"Yeah, there were a couple of things to do with election results and campaign funding. Nothing that stuck. There's been one or two other investigations. Links to a few criminal enterprises, but nothing ever got very far. Oh yeah and his family sound lovely. His uncle and Grandfather were both in the Klan."

"As in KKK?" Brandon asked, his eyes wide.

"Yep."

"Jesus," I said. "Another peach. Anything on Lisa's boss? Crawford?"

"Not yet, but it's on the list."

"Good stuff," I said.

"I got him to run a search on BB too, though, and got a few hits."

"I gave him a few hits," Brandon said, his lips curling into a smile.

Amy gave a brief chuckle then said, "He's never been in *juvey*, but he has had community service a few times and he's been in front of a judge at least twice. Er… petty theft, attempted larceny, possession of an illegal drug and criminal assault."

"Frig me, it's only a small town too."

"I know, right?"

"You might need to add a few more names to your list," I said.

We told her about Zara's revelations. Amy was quiet for a moment.

"Jeez, that's a surprise. I mean, I don't care if Lisa was experimenting or if she's gay or whatever. But… that counsellor? Screw her. That's not cool."

"I guess she's only a couple of years older," Brandon said.

I gave him a look.

"That's not the point," Amy said, with a hardness. "She's in a position of power. Doesn't matter if it hasn't got physical yet. That's not okay."

"Yeah, no, I agree," Brandon said squirming a little.

"I was thinking we'd go pay her another visit in the morning, that okay?" I asked.

The line crackled as Amy exhaled heavily. "Yeah, please. See what she says. I'll have to have a think about how far I want to take that angle."

"Want us not to say anything to Rose about it yet?" I asked.

"No, not yet. Let's wait and see. I'll run a check on her as well."

"And I think you should do one on Samuels. He seemed decent enough, but you never know."

"Who?" Amy said.

"Samuels. Angela Catherwood's boyfriend. The peeler."

"Shit, I totally forgot about that," Amy said, clearly annoyed with herself. "I completely blanked. Geez, I must be tired."

"Of course you are, Ames," Brandon said. "You've had no sleep, got all this stuff happenin' and you drove about a kazillion miles yesterday."

"Yeah, I guess," she said.

We chatted a while longer, then Amy said she was going to turn in.

We said our goodbyes and I grabbed me and Brandon a couple cold beers. I sat down, released a little sigh and lit up a smoke. "Game of Continental?"

Brandon raised an eyebrow. "I can take a few minutes out of my day to kick your ass."

DEATH NOTICE

Chapter 24

He did kick my ass. A lot. Then I showed him how to play five card stud and I beat him a couple of times. It was a moral victory for me. I suppose I hadn't explained the rules all that well, but still.

We agreed that catching Catherwood at lunch time would be a good plan, so we allowed ourselves a lie in. We were pretty beat. The last few months had been quiet; days stretching out with not much nailed down, no commitments. The last five days had been a hectic blur.

We had a quiet morning, got coffee in the motel, watched some news, sent a few texts back and forth with Amy, and went for a drive-through breakfast at McDonalds. It was a crisply cool morning. The sun was hidden behind dark clouds and there was a cold breeze on the air. At midday we were parked outside the college, having a smoke before we went in. Then Brandon's phone started doing its thing. Brandon picked it up and made a face.

"It's a weird number."

"Better answer it," I said.

"Hello?"

I watched Brandon listen, his brow crinkled. "Kate who?"

I tensed.

Brandon continued to listen. His expression was dark. He nodded.

"Hold on a sec," he said.

Brandon cradled the phone in his palm and looked at me. "Mick, it's Kate."

"Kate, Kate?" I asked.

"Yep."

"What's it about?"

Brandon shrugged and passed me the phone. I took a last drag of my cigarette, pushed it out through the crack in my window, and put the phone to my ear.

Kate had been my MI5 handler during my time as an IRA informer. I hadn't exactly been a fully willing participant for them, but I'd always found Kate mostly okay. That all changed last year whenever I found myself being chased by an IRA hit squad. It was in no small part due to Kate's manipulations that I ended up being tracked down.

"What do you want, Kate?" I asked

"Michael, come now, let's not start off like that," she said in her plummy English accent.

"What do you expect? How'd you even get this bloody number?"

The phone crackled as she sighed. "Michael, the combined intelligence services of the western world do not have much trouble in getting a phone number."

"So, what do you want? I'm in the middle of something here…"

"I know you are," she said.

That gave me a slight chill.

"What the hell?"

"We know about Amy's cousin," she said. "I was sorry to hear it."

"I'm sure. Just like you were sorry when you nearly got us both murdered," I said, wishing I hadn't extinguished the cigarette.

"Michael, please. I'm not ringing to hurt you or to ask for anything. I'm actually trying to help."

I gave a mirthless snort. "What do you want then?"

"Okay, Michael, there's no easy way to say this. It's your father. He's had a heart attack… a severe one."

I nearly dropped the phone. "Is he okay?"

"I'm sorry Michael, he's not. He's still alive, but they don't think he's going to make it."

I felt my eyes well up and looked towards Brandon. He looked back at me anxiously.

"Gimme a sec, Kate," I said into the mouthpiece and held the phone away.

"It's my da, Brandon. Heart attack. Doesn't look good."

"I'm sorry, Mick."

I nodded and put the phone back to my ear.

"I'm here," I said, hearing a crack in my voice. "How's my ma?"

"I believe she is doing okay. Your sister's with her."

DEATH NOTICE

"Good," I said. My stomach was heaving, eight years of guilt and pain washing about in there.

"Michael, if you want to go, to see him... before... I have booked you and Brandon two return tickets from Piedmont airport to Dublin. They're yours if you want them."

"What? I can't go... Amy needs me," I said.

Brandon put a hand on my shoulder and gave me a look.

Kate's voice continued and I realised I was holding the phone too far away from my face.

"... please think about it, Michael. I truly am sorry for everything that happened last year. I'd like to help you with this, if you want it."

"I, I don't know," I said, blinking back tears. "I can't just leave."

"If you want to go, we can book seats for a return journey the very next day or the day after."

"I don't know," I said again.

"Michael, speak to Brandon, speak to Amy, and I'll phone you back. One hour?"

"Okay, thanks Kate," I said and held the phone out to Brandon.

He kept his eyes on me but took the phone and ended the call.

"Let's go back to the motel," Brandon said. "I'll drive."

He opened the passenger door and stared at me.

"Okay," I said.

Part 2: Never Apologise Never Explain

Chapter 25

I let Brandon drive my baby and I just stared out of the window and smoked. I didn't even worry for my Hornet's wellbeing. I said very little on the drive and Brandon didn't push me, which I was grateful for. I had a very complex relationship with both my parents. They were both tough, working-class Republicans. My mum had been brought up in a *dyed in the tricolour* family: all nationalist, all passionate about it. My dad hadn't been. His parents had actually brought him up a Prod and a Unionist, but only vaguely. Only with a small *p* and an even smaller *u*. He'd been raised out in the country and his family only paid lip service to both. He was the first in his family to make it to university and when he did, he'd fallen in with some hardline Catholic nationalists, one of those being my mum. Eventually he converted to Catholicism and became a staunch republican. By the time I came along, they were two hardliners.

Looking back, I guess I was fully indoctrinated, but more in the *cause* than the church. When I later joined the IRA, they were thrilled. Yes, they were worried for me, but for them it was like I'd joined the regular army and been knighted all at once. In our community, the IRA were seen as our protection, our guardians. That was the hardest part of me later turning against the war, against the violence. I was turning against my family. For them, having a tout for a son was the unthinkable. There was truly nothing imaginably worse. It would be particularly true for my father. He had a chip on his shoulder, from not being born a nationalist or catholic. To have a son as a traitor, was much worse. That's why I had never spoken to either of them since.

"I'll make us coffee," Brandon said when we got back to the motel.

"Thanks, mate." I eased onto the sofa and lit up a cigarette.

DEATH NOTICE

I lay back and looked at the yellowed ceiling as the kettle bubbled and soon the aroma of fresh coffee drifted through.

"There you go, Mick," Brandon said, setting down my cup.

"You're a good spud," I said and then sighed. "I'm alright now, just a shock you know?"

Brandon nodded. "What are you going to do?"

"I don't know. I suppose I better ring Amy."

"Yeah, see what she says. She'll tell you to go, Mick."

"What do you think?"

"I think you should. You'll regret it if you don't."

I nodded. "I just don't want to let her down."

"I know, but you can just go for a day or two."

"Kate bought a ticket for you too."

"For me?"

"Aye."

Brandon chewed on that. "I'll do whatever you want, Mick. I'll go or stay. It's cool with me."

That kid was getting more mature and wiser by the day.

"Thanks, Brandon. I mean that. I don't know. Let's see what Amy thinks."

Amy answered her phone after three or four rings.

"Is it a good time?" I asked.

"Hi Mick, yeah, yeah fine… are you okay?"

"Em… not so much. But nothing to do with Lisa."

"What is it?"

"It's my da. He's had a massive heart attack."

She gasped. "I'm so sorry, Mick."

"Thanks Amy. They don't think he's going to make it."

"God, I'm sorry."

I told her about the call with Kate and she immediately told me that I should go.

"I mean it. I really mean it. I can't thank you both enough for all that you've been doing, but you have to go. You can still help afterwards. And take Brandon too."

I blew out some air. "I don't know, we're making a little

progress here, maybe," I said. "It's a really crappy time to be up and leaving."

Amy's reply was measured and firm, "Mick, you'll regret it if you don't."

She was right. But I'd also regret it if I could have found Lisa in time and didn't. I also didn't want those local rednecks thinking they'd chased me away. But she was right, and I knew I had to go.

After the call, Brandon made more coffee and told me again that he was more than happy to go with me. I thanked him, sat back down, smoked and waited for Kate to call back. When she did, I told her that we would go. She gave me all the details and told me that our tickets would be waiting at the airport for us. Before she called me back, Kate had sought an update from the hospital. My dad had stabilised, and the doctors thought he would have at least a few days, maybe a week. Beyond that, his odds weren't good.

"Michael, you have to understand that this is… unofficial," she said. "This peace we have, this ceasefire is still very early days. We can't be seen to jeopardise anything. If people like Gerry Adams or Martin McGuinness knew that…"

"…I understand."

"Not everyone is happy about me arranging this," she said.

I chewed on that. I was still bitter about everything last year, but I also saw that she was now going out on a limb for me.

"Thanks Kate, I know you didn't have to do this."

"I wanted to. And of course there are no strings attached here. I don't expect anything in return."

I didn't say anything to that.

"I will have a car waiting for you in Dublin that you can use. Just go to the Avis desk, it will be all paid for. I'm afraid that other than that, I can't offer you any protection. You can't bring your gun and I can't give you one."

"I get it," I said.

"You understand that it's still very dangerous for you there?"

"I do."

"The IRA haven't gone anywhere. There isn't even any real decommissioning yet. And every day we receive reports of new

DEATH NOTICE

factions setting up. Some of those people will still have you at the top of their lists," she said.

"Their hit lists."

"Yes, Michael."

"Well, it's nice to be popular."

After the call, we went about packing a bag each. I reminded Brandon that, "Ireland is miserably wet and cold," and to pack accordingly. We took out our recently printed passports, reminding ourselves of the names on them. Lastly, I packed some snacks and plenty of tobacco. I felt a little discombobulated, but it felt good to have made the decision to go. I was anxious, but still able to keep myself in check. It was a comfort to know that Brandon would be with me. I didn't want him in any danger, but we'd been through worse before. And besides, just as much danger might have been waiting for him alone in Six Mile. Maybe I would even to get show him some of my old stomping ground.

I suddenly remembered about Brandon taking me to an internet café' in New York not long before we'd found out about Lisa. He'd shown me how to get on the Irish League websites and had even printed me out a fixtures list. I rooted it out of a bag and scanned down. Tomorrow night they were playing The Blues. We were up against our old enemy, Linfield. A home game and the semi-final of The Irish Cup. I did the maths of the flight length and the time difference in my head. We'd be getting into Dublin in the early morning. It was then a two hour or so drive to Belfast. I didn't want to try and visit my dad during visiting times and already had an idea for how to get in discreetly the following morning. That would give us the day to get back to Dublin and catch the return flight. Against all odds, maybe I'd get to take Brandon to The Oval and to watch the team that I loved. That was something.

Chapter 26

We informed the motel manager that we'd be away a couple of the days and Amy had already insisted on keeping the tab running. We set off with a full tank of petrol in the Hornet at a good clip. It only took us a couple of hours on the road, and I even let Brandon play another of his new CDs. It was a DJ Shadow album and I thought it was actually class. There were lots of cool old school samples and it had real groove. I told him so and he looked pleased. It seemed to take forever to get through security and baggage handling at the airport, but there were no major issues. We hadn't packed anything we shouldn't have, and our passports didn't bring up any red flags. Once we were safely at our terminal, we had nearly two hours to spend eating sandwiches, drinking coffee and going to the smoking area. We spent most of the time in the smoking area. Brandon already didn't look happy about not having anything stronger in his roll ups. During a lull in chat, I thought things through.

"You get that this could be dangerous?" I said between puffs. "There's many who still want me dead."

Brandon nodded. "I guess. We'll be alright."

"Probably will. But keep that right hook of yours ready. Just in case."

Brandon smiled. "Never been on a plane before."

I raised an eyebrow. "Nervous?"

"Nah."

"Bullshit."

"Maybe a little," he said.

"Only to be expected," I said, grinding out a smoke and starting another. "They hardly ever fall out of the sky," I said with a wink.

"Thanks."

"Of course, lots of other things can go wrong."

Brandon made a face. "Like terrorists? I'm travelling with one anyways."

"Piss off," I said and gave him a playful dig.

"How 'bout you? Are you feeling alright?"

DEATH NOTICE

I blew some smoke into the air, watching a big Boeing through the window, coming in to land. "I'll be fine."

Once we were in our seats, belts clipped into place, I began to relax. I wasn't keen on about having eight or nine hours with no smokes, but what could you do. Brandon looked a little ashen and fidgeted, continually fiddling with his seatbelt, staring out at the wing and engines intermittently.

"You good?" I asked.

Brandon tried a half-hearted smile.

When the plane finally started its run up, engines blaring, racing bumpily along the runway, Brandon near shat. He gripped on his arm rests until his fingers were red and he shut his eyes.

I don't much like take offs myself, but I didn't want to make him worse.

"Have these," I said, passing him a few mints. "It'll stop your ears popping."

He opened his eyes, fed himself the mints and closed them shut again.

Soon enough we had cut through the clouds, levelled out and the seatbelt signs had beeped off. Brandon visibly calmed and released a long sigh.

"Let's get a drink." I caught the eye of a nearby air hostess, and she took our order. Her eyes lingered on Brandon. I saw a smile creep at the edges of his mouth after she sauntered away. He didn't look so worried after that. Distracted. When he took the first mouthful of beer, he looked even better. I got a whiskey on the rocks with a mini can of Sprite. I love a drink on a plane. The novelty of those wee plastic cups sliding into the moulds of the tray.

"Well, that's us up and all. Here we go," I said.

Brandon took another swig of his Bud. "I'm okay now. Didn't like that first bit."

"I noticed," I said.

Brandon stared out at the mass of clouds below us. "Pretty crazy, like ain't it?"

I looked out. "It is," I said.

SIMON MALTMAN

After we were finished with our drinks, I checked my watch; nine thirty. Brandon tipped his cap over his eyes and got himself comfortable. It was far too early to have a sleep. I eased my chair back anyway and shut my eyes.

I went out like a light.

A girl was kissing me. Nice looking, but nobody that I knew. I couldn't focus on her face, but her hair was long, her body perfect. Then she disappeared. I was in some kind of basement, or a cave? The wall vanished. People were being loaded up on trains and pulling away. Then I was in another room. It was dark and there was somebody with me, but I couldn't make out his face. He lit a match, then lit some paper and tried to start a fire on the carpet. I told him to stop. He didn't. Suddenly he was lighting fires everywhere. I tried to put some out with my foot, but it was pointless. Flames began darting up the walls, thick curtains caught, pieces of furniture. I looked for the man, but he was gone. Now there was fire everywhere. I circled the room, looking for a door. There was nothing but faded wallpaper, now catching fire too. The room was getting smaller, I was getting hotter.

Awake!

"Jesus," I said, waking up with a jolt.

"Morning, sleepy head," Brandon said, sipping on a plastic cup filled with coffee.

"God."

"Bad dream?"

"Aye."

I sat up, sweat on my brow, armpits soaked. My back was sore from the awkward position I had been slumped in. I looked around. The cabin lights were on low. Some people were asleep, others reading books or with headphones in.

"How long was I out?" I said, rubbing at my eyes.

"Near on seven hours," Brandon said.

"Jesus."

Brandon laughed. "You must've needed it, Mick."

I looked around for a hostess. One came over and I ordered three coffees. Another for Brandon and two for me. I needed to get myself together. We'd be landing in an hour.

The caffeine did its thing, and I pushed the thickness of the dream away. It had left me feeling hungover. I stared out of the window. We were lower now. Soon enough I could make out the British Isles.

"Look mate," I said.

"Wow," Brandon said, looking dumbstruck. "Looks just like an atlas."

"You've seen an atlas?"

"Screw you, Mick."

By the time my feet were on safely concrete, and I felt the cold, damp Irish breeze on my skin, I was together and primed. I couldn't know what would be waiting for us. Maybe nothing. Those who wanted me dead would suspect I might come back to see my dad. But not for sure. Unless there was a leak, and I knew well that was a possibility.

As we all jostled through narrow corridors like unsettled cattle, I got my passport ready as the procession slowed to a crawl towards *immigration*. I checked my watch, then clicked the buttons, putting it forwards five hours. It was now just after 9.30am, local time. It didn't take long to collect our baggage from the endless revolving carousel. As we came out from *Arrivals*, I tensed and began scanning the faces of groups of waiting families and friends. There were dozens of people waiting and hundreds of others in the general area. The best I could do was to be as cautious as possible. One hitman could look as anonymous as any of the other faces. Besides, it wasn't like the IRA had the resources to have men waiting at the airport at all times, just in case I was to arrive at some point. In saying that, there also weren't many flights coming and going from America. Nothing I could do about it. We pressed on. Brandon looked nervous too. We didn't speak. We headed to the smoking area.

"Jesus, that feels good," I said, blowing a big plume of smoke towards the ceiling. Brandon nodded, doing something similar.

"I'll feel better once we're in the car," I said.

"True. What's the plan?"

"Seeing as we're basically in Dublin, I thought we could take a quick spin into the city? Give you a wee tour?"

"Sounds good," Brandon said.

We had a second smoke, then made our way to get the car sorted. All the paperwork was waiting for us. When I found out it was a small Ford Fiesta, I wasn't thrilled, but it would do fine. Bloody cheap bastard Brits.

We located the little red hatchback, threw our things in the trunk and I had a scan around the parking lot before getting inside.

"Looks okay so far," I said.

I slotted in the keys and started the engine.

"Let's see all what all the fuss about this Ireland of yours is then," Brandon said as we pulled out into the slow-moving airport traffic.

It took no time getting to Dublin. I kept a close eye out for any suspicious cars. Anybody behind or in front for too long, anybody taking too much interest in us. Both my IRA and later MI5 training kicked back into gear. Speaking of gears, the Ford was painfully slow with poor acceleration, but at least easy to handle.

"Now, there's no skyscrapers or anything. It's not that kind of city," I said as we began our journey through the outskirts. The traffic wasn't bad for Dublin. Most employees would have already gone into work. But what did I know? I hadn't been here for eight plus years. I drove a little tour of the city centre, pointing out the Liffey, Trinity College, Dublin Castle. Brandon looked excited, happily smoking out of the window, taking it all in. I told stories about some of the city's writers, poets and freedom fighters, probably indulgently.

"Really cool, man" he said as we crossed the bridge again, now towards the Temple Bar area.

"This is a class part of town. Very studenty and has all the cool record shops, cafes and wee thrift shops."

I found one of the last spots in a dingy car park and we browsed around a few stores. Brandon's eyes were wide as he looked down at the cobblestones and then at all the Georgian doorways and old redbrick buildings. There was nowhere like this in The States, except maybe at Disneyland. The day was dry and cool, but there was a nice buzz in the air. Dublin always had that. The streets were busy, small city noise all around. I saw Brandon staring at two burly men, shouting across the streets at one another in heavy brogue voices.

"This place is dope, man," he said as we passed along a cobbled side street, filled with small pubs; empty kegs stacked outside and barmen smoking at alley doors.

"Check this out," I said as we turned a corner and faced *The Bad Ass Café*.

"It's cracker in here, let's get some breakfast. I'll get you an Irish Fry. Not as good as an *Ulster*, mind, but it'll have to do."

Brandon seemed to like the café with its murals and pictures of donkeys everywhere. It still had an old fifties order track running across the ceiling where waitresses would clip on pages ripped off from their notebooks and zap it across to the kitchen at the back. After we were well fed and watered, we had another dander where I pointed out statues of Joyce and locations from Beckett.

"You know Dracula was written by a Dubliner?" I asked.

"Really?"

"Aye. The whole vampire thing properly started here."

"Everything started in Ireland, right?" Brandon said with a cheeky grin.

"Well, America did, for a start."

"And look how that turned out," Brandon said.

He had me there.

Chapter 27

We had a look in a few more shops, then returned to the Ford and headed out of Dublin, on towards the motorway. It was a little after one and we hit some lunchtime rush hour traffic. But that was okay. We each stared out of the windows, in our own worlds. Both tired, but also in good form. Once we hit the motorway, I opened her up, as much as the Fiord could, my eyes fixed on north and home.

We were speeding along when Brandon started fiddling down at his feet, then took off one of shoes.

"You feeling the heat? It's pretty cold, like," I said.

Brandon gave me a goofy grin and slipped off his sock. A second later he dangled a little baggy of grass in front of me.

"For frigsake."

"What? It's my medicine, man."

"Jesus, do we not have enough to worry about?"

Brandon shrugged. "Didn't get caught though, did we?"

"You know sometimes they make you take your shoes off at security?"

"Do they?"

"Yeah."

"Well, it didn't happen." He began making up a joint.

"I was offered gear twice this morning in Temple Bar."

Brandon shrugged.

I gave him another look and lit up a cigarette.

I felt irked. "Don't be bringing that back to the other side."

"I don't plan on it," he said, grinning.

I smiled despite myself. "Dickhead."

We headed on, me sticking to about eighty, both now smoking. A hard rain began to fall as the sky turned grey suddenly. That was Ireland for you.

"Here, I have to play you a bit of this, seeing as where we are."

"More Irish education?"

"Yep."

I slotted in a CD of Thin Lizzy's *Black Rose* I'd picked up in

DEATH NOTICE

Temple Bar and cranked it up.

Soon enough, Brandon's head was bopping a little and he inspected the liner notes in the jewel case.

"They were Irish, right?" he said.

"Well, yeah, of course."

"All right, some of us listen to music from the last few decades. Their singer was black?"

"Yeah, Phil Lynott. Weren't many black guys in Ireland then, never mind fronting rock bands."

"No?"

"No. Sure I didn't see a black face in the flesh until I was in my twenties."

"You're shitting me."

"I'm not."

It's about a two-and-a-half-hour drive to Belfast. Once we had passed the ominously named town of Black Skull, I knew we were well on the way.

"See how the signs have changed from kilometres to miles?" I asked.

"How come?"

"Means we're over the border."

"Seriously? What, there's no border guards or a wall or something?"

"Not a physical one. That's why it's stupid that it's two countries. It's all just Ireland. You can just tell from the signs... and the roads. One thing I'll say for the Brits, their roads are better."

When we were past Newry and on the final stretch, Brandon's phone started to ring.

"It's Amy," he said.

I turned off the stereo and threw my half-smoked ciggy out of the window.

"Hi, Amy. How are you doing?"

Pause.

"Uh-huh."

Pause.

"Yeah, great. What else's going on?"

Pause.

"Uh-huh."

It went on like that for a while, with me occasionally interjecting and getting Brandon to pass it on. It was a pain in the arse trying to have a three-way conversation on a crappy little mobile phone, while ripping it up the motorway. I was able to glean more from Brandon once the call had ended. Amy had said that her guy had done some checking up on Samuels. He was clean. As far as he could see, anyway, but then even a lot of serial killers don't have any record until they're first picked up. He'd also ran a check on Marcus Crawford. The property developer didn't have a record but had filed for bankruptcy once. There had also been an allegation of some impropriety by a young parishioner at his previous church when he lived in Florida, but the charges had been dropped.

The only other thing that turned up was some sort of scandal in the current church on the internet. Crawford had been accused of being involved with a married woman last year. It was on a social media site called *Six Degrees*. I had no idea what social media was, but apparently the Feds even tracked those these days. Amy also said that data was being analysed of missing girls in the area, to see if anything else turned up. Brandon had asked how Rose was doing, and Amy's mum. Her mum was doing better, and Amy hoped she could come out for a while in the next week if things kept improving. Rose was holding up and had passed on her best to us. Dustin McKeith had been out to visit her and start the ball rolling on more publicity, taking some photographs to pass onto more press outlets. He had also said he rang the Sheriff's Department to add some more pressure. It had helped in keeping Rose's hopes alive.

"Here we are now. The big smoke," I said as we began circling the city of Belfast.

"Looking forward to seeing it."

"Don't expect too much, now. Like I said in Dublin, even more so here, we've little above ten storeys. Remember, it's an outpost

DEATH NOTICE

of the British Empire and it's bombed the hell out of itself for nearly thirty years."

As we slowed down to join the Westlink, I felt a strange feeling inside. It'd been eight long years since I'd been home. Now I was passing the intersect which led to the grubby housing estate I'd grown up in.

"See the flags?" I said, pointing out Tricolours hanging from the notorious Divis flats.

Brandon nodded.

"Now look that way," I said, nodding to the statue of King Billy surrounded by Union Jacks. "See how close they are to each other? Prods on one side, Catholics on the other. That's why we've got peace walls."

"Peace walls?"

"Aye, great big bloody walls dividing up the communities; Protestants and Catholics. We don't have a wall on the border, but we've built plenty up here."

"Really?"

"Yep."

As I turned off and joined the one-way system, I took Brandon on a drive through Belfast's centre. The sun had come out and the city was actually looking well. There were no explosions, no Semtex smoke hanging in the air, no army security checkpoints. There was rebuilding going on everywhere. Cranes were hanging all over the place, as if *Samson and Goliath* had just started a family. It wasn't quite the city that I had known, but it was still my home. I pointed out the grand building of City Hall and The Grand Opera House that I'd a hand in blowing up once or twice. When we passed the recently built Waterfront Hall, I could hardly believe that an almost all glass building had been allowed to be built. Back in the day, it would have been targeted and blown to smithereens as soon as the doors were opened.

"This here's The Ulster Hall. Everybody's played there," I said, as I made a turn past it and up by BBC Broadcasting House. "The Stones, Johnny Cash. I saw The Outcasts and The Undertones there. Led Zep played *Stairway to Heaven* for the first time ever in that place."

Brandon did his best to look interested in that, bless him.

"Charles Dickens performed inside… Sonny Liston boxed in there too."

"Shit, no way." That got him.

In general, Brandon did seem genuinely interested to see where I had come from. It was kind of sweet. I swung past Queens University to finish the tour and then headed back into town towards our hotel. Despite my father's illness, probable assassins and my friend's missing cousin, I felt good. I kept checking my rear view. All seemed okay. Nobody following us. I relaxed. Maybe this was indeed a new city.

DEATH NOTICE

Chapter 28

"Can you guess what The Europa is famous for?" I said, as we walked in through the revolving doors.

"Er... is it where Clinton stayed when he was over?"

"Yeah, I think so, but not what I was thinking."

We started across the plush reception area. I kept my eyes peeled for any signs of danger.

"Tallest building in Belfast?"

"Nope. It's not really for a good thing."

Brandon thought about it as we joined the queue at reception and set our bags down at our feet.

He clicked his fingers, "The most blown up?"

"We have a winner. Yep, most bombed hotel in Europe," I said lowering my voice, "They don't really advertise that. Can you guess how many times?"

"I think I'll quit while I'm ahead," he said.

"Thirty-three times."

"Damn."

"Yeah."

Our twin room was on the system as promised and paid for in full. We made our own way up in the lift without the assistance of the bell hop in his top hat and tails. When we got to the room, I checked around for anything suspicious. I inspected the bedroom and bathroom closely. I didn't expect to find a gunman, but some kind of incendiary device or a bug wouldn't have surprised me from one or other of my former associates.

"All good, James Bond?" Brandon asked, throwing himself down on his bed.

"Very funny."

"So, what now, James?"

I kicked off my shoes, pulled the blinds on the window that looked onto the busy Great Victoria Street and lay down on the bed.

"Don't know about you, but I'm having a nap."

Just before five we were both woken by Brandon's phone giving us a solo performance. The room was dark. Rain beat against the windows. The heating must have kicked in because the room was roasting. I sat up and switched on a lamp. Brandon lifted his phone and answered. It was Amy. As Brandon started up the conversation, I walked over to the minibar and got us both out a can of beer. I got a Harp for Brandon and a Smithwicks for me. I wasn't sure that he'd like either, but beggars can't be choosers. I began drinking, listening to Brandon, piecing together the conversation as best I could. I gave up after a while and figured Brandon would give me the highlights. Lisa had been missing a week now, that would be an unhappy milestone for Amy and Rose.

"Amy wants to speak to you," Brandon said, waving the phone. I took it from him and sat down at the little writing desk by the window.

"Hi, Amy. How are you doing?"

"Good, Mick. You guys get to the hotel with no problems?"

"Just Brandon being a bit annoying. Everything else was good."

Brandon flipped me the bird.

Amy laughed at the other end, then said, "I'm glad. I was worried about you... about both of you."

"We're grand. What about you? I'm sure you're still wrecked?"

"Oh, I'm alright. Mom's doing well. We even went for a short walk earlier."

"Good, glad to hear it," I said.

"So, what's next for you?"

"Well, I don't want to try going into the hospital for fear of bumping into anyone tonight. I'd probably prefer not to bump into my ma even more than the *Ra*," I said with an empty chuckle. "We're going to grab some grub in a minute, then go see the Glens."

"Good, I'm glad you'll get some downtime."

"I still feel guilty, though, I should be over there helping."

"Mick, seriously. It's like two days you're away. You guys have been brilliant. Anyway, Auntie Rose is in good hands. The sheriff even came to visit her today."

"Really? Well, that is good."

"I think the pressure from you guys and now from Dustin McKeith has helped. He's been with my Auntie a lot the last few days."

"McKeith has?"

"Yeah, Auntie Rose thinks he's the business."

I paused, "She... she hasn't given him any money, has she?"

"Well... actually."

"Bollox, I knew there was a bad vibe off him."

"It's not like that. He didn't ask for anything exactly."

"Yeah, just hinted."

"She just wants to find Lisa. She guesses giving him a grand or so…"

"A grand?"

"Listen, Mick. It's towards all the costs. It can't hurt."

Brandon gave me a look across the room, as he licked a cigarette paper and began finishing off making a joint. I was probably irritable from jetlag, I didn't want to piss off Amy, but still.

"Maybe you should add him to your list to check out?" I suggested.

"What? Aww c'mon Mick surely you don't think…"

"It can't hurt either. We don't want Auntie Rose to be taken for a ride."

"Well, obviously," she said, her voice hardening. "I'll think about it."

There was an awkward pause.

"Sorry, I'm a bit tired," I said.

"You're fine, I know you just care," she said, though her voice was a little flat. "Anyway, I'll give you two a call tomorrow?"

"Sounds good."

"Give my love to Brandon."

Then she rang off.

I tossed the phone across to Brandon and he caught it. I took a big swig from my can.

"All good?" he said.

I shrugged.

"Let's go get some tucker."

Chapter 29

The killer had made up his mind.

Enough time had passed. He was ready for another.

The killer was cruising along suburban roads, watching teenagers walking home from schools and colleges. He felt an excitement growing in the pit of his stomach. His brain felt so wired with fresh energy that he nearly pitched forward in his chair. His whole body was vibrating. He shook his head, smiling. The killer wasn't going to do anything now anyway. This was just reconnaissance. But he was closer to the next kill and that always had its own unique sweetness about it. The next one hadn't been chosen yet, but she would be soon. He slowed down, coming up to a stop sign as a brunette teenager adjusted the strap on her backpack, then flicked her hair back.

Maybe it would be her.

There was no rush.

But yes, perhaps.

She walked off and the killer drove on. He eased back against the leather seat, the back of his shirt sticky with sweat. He pointed the van towards the local college. There would plenty of others to pick from there. At least that brash Irish idiot and his sidekick were away for now. They could prove to be troublesome. If they returned, he may have to put off this next kill.

They would need dealt with first.

DEATH NOTICE

Chapter 30

"Go on, try some," I said.

Brandon shook his head. "I'm good with my burger."

"Dear sake. You can have a burger anytime. When d'ya ever see Irish Stew on the menu?"

"Gladly never."

I tsked and spooned up another delicious spoonful of lamb, gravy and veg.

I had taken Brandon across the road to The Crown Bar. It's probably the most famous Belfast pub and one of the oldest; a Victorian *Gin Palace*, not changed much in a hundred years or so. We were seated in one of the original booths, complete with six-foot-high panelled wood and its own door. I was on a Guinness, but I'd had no joy in convincing Brandon to go local with his drink either.

"Y'know, there was a film set in here in the forties?"

"When you were a teenager?"

"Very funny. No, way before my time. *Odd Man Out*. A classic Film Noir. It's about an IRA man, wanting to get out of the organisation, roaming the city and getting in trouble."

"Sounds familiar," he said.

"I hope not. He gets shot and dies in the end."

"Guess there's no point in watching it now. Thanks."

I had finished my stew and lit up a smoke, before swirling the rest of my stout around in the glass. "You should do anyway. It's pretty great. You wouldn't have heard of him, but James Mason's in it."

"From *North by Northwest*."

I gave him a look. "How the heck do you know that?"

Brandon shrugged. "My gran used to watch old movies with me."

"Young Brandon, you really are full of surprises."

At a quarter to seven, we were back in the car, and I was driving us up the Newtownards Road towards East Belfast. I had first checked under the car for any mercury tilt-switch bombs and found none. I also made a few unnecessary turns, just in case, but there were no signs of danger.

"I'm looking forward to this," Brandon said.

"Me too, mate, me too. Hope you enjoy it."

"I'm sure I will. See what all the fuss is about."

"It's a big game. Glens versus Blues. Always a cracker. The lads will be out in force; chanting, tossing flares and all the rest."

"Is there usually much trouble?"

"Aye there usually is some. Always plenty of police about though. Don't be bringing any of that in," I said nodding to the spliff in his hand.

"So, you've always supported them? Glentoran?"

He said it funny.

"Glen-*tor*-an," I said. "It's okay. You'll catch on once the chanting starts. "Yeah, I mean, of course I've always supported them. You can't change your colours. Well, not in football."

I parked up a few streets away from The Oval, just across the bridge over the River Conn. Darkness had come in, but it was a mild, dry evening. I locked up the car and took us on the short cut around the back of the rows of old red brick Victorian houses.

"It's always been right in the heart of the community," I said, as we each lit up a smoke. "Good working-class club. Some of the players even helped build the Titanic."

"Bit old to be playing."

"Very good, Brandon. Seriously though, they did."

"Really?"

"Aye. Worked in the shipyard during the week, played footy at the weekend. The club's been going since 1882. There's some history here. The pitch was bombed by the Nazis too. We rebuilt it after the war. Same stand we'll be sitting in tonight."

"Cool."

We kept going, smoking, chatting. I hadn't been sure if I would ever be home again, if I would ever get to see my family again, get to see my team again. And then, out of nowhere, here I was.

"There she is," I said, as the floodlights of The Oval came into view. We rounded the corner and then could see the back of the grandstand.

DEATH NOTICE

"That's sweet," Brandon said, looking genuinely impressed.

"It's not a huge stadium, but it's got history, atmosphere... especially on nights like these," I said.

We exited the alley, arriving at the front entrance. There were long snaking queues at each of the turnstiles, everybody draped in the green, black and red.

"We'll have to make a wee trip to the shop before it starts," I said. "I don't even have a scarf anymore."

"Not many away fans then," Brandon said.

"There will be. They couldn't come in this way. They'd get a hiding," I said. "The blue bastards come in at the Sydenham end, round there by the City Airport."

I paid us in, and we squeezed through the ancient revolving metal bars to be greeted by the familiar aroma of tobacco and chips, salt and vinegar. I took in a deep breath and smiled.

"Programmes-a-match," shouted burly sellers as we moved into the forecourt.

Brandon looked at me, the accent too thick for him to understand.

"Programmes for the match," I said to Brandon and paid my two quid for a copy. "C'mon, this way," I said, leading us towards the club shop.

I pointed out various memorabilia on the walls on the walk towards the shop and their significance, before we pushed inside the store filled with shirts, scarves, mugs, car stickers and sweaty men. The men weren't for sale as far as I knew.

"I'm getting a scarf and a T-shirt. Not like I'm here all the time. Get whatever you want mate, it's on me."

"Cheers, Mick. That'd be cool actually," Brandon said, scanning around the racks. I selected a traditional scarf in the green, black and red, ordained with GLENTORAN and our emblem of the cockerel sewn into it. I also lifted one of the current home shirts, mostly green, with red sleeves and our sponsor – Smithwicks – etched across the centre.

"I'll go for one of these too. Thanks, Mick," Brandon said, choosing a shirt a few sizes smaller than my own.

Soon we were seated halfway up in the grandstand, right above the halfway line. Just where I'd always favoured. I always liked it because that was where my father and uncle had always sat. Well, my uncle sat there after his playing days were behind him. My father had always been passionate about the Glens too, despite what many of his nationalist friends might have thought. The argument he always gave that we had always had Catholic players, which was true. The same couldn't be said for the ultra *Proddy* Linfield. It felt good to think about my family, to think about my times here as a boy. The excitement I would feel, particularly at these 'big two' matches. It didn't hurt as much as I thought it might. Yes, things had soured with my family, but the memories, the happy memories could never be taken away from me. Most of my oldest memories, at Sunday Mass, at political rallies, I just remember being bored. We never went on many outings. I was taken to Duffy's circus a few times which I loved, but being at The Oval was something else.

As the teams came onto the pitch, there was a roar from the crowd. We got to our feet and joined in with the chanting of '*Glentoran*', Brandon too. The place was heaving and the Glenmen were up for it. Whenever the blue fans could be heard above us, it only made us shout louder. A few of our fans had snare drums, whacking them with even greater force. Brandon grinned, taking it all in. The match hadn't yet started, and it was clearly already exceeding his expectations.

"Fucking hell, man," he shouted over the crowd.

"Yeah. I know," I said, a wide smile on my face too.

It turned out to be a good match. Both teams started off strongly. Many of our players I had only read about, joining long after I had left the country. But they were good. I remembered Justin McBride, a little older, but still able to storm up and down the wings. I was especially impressed with some of the young guys. Paul Leeman and Michael Halliday in particular. Soon enough and we got our first goal, and our stand went nuts. We were on our feet screaming and I was waving my scarf around in the air like an eejit. Both teams got a huge applause at half time. The second half started off slowly and The Blues got an equaliser. Our stand was silent in misery as The Bluemen jeered us. It was sickening. Brandon looked almost as pissed off as I was. The fans soon rallied, and the chants and songs started up again and the team began playing some really nifty football. Soon enough we were rewarded with a header into the top right corner. We went mental. When there was a third goal and we had sealed our place in the cup final, it was pure chaos.

"Unreal," Brandon said as we strode away from the stand on a wave of green; men with ruddy faces, all ordained with wide smiles. The buzz was amazing as we squeezed through the gates, floating on cigarette smoke and shared elation.

"You enjoyed it then?" I asked.

"God-damned right."

"Let's go get some chips."

We broke from the main crowd, off to find a feed.

Half an hour later and we were finishing our gravy chips, leaning on the windowsill of the local chippy.

"They were mega," Brandon said, dumping the polystyrene box in the bin. "Gravy on chips? Weird."

"A Belfast staple, especially after a match. Sorts you out."

"Well, they sure did taste good."

It was close to 11 now and there weren't many people about the streets. Any pumped-up fans wanting a drink or five would be over at the bars on the other side of East Belfast. There were a few stragglers and a few ordinary folks walking a dog or coming back from an evening shift. There were even a few blue-shirted folks to be seen in small groups, heading for a bus or their cars, living dangerously in this part of town. There were a few shouts back and forth of banter with Glenmen, but nothing serious. We took a shortcut down another back alley behind a row of dundering-in terraces. Coming our way were two of the Linfield fans still in the area. They clocked us and the larger one nudged the other. The smaller man was lean, with short, cropped hair, and small eyes. His face broke into a mean smile. We walked on, chatting between ourselves.

When we were a few metres away it began.

"We was robbed tonight," shouted the bigger man. "Ref must have been a dirty Glen-man."

"Not the game I saw," I shouted back.

"Maybe leave it, Mick," Brandon said, looking unsure.

Then men stopped a few yards ahead of us.

"What you say you fuckin' cunt?" growled the smaller man.

I set down my plastic bag with our new shirts inside it.

"I suggest you walk on, dickhead," I said.

I could feel the tensions of the last week congregating together inside me.

"You'd like that, wouldn't ye?" said the big one.

"And a Glentoran nigger with ya too," said the other one.

The big one laughed.

Now I was fit to erupt. Brandon put a hand on my arm.

"It's alright," I said through gritted teeth. "You sit this one out."

"You're a racist couple of wankers," I said to them. "I wonder if you're sectarian too? 'Cause I'm a *fenian* Glen-man."

That stopped them a second. Then the smaller man's eyes grew even narrower. "You serious?"

"Yep."

They pulled off their jackets and threw them on the ground.

I didn't move.

They advanced towards me, the smaller one first.

Suddenly he launched himself at me, trying to catch my jaw with a right hook. I stepped to the side, skipped behind him, pulled off my scarf and wrapped it once around his neck. I swung him around as he gasped. His mate was rushing me and tried a jab, but I swung the first man like a shield, catching his mate's punch on the nose. I let go of the scarf and he crumpled to the dirt, wheezing. The big guy looked down at his hand like it had betrayed him. His face creased and he went to throw another one at me. I swept him with my right leg and he floated in the air for what seemed like ages for a big guy, then he fell down like a sack of spuds.

Brandon gave me a look, let out a sigh, then pushed off the wall he was leaning against. We started to walk away on up the alley, past the men checking themselves over in the dirt, faces dark and flushed all at once.

I looked back over my shoulder.

"Fuck the blues," I said.

DEATH NOTICE

Chapter 31

We both slept okay. Breakfast was only served until ten and we made it down just in time. Everyone else seemed to be dressed in shirts and dresses. Several guests looked to be attending tense breakfast meetings. I didn't care much that we were both wearing only T-shirts and jeans. My Black Crowes T-shirt with two stoned looking cartoon crows was a classic anyway. I ordered for us both; a full *Ulster* each and two pots of coffee. I love it when hotels give you your own pot of coffee with breakfast. Going back to the motel was going to feel like slumming it. Before that, I would have to attend to what I was here for. I had been putting it off mentally and literally.

When the food arrived, it looked fantastic. Sausages, egg, bacon, potato bread, soda bread, tomato, black pudding, white pudding, beans on the side. Perfection.

"I don't even know what half of this stuff is," Brandon said, staring at the big, steaming plate of food.

"Just go with it. It'll harden your arteries, but it'll taste good."

Brandon dug in hesitantly, like someone may be trying to poison him. It wasn't the normal way the IRA would try and get us, so I ate with reckless abandon.

"Jesus, that was good," I said when I was finished. I was stuffed, but still selected a slice of white toast from the little stand and began to slather on some butter from one of the tiny packs on the side.

"I have to admit it, you guys know how to feed yourselves," Brandon said.

To my surprise, he had had a good go at most of it.

"Good lad. We'll have you applying for Irish citizenship yet."

After breakfast, we both stretched out on the beds, our stomachs bursting. After several trips to the bathroom, I wasn't quite so bloated, and I fixed us both an instant coffee from the little teas-made set up in the room. I checked my watch. It was a little after eleven. I aimed to get to the hospital for about midday. Lunchtime would be a busy time, outside visiting hours, when I could slip in more easily, if my little costume did the trick. I really had been putting off focusing on that part of the trip, which was of course the primary reason for coming home. I couldn't afford to embrace my complex feelings on it all. Brandon had offered to go with me, but I had said it would be safer all round if I went alone. I explained to him how to get to the main shops, ten minutes from the hotel. He said he'd go and take a look in the Virgin Megastore and a few clothes shops while I was away.

"Remember though, Brandon, we have to be careful. The 'Ra in Belfast are the ones who'd love to get their hands on me the most. I'm a *tout*, the lowest of the low to them. The ones in internal security... 'The Nutting Squad,' they're known as... they'd torture me for days. You too. I'm serious."

Brandon nodded, finishing skinning up a joint.

I dragged myself up and changed into a shirt and trousers. Then Brandon's phone did its thing.

"Hi, Ames. You're up early," he said.

After a few minutes, he passed the phone to me. Amy asked about the match and wished me luck for the visit to my father.

"Also, Mick, my guy found out a few more things."

"Oh?"

"Yeah. That Sheriff's department is a shambles. The sheriff before Trent Peterson was as corrupt as they come. Peterson ran a ticket on cleaning up the department, but it seems all he really did was to embrace it."

"Figures," I said.

"If anything, Peterson is worse. Half of his men have been involved in some kinds of disciplinaries, or had allegations made against them."

"That makes a lot of sense too."

"Also... I got him to run a check on Dustin McKeith," she said flatly.

Ahh, so she had taken my advice.

"It was pretty clear. I felt guilty even doing it. He's been a lot of help to Auntie Rose," she said.

"*Pretty* clear?"

DEATH NOTICE

She let out a sigh. "Seems he got in some bother with the IRS a while back. He got a hefty fine for fiddling his taxes."

"I'm saying nothing," I said.

"Alright, Mick. So, you know he'd be one to watch maybe a little around money, but he's still doing some helpful stuff."

"Okay, Amy."

"There's one further thing," she said quietly. "The stats came back on missing girls in the area."

"Okay..."

"For a town that size in the state, with similar demographics, you're about one and a half times more likely to be abducted."

"Right, okay," I said, thinking on it.

"And of those missing, you're more than two times less likely to return home safely."

"I'm sorry, Amy," I said simply.

"I know you are, Mick," she said.

"Still though, when you're looking at small figures like these, one or two cases can really skew the percentages. It doesn't mean anything for Lisa."

"But I'm also realistic."

"You're thinking this might be, like... a serial thing?"

She let out some air and then there was a pause.

"Yeah, maybe."

Ten minutes later and I was seated in the Ford, fixing on my new dog collar. I licked my hand and palmed my hair back. I looked in the mirror. I should do okay. Priests in Ireland come in all shapes and sizes. Most importantly, they can roam about hospitals pretty much undisturbed and at any time of day. I just had to hope it worked. I slotted the key in the ignition and paused.

I stopped, my heart suddenly racing.

I had almost started the engine without checking for a bomb.

I took out the key, opened the door and got out, sweating all over. I bent down and checked under the car for a mercury tilt switch.

Nothing.

I cursed myself, then stood up, light-headed. I put a hand to the car bonnet and steadied myself. I got back inside, lit a cigarette and started up the engine.

Just nerves.

It didn't take long to make it to City Hospital. I sat for a moment, breathing deeply, staring up at it. City Hospital is like a giant cube on stilts, fifteen storeys tall- one of the tallest buildings in all of Ireland and bigger than any other hospital in the UK.

"Hello," I said at the main reception, trying my most priest-like manner. "I'm here to visit a Mr Walker. Frank Walker. He's from my chapel."

"Just a second, Father," she said, plugging away at her computer. "Yes, he's up on the thirteenth floor, ward twenty-four."

"Thank you."

Thirteenth floor. Of course it was.

I walked through the bustling ground floor, past the shop, patients in robes, and hassled looking nursing staff. I tried to keep my face passive, but inside I was a mess. My brain couldn't cope with the family situation and checking nobody was there to kill me. My eyes were everywhere. I began to regret my large breakfast. It bobbed about my stomach as if nothing had been chewed. I went over to a machine and bought a coffee, using the refection in the glass to check behind me. Nobody stuck out, but I couldn't be sure. There were people everywhere. I lifted out the plastic cup, took a sip, burnt my tongue, and headed towards the lifts. The first few floors I had the elevator to myself. After that, it was almost at capacity. I kept my head bowed, standing at the rear. My fellow travellers included a doctor, two nurses and one orderly. They all exited gradually; it seemed like a floor at a time. The last floor I had to myself again. I slicked back my hair and tried to breathe normally. I felt sweat bubbling all over, not least on my brow. Wiping it away, I took hold of myself. When the doors parted and the chime sounded, I strode out to the murmur of busy wards and the thick smell of bleach. I threw my empty cup in a bin declaring itself to be for *non-medical objects and no sharps,* then went straight over to the desk.

DEATH NOTICE

There was a nurse standing at the counter, reading from a binder. She was late twenties, brown hair, with a youthful face.

"Good morning, I'm here for a short visit with Frank Walker," I said.

She took in my dog collar, looked me up and down, then peered at a piece of paper on the counter.

The nurse gave me a brief smile.

"Just a sec," she said and hurried away.

I put a hand on the desk, my legs feeling close to buckling.

What the hell am I doing here?
What the hell can I say to him?

"Father... Father?"

I realised the nurse had returned and was looking at me quizzically.

"Sorry, I was a million miles away."

"Mr Walker is rather poorly, I'm sure you know that. He's not well enough for long visits, but you can see him for a few minutes if you would like."

"Yes, thank you."

"He's in and out of sleep, but please come with me."

She led me down the slippery polished floor between bays and then over to a side room.

"Mr Walker is just inside here, please go on ahead."

"Thank you," I said absently as she walked away.

I took a prolonged breath and opened the door.

The blinding light from outside cast a long shadow over the dimly lit room and over my father.

I went in and shut the door.

He lay asleep, in blue pyjamas with stiff white sheets pulled up halfway. It was very hot inside the little room. Hot and stuffy. I stepped across and looked down at the man who had raised me. How small he looked, and old. Small, old and sickly. My father was jaundiced, and his face looked much older than it should have. Indescribably older than eight years before. He looked to be in a deep sleep. I carefully lifted up a chair and set it down beside him. I didn't want him to wake. Maybe this would be best. Just seeing him, nothing more.

A gargle emerged from his throat. I was frightened then that he might come to. I stiffened before he returned to a low thrum of laboured breathing. I let my own held breath escape and leaned back quietly on the plastic seat. I could feel my pulse throbbing in my neck.

I sat that way for some time. I considered taking his exposed hand in mine. The wrinkled hand with a drip fitted to his wrist and a plastic clip on his finger, leading a wire back to one of the machines beside him. Instead, I got up and crossed quietly to the closed blinds. I stared at them.

What am I doing here?"

I tilted one blind open and cast my eyes across the city beyond. It had started to rain, and the sky was fully grey. Some of the dark clouds weren't hanging in the air much higher than where I was stood.

"Am I dead?"

I spun around.

"Da?"

His creased eyes were staring up at me.

"Is that you, Michael?" he said in a low, mottled voice.

"It's me, Da."

He coughed and licked his lips. "Am I dead?" he said again.

A smile came to me suddenly and I crossed over beside him, "No, you're not dead, Da."

He pushed himself up with what seemed an enormous effort. His eyes stayed fixed on me. Then he gave a brief nod.

"Aye, it *is* you," he said.

"I wanted to see you."

He made a croaky noise.

"You want some water?" I said, coming around the bed and lifting the iced jug.

He closed his eyes and reopened them as if to signal that he would. I poured him some into a plastic cup and held it to his mouth. He drank. He began to choke a little, coughed hard and then took another sip. He moved his mouth away.

"Enough," he said in a whisper.

DEATH NOTICE

I set the cup back on the stand and sat down into the chair beside him.

"How are you feeling?" I asked.

He rolled his eyes and tried a laugh that transformed into another bout of coughing.

"Sorry. Stupid question," I said.

"What are you doing here, Michael?" he asked, his eyes focused intently on me once again.

"I told you. I wanted to see you."

"Before I die."

I held his stare.

"I just wanted to see you, because you're sick."

He looked away.

"I went to see the match last night," I said lightly.

He looked back again, his eyes moist. "Against the blues?"

"Yeah. We won," I said.

He nodded. Then there was a long silence.

"Why did you have to do it, Mick?"

A heaviness hung over the room.

I sighed. "Because I had to. It couldn't go on forever, killing random prods, bombing kids, for what?"

"For Ireland."

"Bullshit," I said.

"Don't speak to me like that," he croaked. "I'm still your da."

The last sentiment warmed me.

"Look, what's happening now. Peace... or something like it. It had to happen sooner or later. Truth be known, I didn't want to kill any longer, not for that."

"But you didn't have to betray the cause, betray your mates. Have you any idea what it was like for me and your mother? Still living here?" he said, his voice cracking.

The warmth left me again and my heart felt sore.

He broke into another coughing fit, and I waited until it was over.

"I had to."

"Why?"

"Lots of reasons."

"Like what?"

I sighed again. "Like they were going to put Marie in jail."

His brow furrowed. "What?"

I told him about the safe house. How I got caught. MI5 had threatened to link my sister to the guns and send her to prison. They offered me a deal and I took it. For her, and for me. There were tears in his eyes and he couldn't hold my gaze any longer.

"Why didn't you tell us, Michael?" he said finally.

All I could manage was a shrug.

"You a man of the cloth now?" he said wryly.

"What?"

He gestured weakly to the collar.

"Oh," I said, catching on. "Yeah, something like that."

Suddenly the door opened, bathing us in light.

"Lunchtime, Mr Walker," said a breezy nurse, striding in and setting down a tray. She walked back to the wall and hit a switch. We both squinted as a blaze flickered on from the strip light above.

No.

Not yet.

Not yet.

"Time for your meds too, Mr Walker."

"Thank you," he said in a low voice.

My father turned his head back to me. There was regret there. Maybe something else too. Some kind of acceptance. Of what, I couldn't be sure.

I stood up slowly. "I should be on my way," I said.

"Aye," said my father.

"Take good care of yourself," I said, looking down at him, probably for the final time.

"You too."

I turned and walked to the door as the nurse began setting out a plate, cup and medication. I looked back towards the bed, and he was staring after me.

"Thanks for coming to see me, father," he said.

I swallowed hard, nodded and walked away.

DEATH NOTICE

Chapter 32

The cool water felt good on my face.

I had found a toilet at the end of the ward and locked myself in a cubicle, sat on the toilet and cried. Then I'd dragged myself up, fixed my hair and splashed water on my face.

At least it was done.

It was over with.

It was brief, but we had both said all we had needed to say. The clock couldn't be reset. Those hours, days and years were gone. But maybe we had found something in those last minutes. Maybe we had found a little understanding.

I pulled myself together and went out the door. I kept my head down as I walked through the ward. I nodded to a couple of nurses and to another man waiting at the lifts. I pressed the call button and waited. The man was about my age, dressed in a casual shirt with trousers. The lift doors pinged open, and he gestured for me to go inside. I stepped in and he came in behind and gave me a half-smile, "Which floor?"

"Ground floor," I said.

The elevator was empty save for the two of us. He hit the button, the door closed, and it began to descend. The stocky man looked down at his shoes and I noticed a few beads of sweat appear on his forehead.

Shit.

I braced myself.

All at once, he elbowed the emergency stop button as he pulled out a revolver with a silencer. I threw myself at him, grabbing his arm and pushing it upwards. The gun made a little *pfft* noise as a bullet shot upwards and took out one of the lights. He kneed me in the balls, and I doubled over. As he swung his gun arm towards me, I suckered him in the solar plexus, then chopped him on the wrist and the gun spilled onto the floor. We both took a second to recover before grappling together. I got him up against the metal cased wall and punched him in the stomach this time. I turned and went for the gun, but his knee came up and hit me in the back. I turned to take a punch full in the face. Lights danced in my vision. I shook it off. He was on me again, grappling, jabbing, but nothing very forceful. I got a hand free and rooted around in my pocket. For insurance I'd picked up a pocket-knife in Temple Bar the day before. I took a few more jabs to the jaw, got the knife out and flicked it open. Then I plunged the blade into his chest. He fell away from me, looking down in shock at the blood oozing out over his shirt. He fell back and onto the floor. I caught my breath and stepped backwards, checking myself for blood. I was clean. I stood over him, then bent down and gripped the handle of the knife.

"You shouldn't bring a gun to a knife fight." I pulled the blade free.

The blood began to pump from him as I stepped around, hit the emergency button, then the button for the next floor. The lift started to descend again. I stood at the door, blocking the view of the man. I wiped off the knife and scooped up the gun and stuffed them into my pockets. The lift pinged open where an older couple stood waiting.

"Better find a doctor for him," I said and hurried past along the hallway.

I moved at a steady pace, not wanting to draw attention, keeping my eyes peeled. I followed the signs for the fire exit and turned down a back hallway. There was a hospital bed on wheels and a few bags of laundry on the floor. I headed for the exit door as the sound of shoes running down the corridor came from behind me. I ducked down beside the bed as a silenced shot sparked off the frame. I slid out on my back and plunged off rounds as I sailed away along the slippery floor. One of the bullets took the new guy in the shoulder. I stopped skidding along the floor, closed one eye and shot him in centre mass.

Dead before he hit the deck.

I caught my breath and got my ass up off the floor. I jogged to the exit door, punched the bar and hopped out onto the external fire escape. I registered the many floors down to go, sighed and began my descent. I started off fast, but the hammering in my chest and burning in my lungs meant I had to pause about halfway down.

Stupid cigarettes.

DEATH NOTICE

At around the sixth floor, I leaned against the metal frame, panting, my body aching. I struggled to catch my breath, half-balanced over the railing. I dry heaved. I let myself have about ten seconds rest and straightened up, wiping sweat from my brow with the sleeve of my gun hand. I undid my top button, letting my chest breathe more deeply, and ripped off my dog collar. I tossed it over the side, the wind catching it, floating like a kite for a second before flapping away towards the ground. Just as I was about to go on, the fire door flew open and a large, red-faced man ran at me, firing off silenced rounds. They went wide. I went straight at him. It was only a few feet. I swung the gun and cracked him around the head with it. He went to raise his own gun and I swiped at his arm with the barrel of mine and they both fell with a rattle. He came back at me with a left hook, and I took a few jabs to the face. I got my knee up and hit him in the stomach. Then I hit him with a right. The guy was tough. He came back at me again, smiling menacingly, wrong footing me and sending me up against the railing. He had me by the throat with both hands. I tried to break his hold, but I was being arched over the railing backwards. Out of the side of my vision I could view the many storeys below. I rocked on my heels, building a little momentum, then pulled up my right leg and stomped my foot down as hard as I could, down his shins. His grip eased and he let out a yell. I clasped my hands together and sent them upwards, breaking his hold. Stunned for a second, I hit with a left, then a right. I spun him around and shoved him against the railing. I skipped back, then launched at him with a *clothesline* to his neck that The Undertaker would have been proud of. He toppled over the bar and fell through the air towards the earth below with a scream. I looked away after he made a sickening thud onto the tarmac.

Down below, people yelled and began to run towards him. I changed tac, slotted my gun into my pocket, keeping my finger on the trigger. I went back inside, through the internal door, and found the staircase. I gave up on trying to catch my breath and set off down the echoey staircase, wheezing and dragging myself along. I didn't see anyone and when I got to the ground floor, I walked out into the main hallway, trying to look as inconspicuous as possible. My eyes looked furtively all around. It was even busier now, with people running towards the front doors or pressed up against the windows to see what was going on outside. Several doctors and nurses ran through the double doors, with a bed on wheels rattling along with them. I took a left and found a side door and hurried along the outside of the building. I ignored what was going on beneath the fire escape, kept my head low and aimed myself at the car park. I had a quick check under the Ford, got in and gunned the engine.

Chapter 33

"Brandon, are you okay? Where the heck are you?"

"Mick? What's wrong? I'm in town."

"Shit. Okay. Just be careful. They're on to me. I don't know if they're on to you as well."

"What? How do you know?"

"I just killed three of them."

There was a pause. "Damn."

"Yep. Where exactly are you?"

"I'm uh... just across the street from the hotel." His voice sounded shaky.

"I don't think they know where I'm staying, or about you. Hopefully. They were waiting for me there. They mightn't know about the car for that matter, but I can't be sure."

"What do you want me to do?"

I thought about that. For a start, we still needed our passports.

"Okay, listen. They're probably out looking for me now. Can you go back to the room, quickly grab all the stuff, the passports, and I'll come pick you up somewhere?"

"Okay. How long?"

"How long do you need? 'Bout twenty minutes?"

"Yeah, cool. Look out for yourself, Mick. Be careful."

"You too. I'll swing around the side of the hotel, beside the Opera House," I said and hung up the payphone. I scanned the street. Nobody seemed to be paying me any attention.

I had driven a few circles to check nobody was following me before parking up a side street off Botanic Avenue. I'd walked around the corner to the student area and found a working payphone. At least Brandon was safe, for now.

Twenty minutes to kill.

I wanted to be in the car for as little time as possible. I looked up and down the street. It was filled with students, couples, older folks and a couple of winos who'd started early. I spotted a book shop that hadn't been there before I had left. *No Alibis*, that would do rightly.

I had used a bottle of water to rinse my face and slick back my hair, and had tried to straighten out my shirt some. Not much could be done about my battered face. I still looked a bit of a state, but that couldn't be helped. My knuckles were throbbing and cut, but at least I hadn't been stabbed or shot. I marched up to the shop door and the bell gave a little *tring-a-ling* as I entered. The man behind the desk looked over his glasses at me and gave a little nod.

"How's it going?" I said and began to pretend to peruse one of the aisles. I didn't take in any of the names or titles, I was just glad to have a moment to slow my heart rate down and to plan our next move. I fingered a few books and picked a couple up as if I was interested, then switched to the other side. The ceiling caught my eye as I moved across. There was a large portrait of Columbo hung there on the ceiling. The owner saw me notice.

"That's our store detective," he said, with a thin smile.

"Ah right, cool," I said, forcing a smile of my own.

I went back to my fake browsing, but noticed I was in the Crime Fiction section. That was rather apt, considering. I did like to read some crime. I spotted a couple of Colin Batemans I hadn't read and lifted them out. I checked my watch. Still plenty of time. I started looking properly through the shelves and found a new Robert B Parker I hadn't read yet either. I took the books up to the counter and paid for them with cash.

"See you again," the owner said as I was leaving.

"Yeah. Hope so," I said and left.

Ten minutes later and I was idling the car at the side of The Grand Opera House. After a minute or so, Brandon came hurrying around the corner. He spotted the car and ran across, throwing our bags in the back and hopping in. He lifted the books and threw them on the floor.

"Careful. They're new," I said.

"Glad you had time for some shopping first," Brandon said and the slammed the door.

I pulled out into traffic and headed towards the Westlink.

"What the hell happened?" Brandon asked.

"Just gimme a sec to get off here, then I'll tell you."

DEATH NOTICE

Brandon rummaged in his pockets, then began building a spliff.

Once we were on the main road out of the country, I felt the pressure ease a little. I'd spent twenty minutes telling Brandon everything that had happened as we both smoked.

"So, what's the plan now?" Brandon asked.

I blew out my cheeks.

"The plan is 'we get the hell out of dodge.'"

"Well, yeah, but anything else?"

I offered a weak smile.

"Great. So, the plane isn't for hours yet. Where will we go?"

I checked my watch. "True. We've got a lot of time to kill and we don't want to get killed while killing it."

"Nice."

"So, we go a good ways, then find some place quiet to keep our heads down. The only way out of the country is through Dublin. They know that's where we're headed. Maybe they're done for now. Three men killed and us on the way to the airport. They might just cut their losses."

"You really think that?"

"No."

I figured we'd be best to keep off the beaten track for as long as possible. I constantly eyed the cars around us for any signs of trouble. We seemed clear still by Newry, but if we went straight to Dublin, we'd be stuck waiting around the airport for hours and hours, an easy target. I turned off from the main road and took the signs for Warrenpoint. It's a remote coastal town, not on the main through-way to anywhere much. It would do fine to stay low and pass a couple of hours.

"The next part of your Irish tour, Brandon. Chips by the sea."

Chapter 34

The sun had tried to come out and we enjoyed the mixed results. At least the clouds had remained zipped shut. We were sitting on the stone harbour, smoking. Our chips were already eaten and the newspaper wrapping lay balled up beside us.

"I didn't get to ask you how it went with your dad. What happened, Mick?"

I flicked some ash off my ciggy and wiped my fringe away from over my eyes.

"Yeah... it was okay."

"Was he awake?"

"Kind of. He thought I was a ghost at first."

"A ghost?"

"Well, yeah, kind of. For a minute anyways. Then he came around. We chatted some. Not for long."

"Were you able to... I don't know... clear the air a little?"

"Actually, yeah... a bit."

Brandon nodded.

"Don't know if it was worth getting shot over. Certainly not worth *you* getting shot over," I said.

"We'll be okay."

We walked about the little village, kicking our heels, killing an hour or two. I decided we best hit the road soon enough. We still had the guts of a hundred miles left to drive. We didn't want to be too early, but traffic around Dublin was unpredictable and the last thing we'd want would be to miss the flight and have to stay another night or two, left even more exposed. An hour later and we were across the border again, miles turning to kilometres. I mixed up speeds, mixed up lanes and kept a close watch on all the cars around us. It was going fine, and I was thinking of putting on some music, when I noticed a dark coloured Range Rover come into view a few cars behind us. I'd seen it before a few miles earlier. I moved into the left lane and let a few cars pass us. The Range Rover got tooted by a Merc when it slowed down too much, and it had to pull into the space right behind us. The man driving had big black sunglasses, with another guy beside him on his mobile phone. They both wore dark expressions, both had hard faces.

"Problem?" Brandon asked, looking in the mirror.

"Might be."

I accelerated out past another Ford, then moved back into the left lane. The Range Rover moved out quickly too, saw I'd reduced speed and moved back in again.

I sighed.

"I think we've got a tail," I said.

"The Range Rover?"

"Yep. Hold on."

I swung out again into the outside lane, the road clear up ahead. I floored it.

Seventy, eighty, eighty-five…"

I kept watch in the mirror, watching the Rover pull out, dust spraying, as it flew up behind us.

"Fuck," I said. "It's them."

"What are you going to do?"

"Don't know yet."

I pushed the little Ford up to ninety, wishing I was in the Hornet. We were on a long stretch of motorway, about twenty miles south of the border. I weaved in and out of lanes, keeping my speed up, the Rover in close pursuit. A sign appeared for a turnoff half a mile away. I craned my neck to see ahead. There was a slip-road, then what looked like a few miles of country road.

"Open the glove box," I said.

Brandon flicked it open and pulled out the two guns I'd collected at the hospital.

"Check them, will ye?"

"Okay, Mick."

"Just watch out. I'm going to take this pretty tight."

Brandon checked the weapons and I slowed to about forty in the left lane.

"All okay."

"Good," I said. "Hold on."

"Shiiiiiit," he said as I swung the wheel and took the bend sharply, us both rocking about in our chairs and the Ford skidding wildly around the corner. It took me a second to right the car, nearly sliding into an oncoming lorry. I slipped into fourth, then fifth and ripped off along the country road. I checked behind. They had missed the late turnoff and were now recklessly making a U-turn, their tyres screeching as they flew around, turning in the central reservation.

I put my foot down.

They had to wait for a few cars to pass before joining the country road and were well behind. But their engine was twice what ours was. We rattled along, Brandon clinging to the dashboard, the guns in his lap. There was nothing but barley fields either side of the road.

My brain worked overtime.

Very soon and they would catch up with us.

It was inevitable.

Then I spotted an old barn up ahead, on the left down a dirt track. I pushed the pedal to the metal and slowed just before the turn off and swung us around behind the building. I braked hard, mud ploughing up and spraying all around us.

"What're you doing?" Brandon said urgently.

"Keep her idling. Hop into the driver seat. I'm going to try and slow them down.

I grabbed one of the guns, got out and took part cover around the side of the dilapidated barn. The Rover was hurtling along towards us.

I closed one eye and raised the gun. I began plunging off shots, aiming for the tyres. The first few went wide, and the Rover continued on, dust spewing up all around it. I stepped out further onto the track. I raised the gun. Two shots sank into the front right tyre with a bang and the car skidded around, almost toppling over, before tearing up into the field. It came to a halt. I paused, closed my eye again and sent a round into another tyre. Suddenly one of the men was out and striding towards me with a Beretta, spraying bullets my way. I ducked around the corner, got to my knees, then inched back, firing off two shots. They both hit the man in centre mass. He went down. All at once, the second man was out too, with an assault rifle in his hands. A blast of bullets came my way, ripping plaster and brick out of the wall.

"Sod that," I said under my breath and got to my feet. I ran around to the car and jumped in.

"Bloody floor it!" I shouted.

Brandon didn't need to be told twice and gunned the engine and sent us careering across the gravel and away towards the other fields.

I looked back to see the guy running our way.

"Keep going. Do a big loop. Just keep us away from that feckin' gun," I said. "He's not going anywhere."

As we appeared around the far side of the barn, a stream of bullets came very close. I turned in my seat to see the stocky man planted to the ground, like Rambo, his gun still roaring at us. Brandon raked it, taking us in a wide arc, trampling crops as we went.

"That should be enough," I said, "Get us back to the main road."

Brandon swung the wheel, and we ploughed across the fields and out towards the motorway. He crunched the gears, the tyres spinning for a moment, and the engine giving a growl of disapproval.

"I hate driving stick," he said.

"You're doing great. Just remember when we hit the road, you need to drive on the left."

Chapter 35

"You wanna take over? You think we're far enough away yet?" Brandon asked.

"You're doing fine."

"No, Mick. I want you to drive. I need a smoke."

It was half an hour later and I got Brandon to pull off at the next services. We swapped over.

We got back on the road, and I tried to stay around eighty as much as I could. We both smoked, deep in thought.

"That was close back there," Brandon said after a long smoky brown exhale. There was no way the Brits were getting their deposit back on the car.

"I reckon we just go straight to the airport now," I said.

"But they'll know that's where we're going."

"Yeah, but there's nothing we can do about that. If they send somebody else, we're still sitting ducks. If we can get into the airport, we've a better chance."

"A better chance?" Brandon said pulling a face.

"We'll be fine. I just want to play the odds as best as I can. There's a good chance we'll be first there and that gives us an advantage. Also, airports have a lot of security. These guys don't want a shoot-out with security guards and cops everywhere."

"I guess."

"And if we get through passport control, they'll need a ticket to get in and they won't be able to get any weapons through security either."

"Okay, Mick. Makes sense."

About an hour later I was pulling into the short stay carpark at Dublin Airport. I didn't want to waste time checking the car back in. I just left it with the keys on the seat. The powers-that-be could worry about chasing their deposit. We got our bags and crossed through the carpark carefully. There were people everywhere. It wouldn't take much to pick us off. My heart hammered in my chest. I just wanted to get us inside the terminal.

DEATH NOTICE

"We can't get caught with the guns. We have to dump them."

Brandon nodded but didn't look happy. I knew how he felt. We'd feel naked without them, knowing that enemies had us in their sights. We stuffed them in a bin and walked at a pace on inside.

It was a tense forty-five minutes, walking through the terminal building, waiting at ticket collection, queuing through passport control. Once we were though and I hadn't seen anyone looking too suspicious, nor the guy from the Range Rover, I felt better.

"Up there," I said, gesturing to the second floor.

There was a café with tables near the escalator that looked down on the entrance from passport control. We could watch everyone who came through from the café's vantage point. If there were people wanting to harm us already inside, I couldn't do anything about that. All there was left to do was be cautious and play the best hand we could.

We got the table with the best view and Brandon went away to buy the coffees while I took first watch. When he returned and set them down, I thanked him, but kept my eyes fixed on the entrance. There was a fairly steady stream of passengers coming through and my eyes were already starting to burn. It had been a hell of a day.

"So, has this been a fairly typical holiday to Ireland?" Brandon asked with a thin smile.

I glanced at him and smiled back. "Yeah, pretty much."

"I think we could do with another holiday after this."

"Yep. Instead, we need to go back and try and find Lisa."

That hung in the air, and we were each lost in our own thoughts for a few moments.

Soon the conversation lightened some and we chatted, taking it turnabout, swapping seats. After about an hour and a half, many cigarettes, and on our third coffee each, I spotted them. It was Rambo from the car and another guy, taller and a little thicker around the middle, but stronger looking too.

"We're on," I said.

Brandon swivelled around in his chair and looked down at the two men, stalking along below us, their eyes everywhere. We watched them closely. They stopped, spoke to one another, then separated and began weaving back and forth between the shops and newspaper stands below. At least we were pretty well concealed behind a couple of tall, fake plants.

"Alright, let's do like we spoke about. Gimme your phone."

He passed it to me.

"Be careful, Mick."

"Always," I said.

"I'll sort the toilets, go over to the payphones. Ring you in ten?"

"Good," I said, keeping my eyes on the men below and getting up from the table.

I took the escalator downstairs, making sure to be looking away from the men. I turned away to the right and went over to a stand of books outside a WH Smiths. I lifted a few up and leafed through them. The hairs on my neck pricked. This time I hoped that my *spider-sense* was tingling for a good reason. To make certain, I walked slowly across to the shop opposite and queued and bought a bar of chocolate. I clocked one of them with my peripheral vision, stood outside, looked up at an electronic departures sign and ate my Twix. It tasted good. I'd missed them in America. I threw the wrapper in a bin and checked my watch. That should be enough time. I felt Brandon's phone vibrate in my pocket as I strode across to the nearest toilet block. I ignored the buzz. Tried to look casual. As I approached, I saw that Brandon had managed to put the 'cleaning in progress' sign on the door to the men's room. I went through the door and let it swing shut and pulled out the phone. It was an Irish number.

"All good?" I asked.

"Yeah," Brandon said. "I just saw you go in. I don't think they've made me."

"Okay, good. It'll be fine."

"If they go in and you don't come out in five minutes, I'm going in too."

"No, Brandon," I said firmly. "If I don't come out, you get the hell out of here and go to the police. If I don't come out, you'll have no choice."

DEATH NOTICE

"But, Mick…"

"No."

Brandon sighed.

"Where are they now?" I asked.

"They're ten yards in front of me, talking. They're staring at the toilets."

"Hurry up, you feckers," I said with the phone balanced in the crook of my neck. I went into the second to last cubicle and removed the ceramic lid from the cistern. I came out and set it around the far side, where there was a small, concealed gap beside the urinals.

"They're coming!" Brandon hissed.

"Okay," I said, hanging up and stuffing the phone in my pocket. I went back into the cubicle, snibbed the door lock, then stood up on the toilet seat and climbed out, jumping down onto the floor. I hopped around the side of the cubicle door, just as light and noise flooded into the room for a moment as the outer door opened and then shut. I pushed myself up against the bleachy smelling wall, the stench of piss coming at me from the urinal on my other side.

There was a shuffle and scuff of feet. Shadows moved above the urinal as the men walked through. They stopped outside the closed cubicle.

Then there was nothing.

I held my breath.

Suddenly there was a massive crash as one of them kicked open the cubicle door. I came out, swinging the cistern lid as I did. The second man was standing back, with a shard of broken glass in his hand, gripped by his sleeve. I swung the cistern into his face, breaking his nose and probably his skull too. He crumpled to the floor. I dropped the heavy piece of ceramic onto his head to finish the job. Rambo was standing with his mouth hanging open, his leg only just returned from kicking the door in. He had a shard gripped in his hand too. He regained his composure quicky, skipped to the side and swung the shard at me. I danced away and popped him with a right hook. He came at me again. I got around him and kicked him in the balls. He doubled over and I got both my arms around him and forced the shard out of his hand onto the floor. He elbowed me in the jaw and I let go. Then he hit me with a big punch to the stomach. My three coffees near came up. He swung again and I got out of the way of it. Then I was on him; left hook, right, left again. He had no place to go but backwards into the cubicle. I hit up again and he fell to his knees, almost out. I got down with him, grabbed his collar with one hand and lifted the toilet seat with the other. I pulled him over the bowl and forced his head down into the manky water. I gripped his hair, wedged my left forearm above for support and kept him under. He gargled and his legs kicked, but not for long. When I was sure he was done, I flushed the chain and got up on my feet. I stumbled out of the cubicle, trying to catch my own breath.

Suddenly the toilet door flew open. I near shat my pants. At least I was in the best place for that.

It was Brandon. He was breathing hard and brandishing a half bottle of duty-free whiskey over his head.

"What were you going to do with that? Make them drink themselves to death?"

He blinked, lowered the bottle and started to pant. "Damn," he said.

We looked at one another and nodded.

"That it?" he asked.

"Think so."

He looked down at the bloodied body on the floor.

"He wasn't feeling very well," I said, "You should see the other guy. His head's still down the toilet."

DEATH NOTICE

Chapter 36

"Take-off not as scary this time?" I asked.

"Nope. Seen some scarier stuff than that this vacation."

"True enough."

"You think we're clear of them?" Brandon asked.

I blew out my cheeks. "I think so. I can't see any of them flying over to America to make a move. It was different last time when they had my address, and they all already had men on the ground," I raised a bushy eyebrow. "We took care of their men on the ground."

"We did."

"Besides, they don't even know the names we're travelling under, or where we're going to."

Brandon nodded and laid back in his chair, looking out at the wing of the plane soaring up through the clouds.

"You glad we went, Mick?"

I let out a little sigh. "Yeah, all things considered, I am."

"Did you get what you needed?"

I thought about that, and Wilde came to mind. "'No man is ever rich enough to buy back his past.'"

Brandon broke into a grin. "You know, you didn't do that the whole time we were away."

"Do what?"

"Quote your old Irish stuff."

"Did I not?"

Brandon shook his head and smiled.

"I'll have to think about that too."

The journey was uneventful. We slept on and off, had a few drinks. We got through security at the other end quickly and the traffic was light on the route to Six Mile. I fell into bed about one am local time and slept the sleep of the righteous.

"Got you a coffee, Mick."

I opened one bloodshot eye. "I knew there was a reason I kept you around. Cheers Brandon. What flipping day is it even?"

"Saturday, I think."

There wasn't much we had in so after a couple of coffees, we went for a McMuffin or two each. We were parked up finishing off our breakfast by the playing fields when Brandon's phone rang. There had been some texts back and forth with Amy, but we hadn't told her about our adventures over the last half a day or so yet. After a brief chat, Brandon passed the phone and let me fill her in on it all. She listened attentively, making all the right noises in the right places.

"Good Lord," she said finally.

"Yep."

"And you're both really okay?"

"We're fine, Amy," I said.

"Thank God."

"A little bruised maybe, and very jetlagged."

"I'm sure," she said. "Just rest up today, don't try doing much… you know?"

"We're fine, Amy. We're back here for a reason. We never made it to see Angela Catherwood again the other day, so we're going to pay her a visit at home today."

"Are you sure?"

"We're sure."

"Well, my mom's doing much better, so I hope to come out on Monday and stay for a while."

"For a few days?"

"That's the plan. Maybe even for a week or so."

"That's great, Amy."

"Oh, and there's been a few good things happening. McKeith got some more coverage in the local papers. He even got Auntie Rose an interview on the county TV news channel."

"That's good," I said.

"Even Marcus Crawford has got his act together. His congregation went out delivering leaflets yesterday and they're having a special candlelit service tomorrow night."

"At least they're doing something," I said.

DEATH NOTICE

Afterwards, Amy texted through Angela Catherwood's address, and we went straight there. She lived on the edge of town in a smart new block of eight apartments. Hers was on the ground floor and her name was written beside the bell. I gave it a ring and we stepped back. After a few moments, the door was opened by a man in a white T-shirt and boxers. It was James Samuels.

"Oh... hi," he said with an awkward smile.

"Sorry, Officer Samuels," I said. "We were just looking to have a wee chat with Angela."

He glanced back and bit his lip, "Er... yeah of course, I was just going to grab a shower. Come in," he said and pulled the door back.

"You guys just grab a seat in there." He gestured through an open glass door into a modernly furnished little living room.

"Sorry to interrupt at the weekend," I said.

"No, no it's no problem," he said and jogged off down the hallway.

We went in and sat down on a black leather sofa and exchanged a look.

"Whoops," Brandon said.

The room looked like something out of an Ikea catalogue and perhaps most of the furniture was just that. There was stained wood for a floor and a shaggy rug in front of us, with a glass topped coffee table on top of it. It was several minutes before Angela came padding along bare footed and appeared in the doorway.

"Good morning both," she said, a questioning look on her face. "I wasn't expecting you." She had a towel wrapped around her head and she was wearing jogging bottoms and a black t-shirt.

"Yeah, I'm sorry. We can come back?" I gave her my most honest smile.

"No, no it's fine," she said, a little irritably, sitting down on the seat opposite us.

"Sorry 'bout that," Brandon said.

"What can I help you with?" she asked.

Just then, Samuels appeared at the doorway, now also wearing jogging bottoms.

"Can I get you guys a coffee or something?"

I raised a hand. "No, we're fine cheers."

"Okay, I'll just go grab a shower then," he said, glancing at Angela before ducking out again.

Angela gave us a tight smile.

"Like I said, sorry for barging in. I wanted to speak to you the other day, but I had to go out of town unexpectantly," I said.

"Yes, I heard that," she said.

I wondered how she had known.

I decided to dive right in. It was in our favour anyway that we'd caught her off guard.

"There's no easy way to put this," I began. Brandon instantly looked very awkward. His eyes settled on the shaggy rug. "We know that you were lying to us the other day."

Angela scowled, her beautiful face changing suddenly. Then her eyes widened. She looked indignant. "Pardon? What are you talking about?"

I leaned forwards and lowered my voice. "I'm talking about your relationship with Lisa."

She met my stare, then looked to one side. She took in a breath of air, then got to her feet and shut the door. She looked stiff as she crossed in front of us again and sat back down.

"We don't have a relationship. Nothing beyond a professional one."

"Oh, come on now Angela, you know what I'm talking about. You had a relationship with her. Something very different than professional."

She looked nervously off at the door, then said quietly, "Please stop saying that."

"Okay, well tell me what it was then."

"It was nothing," she said, with a forced smile, raising her hands. "She is just one of my students."

"Do you have romantic feelings for all of your students?"

Brandon nearly choked on his own saliva.

"Of course not," she said sharply. Again, the look towards the door.

"We know you were with her the night she disappeared," I said. "You lied to us about that."

DEATH NOTICE

"Jesus," she said and covered her face with her hands. A few tears began to fall. "It wasn't like that." Then she stared at me suddenly, fear in her eyes. "You don't think that *I* had anything to do with that?"

I shrugged.

"Tell us how it was," Brandon said calmly, taking the good cop role.

"God. Oh, God."

"Come on," I said. "Better us than the cops," I said, nodding at the closed door.

"This is just between us… right? I could lose my job. I could lose…" She sobbed a little and scratched a hand up and down her thigh.

"We don't want to hurt you. We just want to find Lisa," I said.

"But you won't tell anyone?"

"Not if we don't have to."

Her eyes looked pleading. "I swear, we never did anything. Nothing at all."

"But you did meet up sometimes?" I asked.

"Yes," she said with an exaggerated shrug. "Sometimes we'd go for coffee or something."

"But you knew she had feelings for you?" Brandon said.

A little nod.

"She told you?" I asked.

Another nod.

"And you had feelings for her too?" Brandon said.

"No… no. I don't know… maybe."

"Why did you lie to us about it? Why did you lie to the police?" I asked.

She wiped some tears away from her eyes. There was no make up on her face yet to smear.

"I don't know… I panicked…. because I knew it was inappropriate," she said.

"What happened that night?" I asked.

"Nothing!" she said loudly, then put a hand to her mouth before lowering her voice again. "*Nothing* happened. We went out for a coffee, then I dropped her back outside Zara's house."

"That's it?" I asked.

"That's it. We had a coffee in a diner outside of town, then I dropped her and came back here."

"You came straight home?" Brandon asked.

"Yes."

"You didn't see anyone else around? No cars, no vans?" I asked.

"Not that I remember. It was very quiet. I don't remember seeing any other cars. I mean there might have been. I just didn't give it any thought at the time."

"And when did you hear about Lisa disappearing?"

"Not until the next day. I heard she hadn't gone to any of her classes, then later I heard she hadn't come home either."

"Was Officer Samuels staying with you that night?" I asked suddenly.

"What?"

"Was he staying with you the night of the disappearance?"

"No... no he wasn't. I think he was on shift." A glance at the door again.

"And does he know anything about any of this?"

"No!" she hissed. "And I want it kept that way. Besides... nothing happened... never. I swear it."

"You're sure he doesn't know anything?" I said, holding her gaze.

"No."

We wrapped up the conversation a few minutes later, still difficult and heavy. Brandon practically sprinted out the front door. When we were safely back in *The Orange Beast* and heading off towards town again, I turned to Brandon. "Again, you did really good man."

"Thank you. Do I get a promotion?"

"Well, let me see. What I will do is say our dynamic is now more Riggs and Murtaugh."

Brandon looked thoughtful, then said, "*Lethal Weapon*?"

I smiled. "Good work, Sergeant. See, they were even both the same rank."

"But Mel Gibson was still the star. The cool white guy with his black sidekick."

I made a guffaw and gave him a wink. "Not my fault."

Her gave me a dig on the arm. "Dick. So anyways, what you think. She still lying?"

"I don't think so. I think this time it was the truth. Or as much as she's even admitted to herself."

"So, you think Catherwood and Lewis are in the clear? Nothing to do with Lisa?"

I shook my head.

"She maybe is. But just because she thinks Samuels doesn't know about what was going on, doesn't mean she's right."

Chapter 37

We stopped for a quick bite and caffeine refuel before going over to Auntie Rose's. She greeted us warmly and brought us through to the living room.

"Gentlemen," said Dustin McKeith, getting to his feet.

"Oh, hello, Dustin," I said, taking his offered hand.

Brandon said hello and shook too.

"I was about to get on my way," he said. "Just checking in with Rose." He gave us one of those smiles I felt were too smug.

"Aww, sure you can stay another few minutes, can't you?" Rose said. "I was going to brew another pot."

"Well, alright," he said with a broad grin now. "You've twisted my arm," he said as Rose hurried off to the kitchen.

We all took a seat.

"I hear you've been making some progress," I said.

"Yes, well we've managed some publicity, but sadly no leads as yet."

"No, but at least there's more people aware of Lisa being missing," I said.

"Can't hurt," Brandon added.

"Indeed, indeed," said McKeith thoughtfully. "My heart goes out to Rose, a lovely woman. A real trooper."

"She's great," I said. "I'll be keeping a close eye on her, now I'm back. So, do you have anything next in mind?"

"Well," he said shrugging up his hands and letting them fall onto his well pressed striped trousers. "Hopefully the publicity will bring us in a few fresh leads. After that, I plan on putting a little more pressure on our dear Sheriff," he said, with a twinkle in his eye.

"Good luck with that," I said.

"How about yourselves? Any progress your end?"

"We had to leave for a few days, but we're back at it again. There's a few threads come loose. Just have to see if they go anywhere."

"Oh?" he said.

DEATH NOTICE

I didn't get to elaborate as Rose appeared with a tray of coffee and biscuits. She seemed quite upbeat, and it didn't feel the right time to get onto anything too deep in the case. McKeith said his goodbyes after a brief chat and coffee, and we stayed on for a little while before heading on ourselves.

It wasn't even dinnertime, but I was knackered. Brandon looked wrecked too. We picked up frozen pizzas and a sixpack, then took them back to our motel. As soon as we arrived in, a heavy rain began to pour in sheets outside. The sky was dark. We needed to turn on the lamps and the little blow heater too. It felt good to be in our home-from-home. It was cosy in its own way. And we didn't have much of a real home anyway. We put on the telly, had some pizza, and didn't pay attention much to either, or even to each other. But that was okay. We both needed some downtime, some unwinding. The beers helped with that too. The good thing about me and Brandon, one of many things, was that we felt comfortable in each other's company, loud or quiet. Around eight-ish, Brandon suggested a game of cards and I switched off the TV. I fetched Brandon a beer and myself a whiskey with lemonade on the rocks.

"So," Brandon said, shuffling the cards.

"So."

We both laughed.

"Where are we at now?" he asked.

"Frig knows."

He began to deal.

"Seriously, though. Anybody jumping out at you yet?"

"No, not really," I said. "For all we know it's somebody we haven't met or even heard of. What about you?"

Brandon gave a little shrug as he dealt out the last cards. I scooped mine up and began sorting them.

"Well, who have we got? Let's see," I began absently. "We've got her boyfriend, BB."

"His Dad too?"

"Yeah. I'm near sure he was one of the ones who jumped us. Then there's the Sheriff, dickhead Lester…"

"Samuels too."

"Yep, he's certainly on the list. Then there's McKeith, Marcus Crawford... is that it?"

"Can't think of no one else," Brandon said.

"Not a lot to go on."

"Nope."

"Seven men."

"Seven *white* men," Brandon added.

"True. But black guys can be bad too sometimes."

"All the brothers I know are peaches," Brandon said with a wry smile.

"Sure. Still, it does seem to be men at the route of most crimes." I said, leaning back in my comfy chair and firing up a cigarette. "What's the matter with us?" I smiled. "Seeing as you said I'm down on my quota of literature, here's some Oscar Wilde for you."

Brandon rolled his eyes, flicking the ring pull on his beer.

"'Men become old, they never become good.'"

DEATH NOTICE

Chapter 38

I had some bizarre dreams that night. My dad was in one of them. He seemed to be asleep in his hospital bed, though it also appeared to be floating on the sea or maybe hovering in the sky. Something weird like that. I was floating too, or swimming. Whatever it was, I couldn't catch a breath. I started to panic. Then I was chasing somebody through a dark park, but then it changed, and I was the one being chased. My heart was racing, and I couldn't keep up the pace and whatever was happening, I started slowing down. The harder I focused on trying to speed up, the less my legs did what I wanted. They were gaining on me. Finally, I stopped moving altogether, turned around and Amy was standing there. We stared at one another, then we disappeared into the next dream. That was one of the few dreams from that night that I could describe. The rest were like listening to *Trout Mask Replica* on acid.

Sunday didn't begin very actively. The continual cycle of dreams made me feel like I had barely slept. We both were sluggish and had a slow start. About a gallon of coffee helped. Neither of us showered until after lunch. We had a call from Amy in the early afternoon, then Brandon and I chatted through our next steps for a while. We had already decided to attend the special church service to see if anything shook loose. With the tiredness we both felt, that seemed like a reasonable goal for the day. We also didn't have a lot of other ideas. We certainly weren't mentally prepared for what would be waiting for us that night.

Dressed in smart-casual shirts and black jeans, we arrived at the church at ten to seven. It was a modest-looking church: white painted brick and a small spire above a long rectangle, it maybe would seat five or six hundred at most. It was clear from the congregation and their appearance that the church had money. There wasn't much money about where I grew up, but the chapels were enormous. Go figure that out.

"You ever go to church much when you were a kid?" I asked Brandon as we climbed the church steps, weaving in and out of members chatting to one another.

"Nope. How 'bout you?"

"Well, yeah. I had to go to chapel a lot. It was expected. Being Catholic and Nationalist went hand in hand. I'd have been shot for going to a Protestant church," I said. "And I'm not even speaking figuratively."

"Mick, Brandon," said a voice from behind us.

Marcus Crawford was climbing the steps below us, wearing a navy jacket, casual shirt and chinos.

"Marcus." I shook his hand.

"Thanks, both of you, for coming. Nice to see you here," he said, giving us an uncertain smile.

Perhaps it was strange to him, seeing us on his home turf. Maybe he could tell that I was a Catholic. Maybe my eyes were too close together.

He chatted enthusiastically for a couple of minutes and introduced us to a few folks as he ushered us inside. He found us space in a pew near the back and then went to sit with his family, saying he would see us afterwards.

We sat there quietly, taking in our surroundings.

"Religion is pretty weird," Brandon whispered to me.

"You don't need to tell me that," I said.

I looked down at the order of service we had been given. Prayer, hymn, reading, prayer, hymn, reading. Sermon... prayer, reading, hymn. They mixed it up at the end there. I turned to the back page and was a little taken aback by a large colour photograph of Lisa looking back at me. There were a few lines about Lisa's disappearance and some contact numbers. It said that the collection would go to the fund for Lisa and details were given of the candlelit walk through the grounds at the end of the service. All were welcome.

Soon enough, the organ groaned into life and the pastor entered stage left. I wasn't disappointed by the running order. They stuck to the script. I'm not sure I could say the same about the content. I zoned in and out. Brandon was right. Religion *is* weird. It was a conservative service, I thought, from my very limited frame of reference. I was relieved that I didn't burst into flames for being seated there. I was actually thankful for the quiet time. A few times

DEATH NOTICE

the peace of the church made my mind wander all over the place. I thought of my da. I wondered how he was doing. Was he really so close to death? Had he told my mother that I had come and visited? If he had, what would she think of that? Would his body soon be resting at a service somewhere like this?

It wasn't the time. I pushed those thoughts to one side. I was here for Lisa.

My eyes scanned over the few hundred people in attendance. Everyone was smartly dressed. Nearly everyone was white. They were of all ages; the recently indoctrinated and those closer to heaven, sitting side by side. Was there a killer in here with us?

At the end of the service, candles were lit and handed to everybody on the way out of the church. It was the first time I had spotted Auntie Rose. Maybe she had been seated on the small first floor balcony at the back of the building. We spoke a few words outside and Brandon and I gave her a half hug on the way down the steps, while carefully balancing our candles. Crawford approached us, his expression solemn, and after a few seconds, he led Rose away to speak with the pastor. We shuffled on, joining the flow of floating candles, taking up a position in the church yard as part of the rough semi-circle. Once everyone was outside, the minister broke away from Rose and Crawford, and stood in the centre, arms raised. Rose stood off to one side with Crawford, looking uncomfortable and a little lost. I wanted to go over and put an arm around her, but I didn't know what was appropriate.

We stayed where we were as the pastor began his address. We'd already had a sermon inside. Something about the water into wine and the metaphorical significance of this. I'd always thought that Jesus had just been helping out a mate who didn't want to have a dry wedding. A few mentions of Lisa had been given in the service, but now she was front and centre. What the minister actually said was fine as far as it went for someone who didn't know her. He was only late twenties or early thirties. Maybe his age made it hard to take him serious as somebody who was particularly good buddies with the God and creator of the universe. Or it might have been the carefully put together preppy look, and the affected timbre of his voice, I don't know. Ten minutes later and there was a final prayer before we were all invited to leave our candles lit around the church walls. After that we hunted out Auntie Rose again, hugged her and said our goodbyes.

As Brandon and I left through the gates, we hoked out our smokes and lit up.

"I'm glad that's done," Brandon said.

"Yep," I said, releasing a plume. "Thank God."

DEATH NOTICE

Chapter 39

The heating system in the Hornet warmed up quickly and made the inside nice and toasty. A flood of cars exited at the same time as us and then the flow reduced as we made our way across town, under the Ranfurly Bridge and moving south. We came off the outer circle and were on a small country road about ten minutes from our motel. The road was empty until I saw a dark coloured van appear in the rear view. It was accelerating hard.

"Someone's in a hurry," Brandon said, clocking it too.

"Yeah." I slowed a little and moved close to the verge in case they wanted to pass. I already had a feeling that that wasn't the intention.

The van's lights were now glaring into my mirror, the beams on full. I gripped the wheel.

The van wasn't slowing down.

"Watch out," I warned Brandon as the van pushed on further and smashed into my rear bumper, just as I tried to swerve away.

"Fuck!" Brandon said.

I accelerated, but the van had barely slowed. It cracked the back of my sweet baby again, this time on the right-hand side.

"Wanker," I muttered.

"He trying to kill us," Brandon said bobbing about beside me.

The road was narrow. I was now doing a fair pace on the wrong side of the dividing line, whipping over blind brows. The van came alongside me. The inside of the cab was dark. The driver had a baseball cap pulled low over his face. He swung the wheel and glanced the side of my car again.

"Right, you wee hallion," I said and took my foot off the accelerator and pumped the break. The van swerved and slowed but was now a few metres up ahead. The driver began to try and accelerate away.

"Who is it?" Brandon asked, his spliff dangling crookedly from his lips now.

"Don't know. But let's see how *he* likes it."

I let the Big Orange Beast off the leash and lunged forwards. Seconds later I was right behind the guy.

"I'm sorry," I said, patting the dashboard. "In for a penny..."

I swung the wheel and crashed the front of the Hornet into his nearside. The van swerved, skidded, and then tried to pull away. We were now both driving at a ridiculous speed for the width of road and lack of visibility up ahead.

"Sorry, baby." I patted the dashboard again.

I accelerated harder and this time hit him an almighty shunt square on his rearend. I winced as I imagined the dents in my pride and joy. The van did a full one-eighty as its breaks screeched and moaned, tyre marks burning across the asphalt. I slowed and took a sharp turn, spun around and stopped. We were facing the van now, almost square on. Steam was pouring out of both vehicles.

We sat for a few seconds, staring at the van. Our headlights lit it up and the opposing full beam glared back at us. Suddenly the driver door popped open. A man appeared with a shotgun in his hands. He cocked it and sent off a round.

"Shit!" Brandon shouted as I threw it into reverse. We screeched backwards and a second shot went wide.

The man jumped back in the van, made a sharp turn and shot away in the opposite direction.

"You alright?" I asked.

"Yeah, I guess, you?"

I stared out the front window at my steaming engine, thick black smoke now joining the plume.

"No, I'm pissed."

DEATH NOTICE

Chapter 40

We didn't need a tow, but it wasn't an enjoyable trip back to the motel.

"Damn," said Brandon, sidling up beside me.

I stood staring at the damage to the Hornet. I had already walked around it a few times, seething.

It was late Sunday night. No mechanic was going to look at it now, so I'd have to wait.

"What about the cops?" Brandon asked when we sat down, each with a cold beer.

"Sod it, I'll speak to them in the morning," I said, while chewing on the end of a fresh cigarette.

"Do you think he was one of the guys from the last posse?" Brandon asked.

I shook my head. "Not with the gun. He was trying to kill us, but those other guys were just trying to put a scare into us."

"You think it's whoever's taken Lisa?"

"Yeah, I do."

My mood was pretty black. I didn't feel much like talking, but I didn't want to take it out on Brandon. I told him I was going to turn in, taking the rest of my beer to my bedroom. I pulled the curtains, switched on the lamp and sat on the bed; stewing, beer in one hand, ciggy in the other. I breathed out heavily. I thought I'd been coping pretty well with everything. Sometimes it's the little things that get you. Not that's it's little to have my pride and joy all smashed up. And more than that, I was kind of sick of people trying to kill us all the time.

The next morning and a decent sleep later, things looked a little better. Still fairly terrible, but better. After some breakfast, we were on the road for after nine. I got the Hornet going, though she was reluctant at first to start. As we headed out of town towards the Sheriff's Department, an ever-growing spiral of smoke wafted from under the hood. I ignored the visitor parking area and drove into a space reserved for law enforcement. I didn't care, and besides, I was helping with law enforcement in my own way. Sort of. I sat for a moment, staring at the smoke. I shook my head. Brandon gave me a reassuring pat on the shoulder.

"C'mon, Mick. Let's go," he said.

As we approached the door, a blue and white pulled in and parked beside my Hornet. Inside was Officer Samuels. He clocked the car and scowled. He got out and tilted his head, inspecting the damage. I doubled back and strode towards him. He turned around when he saw me coming his way.

"Y'know this is reserved for cops?" he asked.

"I thought you lot would want to see it, seeing as a psycho tried running me off the road and then started shooting at me."

He raised both eyebrows. "Shit, really?"

"Yeah."

"You coming in to make a report?"

"Yeah."

Samuels nodded and moved off again, walking a circle around the car. He sucked in and made a high whistling sound. "Sure did do a number on it."

"Yeah," I said again.

Samuels led us inside and even got us a couple of coffees. The coffee was bad, but the thought was nice. To our surprise, it was the Sheriff himself who agreed to see us.

"How you doin', fellas?" he said as he ushered us into his office and shut the door.

He was once again in full tan uniform, Stetson and cigar chomped between his teeth. We got settled, exchanged pleasantries, and he got behind his big old desk and crossed his legs up on the end of it.

"James tells me you've had a problem with your vehicle?"

He said vehicle like *vee-hick-el*. He made a pained expression and I'd have sworn there were a few more horizontal lines across his brow than there were the last time I'd seen him.

"Yeah, the problem was somebody tried running us off the road, then emptied a shotgun at us."

DEATH NOTICE

He shook his head. "My, don't some folks have terrible road rage," he said and made a throaty laugh. He stopped when he saw we didn't find it very funny.

"And you didn't recognise this fella? Didn't get a plate number?"

"No." I said, lighting up a smoke without being offered it this time. "He had a cap on pulled low and the licence was all muddy. But it was a dark van, like the description of the one seen before Lisa was taken."

"Now, hold your horses there. Let's not get too carried away," he said, swinging his feet down onto the floor and raising a hand up. "We don't even know yet if Lisa was taken, and if she was, if it was anything to do with that particular vehicle."

He did again. *Vee-hick-el*. It was kind of annoying.

"And all that being said, we sure as hell don't know if that there vehicle was the one you had your altercation with."

I took in a lungful of smoke and tried not to wince. Brandon fumbled in one pocket, made a face, then went into the other side for his ordinary smokes.

I exhaled and hooded my eyes. The Sheriff stared back.

I gave a sigh. "Right, so what about what happened last night? What are you going to do that about that?"

"Well sir, I'm gonna get one of my best deputies to sit down with you two fellas and take a statement from you both. Then we'll go check out the scene and we'll make our enquiries."

"I hope your boy Lester isn't part of it," I said, and let it hang in the air.

Peterson had a little puff on his cigar, then put his feet back up on the desk. "Now, why do you say that?"

"Because a couple nights ago, he stuck on a hockey mask, got a couple of good old boys to join him, and tried to knock hell out of us," Brandon said.

I smiled. "Yeah, what he said." I gestured my thumb towards Brandon.

Peterson gazed out of the window for a moment, then looked from Brandon to me with a solemn expression. "I heard about that."

"You heard that one of your cops turned vigilante?" I asked.

He did the hand thing again. "Now please, again, let's not go off cock-eyed here. I've heard some things and we're looking into it," he said, his voice more brittle than I had heard before.

"And what about Lester and our case?"

He shook his head and made a throaty half cough, setting the burning cigar on the end of the glass ashtray. "He won't be working here for a while," he said.

Brandon gave me a look.

"And, Michael," he said, leaning on the desk with one arm. "The department will cover the cost of fixing up your car. I know a good mechanic."

That took me back a bit.

"All of it?" I asked. "I don't need to use my insurance?"

"No, we'll see to it all," he said.

"It's a bit of a classic, you know? And it got pretty messed up last night."

"We'll have it looking like it just drove out of a lot."

"A second-hand lot?"

"Well, yeah," he said with a chuckle and a twinkle in his eye. "I know a good mechanic, not a magician."

DEATH NOTICE

Chapter 41

The killer slipped on his outdoor shoes, opened the backdoor and headed out to the garage. He rolled up the shutter, then pulled the cord for the light. He stared at the van. It was in pretty bad shape. He kicked one of the tyres. Then he landed a couple of punches on the side panel before thinking better of it.

He was breathing hard.

He stood back and caught his breath, regarded his reddened knuckles.

The killer ran a hand over his head, patting down his hair.

No need to lose his cool. That just wouldn't do.

This was not the time to let things fall apart. It was not the time to let his focus slip.

There was somebody inside the house that needed his full attention.

Chapter 42

"I can't believe he's going to pay for the car, Mick."

"Yeah, me neither," I said. "Don't know what to make of that."

We had been dropped off at a little café in town by Samuels. He was his usual pleasant self; wished us well and said they'd be in touch in a few days about my car. Amy had texted back and forth and was due to arrive. When she did, we hugged and ordered coffees. She had rings around her eyes and her hair was uncharacteristically messy. But she still looked beautiful to me, and she still managed to be in good form somehow.

We told her about what had happened the night before.

"Oh my God," she said, open mouthed.

Brandon laughed into his coffee, then took a sip.

"You know how we roll," I said, reaching for my ciggies.

"How you roll, is every time I speak to you, somebody's tried killing you," she said.

I shrugged. "Not everybody's born popular."

"Who do you think it was?" Amy asked, looking at me intently with those big brown eyes of hers.

"Can't be sure, but I think it was our man."

"Whoever took Lisa?"

"Yeah, that's my best guess. It wasn't just a scare from some local yokels this time. This was serious. Serious as a shotgun. Then there's the similar-looking van too."

Amy nodded. "I think so as well." She let out a long sigh. "I'm just glad you guys are okay." She stared off into the middle distance.

"So, what about your mom?" Brandon asked.

Amy carefully wiped a little bit of foam from her mouth, set down her cup and smiled. "She's actually doing really well. I'm pleased. This time I don't need to worry as much. She's up and around, able to make coffee and snacks; much steadier on her feet."

"That's good, Ames."

"Great to hear," I agreed.

DEATH NOTICE

"Yeah, she's got great neighbours and they're checking in on her. There's a nurse still coming out every couple of days, too."

"And she doesn't have to cope with your home cooking for a while," I said.

Amy gave me a dig on the arm. "You've tasted some of my cooking. It's not so bad. And I've tasted *yours*."

"Yeah, okay. Fair point."

"Listen, guys. I've some things to show you," Amy said, reaching down, unbuttoning her satchel and taking out a folder full of printed paper.

"What are these? Some of your recipes?" I asked.

"No. Have a look. My buddy in the Bureau sent me these yesterday."

Amy pushed some of the pages across to us. We took a sheet each and began reading.

"These are some of the missing girls from the local area over the last couple of years," she said.

I nodded and read one of the overviews of the missing person's report.

"They're all within a fifty-mile radius from Six Mile. These are just ones who are female and between twelve and eighteen," Amy continued.

Brandon looked up, shook his head and went back to reading. I finished one, then lifted up another and scanned it. There were six reports altogether spread over the table. Amy watched us and quietly drank her coffee. I finished leafing through the second one and set it down.

"What happened to the girls? Were any of them ever found?"

Amy shook her head. "Not one of them," she said quietly.

I ran a hand through my hair and lit up another cigarette. Amy bent down to her bag, lifted a stapled bunch of papers and pushed it across the table towards us.

"This one's from a few days ago," she muttered.

"Shit," Brandon said, looking at me.

I picked up more of the papers and began reading. Stacy Vanucci, sixteen, lived a couple of towns away. She had been walking home about seven in the evening. Stacy had popped around to the local store for her mother, to get milk and eggs and didn't come home.

"Damn," I said.

Amy nodded again. Her eyes were glistening. "I spoke with the Sheriff first thing about Stacy. Her case was in his jurisdiction too."

I gave her a look. "Maybe that's why he was being extra nice to us. He never mentioned it."

"He told me there was already a large investigation regarding Stacy. But much like with Lisa, there wasn't much to go on."

"You don't think Sheriff Peterson's doing much?" I asked.

"I don't know. He sounded serious enough," she said. "He sounded… different."

I chewed on my cigarette for a moment. "Maybe he's starting to see this mightn't just be a string of coincidences."

"Maybe," she said.

"So, what do we do now?" Brandon asked.

Amy looked at me, nodded slightly, then looked at Brandon. "I think we go and speak to Stacy's family."

DEATH NOTICE

Chapter 43

Amy drove to the motel and dropped off her things. Then we set off in her car. I wondered where my Hornet was. Was she at a garage yet? Were they looking after her? My poor baby.

Amy rang the girl's mother before we set off. The lady said that she would be pleased to meet with us. She was another single mother, but much younger than Auntie Rose. Mrs Vanucci was divorced, with one older son at university. She lived in a big house in the small town of Morton. It was a red-bricked affair with a double garage. Pure suburbia. Somewhere where this sort of crime shouldn't have happened.

After introductions, we were brought into a formal living room with plush sofas, a roaring fire in a huge hearth, and expensive looking wallpaper. Mrs Vanucci wore a patterned blouse, beige cardigan and a long black skirt. She emanated a quiet strength and overriding decorum. She was clearly upset and troubled, yet she couldn't be described as going to pieces. Once we were seated with drinks in front of us, Amy went into more detail about who we all were exactly. Mrs Vanucci nodded along, legs crossed, hands in her lap. I peered about the room as Amy continued. It was a beautiful house, but there was something lacking in it. Something perhaps a little stale. It may have been a warm and elegant house, but it seemed like a cold home.

"Could you tell us a little more about the day that Stacy went missing?" I asked, once we were further into the meeting.

"Of course," she said, carefully setting down her teacup on its saucer on the mahogany sideboard to her left. She pushed back her hair from her lightly made up, and still very attractive face. She appeared to be of Italian descent, with dark features, but bright blue eyes. "Stacy had gone around to our local store. As you can see, we live in a quiet part of town. The schools are a few miles away and we have very few businesses in the area. Not much traffic. We do have a little shop where we can pick up little things. Stacy goes there all the time. It's a family run place. Nice folks."

Her voice was steady, but she blinked away a tear and uncrossed and recrossed her legs several times.

"And how long was it before you phoned the police, Mrs Vanucci?" Amy asked.

"Well, after maybe forty minutes I went out in the car to check on Stacy. It's only about a minute away in the car. When I got there, there was no sign of my daughter. I spoke to the owners, and they said she had left almost half an hour earlier. I started to worry and drove around all the neighbouring streets. Nothing."

Her voice cracked a little. Brandon offered her a reassuring half-smile.

"And that's when you called the police?" I asked gently.

"Yes, yes that's right. I suppose it was about an hour before I rang them, once I got back here. They came very quickly."

"Did they?" I said, surprised.

"And that's when they found the bag of groceries?" Amy asked.

"Yes," said Mrs Vanucci, now visibly struggling to hold things together. "They were dumped over a garden wall, just a street away from here."

"I'm sorry," Amy said.

"And you think this may be connected to your cousin's disappearance?" Mrs Vanucci asked, blinking a few times.

"We don't know for sure," Amy said. "We're really trying to consider all possibilities. But we think it's a strong maybe."

"If we can help you and your family, we will," I said.

"Thank you," said Mrs Vanucci, before she broke down in tears.

Afterwards we went for an early dinner at a place in town called The Roost. It was a nice spot. Their speciality was locally sourced steaks, with their signature sauce, onion rings and fries. We all went for that. It was pretty great. Once we were onto desert and a few drinks down, we were all talked out about the cases. You can only go round and round in circles so many times. Especially in Amy's case; Lisa being one of her own. The meeting about another missing girl and another mother's heartache did not help the mood. But I think all of us needed to stifle the tap that pumped out adrenaline and anxiety. We needed a break.

DEATH NOTICE

Eventually, we started to relax and talk about *ordinary* things. I slagged off Destiny's Child who Amy quite liked. She talked about how she had hated *American Psycho*, which had recently been released. And Brandon generally made fun of us both for being over thirty. He also spent quite a lot of time texting on his phone.

"I really needed this," Amy said. "I missed you guys."

"Us too," Brandon said, looking up from his phone.

"I really wanted to be at the service yesterday. There was just too much still needed done."

"You can only do so much at once. And Rose was fine," I said, knowing Amy would have been worried about her.

"Good." She gave my hand a little squeeze, then slid her hand back and took a sip of her drink.

"What's with all the *texty texty*?" I asked, looking at Brandon.

Brandon squirmed.

"Nothing," he said.

Amy raised an eyebrow and a smile played at her lips. "It's a *girl*."

"Brandon, you dark horse," I said.

"Racist," Brandon said under his breath, still looking uncomfortable.

"Go on, spill," Amy said, putting her elbows on the table, staring across at him.

Brandon sighed and set his phone on the table. "Shut up, it's nothing… Just might meet somebody for a drink later," he said, reddening. "That's all."

"Someone around here?" Amy asked. "Who is it?"

Brandon rolled his eyes. I lifted my beer, smiling widely between swigs.

Brandon gave another heavy sigh. "It's Zara, okay? Just a drink."

"Oh… well that's lovely," Amy said, a little uncertain.

"Brandon, you child-snatcher," I said with a smirk.

"Be cool, Mick," he said, giving me a dig on the arm. "She's like three years younger than me."

"I'm only messing. Good for you, mate," I said.

He rolled his eyes again. "It's just one drink."

There was an awkward silence. Amy and I exchanged a schoolyard grins.

Amy put a hand over her mouth, her eyes dancing a little.

"Is there not a conflict of interest here, Brandon. Seeing as she's a witness and all?" I asked playfully.

Brandon scowled and took a drink of his beer. Amy's smile dropped. Damn, that was a little much maybe.

Stupid.

"Sorry, Brandon," I said. "Only mucking about."

"You just ignore him, Brandon," Amy said, with a mocking glance towards me.

That was a relief. I hadn't annoyed her too much.

I raised my hands. "She's great."

"Zara's a nice girl," Amy added.

"Can we change the subject now?" Brandon asked, a little sullenly.

We did change the subject, though I couldn't help sprinkling in a few winks and comments through the rest of the conversation. He took it okay. About forty minutes later, Brandon left to go and meet Zara.

"Just mom and pop left, now," Amy said, leaning back and taking a sip from her glass.

I smiled at her. "*I'm* too young to be his dad," I said.

She gave me a whack on the arm.

"People need to stop doing that," I said.

"You need to stop deserving it. It's nice for Brandon, though, isn't it? I hope he has a good time."

"He'll be grand," I said. "I've taught him everything he needs to know."

"That's what I'm worried about."

"Another drink?" I asked, getting to my feet.

"Why not?"

We had a few more. No, a lot more. We stayed there until chucking out time. The conversation flowed well and so did the drink. We talked about everything but Lisa. And that was much needed for both of us. I told her more about our trip to Ireland, then I waffled on about Ireland in general. I suppose I have a habit of doing that. Amy talked about her mum, their life together, and even about her getting back into sketching. We decided it was best to leave the car and stumbled up the road in the direction of the motel. The roads were quiet, and the night was still. No breeze. Not too cold out. We were both solidly drunk, probably the most I'd seen Amy, but she was smiling, enjoying herself. Despite everything, we'd had a great night. We continued on up the road, not very steadily.

"You want to see some of my sketches sometime?" Amy asked, threading her arm through mine, a goofy smile on her face.

"Yeah, of course. But I won't try showing you any of mine. Unless you like stickmen."

"I'm sure you're not that bad."

"I really am. Three-year-olds would be better than me. I'm better at modelling," I said, striking a pose for a second. "You could draw me."

Amy looked away, a smirk lingering.

"What?"

"Nothing."

"Go on," I said with a quizzical look.

"Maybe I already have," she said quietly.

"Sketched me?"

Her eyes narrowed, mock angry, "I sketch *lots* of things. C'mon, race you."

She took off along the road at pace.

"Jaysus," I said, and set off jogging.

She sped along the dirt track that cut across the field beside the motel. She was going at some pelt, though not quite as gracefully as when I'd seen her run before. Even so, I gave up after about twenty seconds and followed her the rest of the way walking, wheezing and starting to sweat. Eventually, I caught up.

"You need to cut down on the smokes," she said, panting gently, leaning against the outside of the building.

"Aye, that'll do it," I said, trying to catch my breath.

We had lowered our voices, most of the buildings in darkness or at least semi-darkness.

"You're mental, you," I said, coughing and wishing my heartrate would slow down.

"Maybe just a little bit," she said, smiling and leaning back against her door, stumbling a little. She giggled.

"You're pretty shitfaced," I said.

"Am not. Well, maybe."

We looked at one another and smiled. The night air smelled nice. Clean and fresh.

"You want a nightcap?" she asked, gesturing her head towards her room.

She locked eyes with me. There was no chance of getting my heartrate down now.

I couldn't be sure what she meant.

I knew I wanted to.

I also knew that I shouldn't.

"Better not, I'll be in no fit state tomorrow," I said reluctantly.

"You sure?" She took a step closer to me, her eyes still on mine.

Amy touched my coat sleeve for a moment and fiddled with the button.

"I'd like to…" I said carefully. "But better not."

She looked away and her mouth hardened.

"You're probably right," she said, and slid her key in the lock. "See you in the morning,"

And then she was gone.

Eejit.

DEATH NOTICE

Chapter 44

I went through my own door, cursing under my breath. My mind was running overtime, and I was taken aback to see Brandon standing there on the other side of the door. I'd forgotten I had a roomie.

"God," I said with a jolt.

"Easy there, Mick," he said.

"Sorry."

I had managed to pass myself, asking about his night and getting to my bed as quickly as possible. I had lit a cigarette and cursed myself quietly into my pillow.

Shit.

Shittity, shit.

Had I just knocked back the most beautiful, most intelligent, kindest woman that I knew? The girl that I quite possibly loved.

If I had, I knew it was the right thing to do.

She was drunk. Whatever she did think or didn't think about me, I didn't want anything to happen that way. If it wasn't bad enough that she was drunk, her cousin was missing, and her mother was sick.

Okay

Okay

Okay

I puffed frantically at my cigarette.

And maybe I was flattering myself anyway. Maybe she wasn't interested that way at all, and I had just turned her down for a last drink. Maybe it was even just a little drunken flirting.

But it didn't seem that way.

My sleep at best, you could say, was fitful. I remembered checking the time at 3am and again at four. Daylight finally creeping in through my window was almost a relief. I got up after six, no longer interested in the futile dance with sleep. I drank coffee and smoked cigarettes. Brandon got up about eight, just as I was starting to nod off in front of CNN. Typical.

"You look beat," he said. "You two must have hit it hard?"

"What? Oh yeah, we had a few drinks."

"A few?"

"Yeah. Who are you, my mother? So, your date went well?" I said, quickly changing the subject.

"It wasn't *a date*," Brandon said, pouring the remnants of the coffee pot into a cup.

"If you say so."

"But yeah, it was alright," he said with a little sideways smile.

"Good man, yourself," I said, and turned back to CNN. I didn't pay attention. I only thought about what might have been the night before.

After we were showered and Brandon and Amy had exchanged a few texts, she arrived at our door, knocked and came in.

"Morning," I said, getting up off the sofa. "Coffee?"

"I'm okay. We'll all get something at the café," she said breezily.

She went over and gave Brandon a hug and asked him about his night. She was very upbeat. Maybe too upbeat.

"You don't do hangovers?" Brandon asked. "You should have seen Mick when he came in last night."

Amy flitted her eyes to me. "I obviously can handle my drink better. Will we get going?"

We set off on the short walk into town. Amy continued to seem fine, as if nothing had happened. Maybe nothing *had* happened. Or maybe she'd been too drunk to remember. But she also didn't make much eye contact with me and spent most of the time talking to Brandon. We had breakfast at a greasy spoon. I had lots of bacon, lots of syrup and lots of coffee. We all chatted along fine, but there was a tenson that I felt only I noticed. There was nothing else for it, so I attempted to carry on like nothing had happened too.

We had an arrangement to meet at Auntie Rose's with her and Dustin McKeith. The plan was to go over everything with Lisa's

DEATH NOTICE

case and discuss the new disappearance too. McKeith was already there when we arrived. The coffee and cookie tray were in place as well. After the formalities, we got down to talking about it all and brainstorming anything else we should be doing. McKeith was dressed in an expensive looking polo shirt and trousers, well turned out as usual. He listened attentively, as usual, and this time it seemed genuine to me. Maybe I'd misjudged the guy. He had lost his son, so he knew how people like Auntie Rose felt. If he made a living off it too, maybe that wasn't so bad.

"Michael," he said after a short lull as Rose poured fresh coffee. "I heard about your bit of excitement the other night." He looked at me with a furrowed brow. "After the service."

"Yeah, fucked up my car pretty good," I said.

Amy shot me a look.

"Sorry," I said, gesturing a hand towards Rose.

"Come now, don't you think I've ever heard any bad words?" she asked with a twinkle, placing a hand on Amy's thigh. "I bet I know one or two you've never heard."

"I bet you do too," I said.

"So, do you think it was our man... the other night?" McKeith asked, bringing the conversation back around.

Brandon shrugged. "Don't see who else it could be."

"Yeah, I think so," I said.

McKeith nodded, his thick forehead frowning. "Terrible business, terrible. At least you're both unharmed. I should tell you, I've made contact with the other missing girl's family. The Vanuccis. They would like some help."

"Good of you to get in touch so quickly," said Rose, looking at him warmly.

"It's what we do. I only wish I could do more. I'm meeting the mother tomorrow. What you told me so far about the case," he said looking at Amy, "that will help me get a head start. Then we can focus on other things. A little knowledge is always better than none," he said with a light chuckle.

Amy nodded. She glanced towards Auntie Rose, then said gently, "If somebody is taking these girls, he has to be stopped."

"Amen to that," I said.

Chapter 45

After more coffee and a plate of cheese and tomato sandwiches, we were getting ready to leave. Then the doorbell sounded.

"Who's not already here?" Rose said with a forced little smile, then went out to answer the door. On her return, she was joined by Officer James Samuels.

"Afternoon, all," he said, tipping his hat. He was in full, well-pressed regalia, his hair freshly buzzed beneath his hat.

We all said our hellos before a cup and plate was forced upon Samuels and he was given a chair by Rose.

"Thank you, Mrs Kendrix. I was just coming to check in with you. Discuss any developments."

"Has something happened?" Rose asked, her face growing pale.

"No, no. Nothing like that," he said, struggling with his cup, plate and saucer. "Sorry, I just meant I wanted to talk things through.

"So, there's no news?" she asked, her voice hardening.

"I'm afraid no, not an awful lot."

"I was just going to be on my way when you called," said McKeith getting to his feet.

"We were too," I said, standing as well.

Amy and Brandon followed suit. Amy bent over and hugged her aunt, still in her chair.

"Do you want me to stay a while, Auntie Rose?" she asked.

"No, no, you go on, dear. I'll be fine."

"Alright, but I'll call you later," Amy said.

"Mick, can I just have a quick word?" Samuels asked me quietly.

We all proceeded to the front door, McKeith going out to his car, and Amy and Brandon getting into hers.

"Just give me a sec," I shouted after them. "What's up?" I asked Samuels.

My first thought was that Samuels had found out about Lisa and her girlfriend. What would I say to him about that? But his face looked serious, yet open, so I guessed maybe not.

"It's about the other night. We visited the crime scene and found a few bullet casings. We've sent them off to the big smoke for testing." He shrugged. "Not sure they'll tell us anything. It's worth a try."

"What about my car?" I asked, admittedly more interested in that.

He made a face. "Not great. The mechanic we took it to said he couldn't fix it. He wouldn't have the parts. It's getting towed to another place later today, out of town."

"Damn. Okay, cheers," I said, trying not to sound too heartbroken. "Any idea how long it'll take?"

He blew out his cheeks. "I guess we'll see what they say when they take a look at her."

"Okay, thanks," I said.

"Look after yourself," he said, and went back into the house and shut the door.

"She's a tough lady," I said, as we headed off up the road in Amy's car.

Amy nodded. "Did she seem okay to you?"

"Well... as much as she could, considering everything," I said.

"She looked a little upset at the end there," Brandon said from the back seat.

Amy nodded. "Yeah, I thought that too," she said. "I don't know. I'll ring her later and maybe call back in tonight."

"You're good to her," I said.

Amy shrugged. "She's family."

Amy had an appointment in Mount Greer, a couple of towns over with her old FBI colleague, and Brandon was meeting Zara for a coffee. Not much else was needed right then, so I just got Amy to drop me off in town. I said I could do with the walk. It was unusual to have some free time to myself. I headed to the nearest bar and ordered a pint and a chaser. I'd always liked bars in the afternoon. The artificial darkness, the quieter atmosphere, the feeling that you should really be out working, but were instead tying one on. This was a nice wee place. It had a local vibe about it. Old men were balanced precariously on bar stools like extras off *Cheers*. A few people were at tables eating grilled sandwiches. I didn't recognise anyone at first, until I did. There was Officer Lester, by himself at a table in the corner, nursing a pint. He looked like it wasn't his first of the day. I thought *sod it*, downed my short, lifted my pint, and got up. I crossed the room, set my pint down on his table and sat down beside him. Even when he saw it was me, his eyes looked all but vacant, his expression unmoving.

"What do *you* want?" he mumbled.

"I thought you might offer me some stimulating company." I picked up my pint and took a swig.

He hooded his eyes, then looked right at me. "Haven't you done enough?"

"Like what?"

"Like get me canned," he said with some grit in his voice. He picked up his glass, swilled it around and took a long pull.

"And how do you reckon I did that?" I asked.

"Doesn't matter," he said, looking away.

"Oh, you mean because I didn't like you getting a posse together and jumping me?" I put a bit of grit in my own voice and dropped the jocular tone. "And jumping my friends too. A kid and a woman."

Lester made a noise that sounded like *bah* and took another drink.

"I know it was you, and by the looks of things, so does your boss," I said.

"And what of it, if it was me?" he said, sitting up straighter, his voice rising.

I laughed. "Don't you think it reasonable for me not to be so happy about it?"

"Then you shouldn't have gone making trouble. Fighting with teenagers."

"So, it was over that. I thought I recognised that dickhead's da. And you're meant to be a cop. Serving and protecting."

"I *do* serve and protect," he said through clenched teeth, his clasp on his pint nearly breaking the glass.

"Is that what you call it?"

"Sometimes, yeah."

DEATH NOTICE

I lit a cigarette and leaned back in my chair. I looked about. Nobody was taking any notice of us. A baseball match was quietly buzzing away on a couple of TVs and a group of men in the other corner were having a seemingly very humorous conversation. Lester was looking into his glass. Apparently there was something very interesting inside it.

"Are you saying that jumping citizens is not your usual thing?" I said finally. "The first night we met, I had a fair idea of what you were like."

"I'm a good cop," he said, his eyes suddenly blazing. He thumped his fist down on the table and this time we did receive a few looks. His eyes darted around, then he lowered his head and put his hands on his knees. "Sometimes I've got to do things I'd rather not have to do."

"I think you liked it well enough."

"Think what you like," he said sullenly.

"Maybe I think you had something to do with Lisa's disappearance."

"What the fuck you say?" he said, leaning forwards, both fists now up on the table.

"You heard. So did you?"

"Bastard. What do you think I am? Some sort of damned pervert?" He was struggling to keep his voice low as it quivered with rage.

I leaned back again and lit up a smoke. I shrugged. "You tell me."

"I don't have to explain myself to you. I've never, *never* done anything that wasn't to protect somebody else. I don't mind getting my hands dirty sometimes, not like his high and mighty up there," he said gesturing his hand vaguely. "But if you ever suggest I'd be involved in something like that again, I'll break your fucking neck."

"Then next time you'll need a few more buddies. And a bigger stick."

Chapter 46

I went to a bar across the street and had a few jars in there, thinking everything through. Nothing much was breaking loose in my grey matter. Though after talking with Lester, I didn't like him any better, but I liked him less as a suspect for taking Lisa. Then I began the walk up to the motel. It was after dinnertime, and I was starting to feel peckish. As I was approaching the buildings, Amy appeared, hurrying out of the door of her room, locking it and starting towards her car.

"Amy," I shouted.

She looked up, distracted.

"Are you okay?" I asked.

"Yeah... yeah, think so."

"Did your meeting go okay?" I asked, stopping up beside her.

"Yeah, fine, not much from it. It's not that. I've been ringing Auntie Rose on and off the last few hours. No answer. I'm heading over to check on her."

"Maybe she's out seeing a friend or something."

"Yeah, but she's not answering her cell either," she said, unlocking her car and starting to get in.

"Want me to come with you?"

She gave a little smile. "Yeah, thanks, Mick."

We didn't talk much on the short journey. The sun had gone down and the streetlights were on, even though it wasn't very late. When we pulled up outside, the house was in darkness, but Rose's car was in the drive.

Not a great sign.

Amy visibly tensed up.

She quickly got out and I followed. We rushed up the pathway and saw the door was lying a few inches open. Amy pulled out her Glock from her back pocket and I regretted leaving my Colt at the motel. Amy widened her stance, raised her gun, and kicked the door wide open. She went in, aiming the gun around the hallway as I came in close behind.

"Auntie Rose?" she shouted. "It's me... Amy."

DEATH NOTICE

Silence.

We headed towards the kitchen where a faint smell of coffee lingered. It was dark, but we could see she wasn't in there. We crossed to the living room. The door was closed. Amy nodded at me and aimed her gun at the door. I eased around her, pressed down the handle and flung the door open.

The room was only illuminated by the moon's rays, breaking through the blinds in stripes across the wall. Rose was slumped in her chair in an unnatural position. It looked like something black was oozing from her chest and left knee.

"Oh my God!" Amy hit the light switch and ran across to her, tossing the gun on the floor.

The new light made everything worse. Rose was very pale, eyes shut, and it appeared that she had been shot in both her chest and leg.

"Auntie Rose, Auntie Rose!" Amy shouted, giving her a gentle shake before putting pressure on the wound in her chest. I ran over and examined her knee. She'd lost a lot of blood from both wounds. Amy looked at me helplessly as she kept her hands pressed to Rose's chest. I stood up and put an ear to Rose's mouth.

"There's a faint breath," I said.

"Thank God. Ring 911," Amy said, nodding to the portable phone in its cradle on the coffee table. I picked it up, dialled, and scooped up the gun with my other hand. I did a quick scout around the rest of the house as I placed the call. By the time I had been all over the house, confirming it was empty, there were sirens in the distance. After that, it's all just a horrible blur.

Chapter 47

Amy went with Auntie Rose in the ambulance, and I followed behind in her car. I'd have been many times over the limit, but any drunkenness was long gone. I found Amy in the ER after she had been chucked out while a team worked on Rose. Amy was crying and being led away by a nurse. Then she threw up on the floor.

I helped get Amy cleaned up with some blue paper towels as an orderly mopped the floor stoically.

Then began a terrible and endless haze of waiting, tears and asking for news.

It was all bright lights, bleachy smelling floors, white coats, noise, crying.

I did my best in comforting Amy, but to be fair, I was in a bit of shock myself.

Back and forth, different seating areas, somebody else crying… someone screaming. Police escorting a woman past in handcuffs… family members crying… Patients ushered past on beds, drips in their arms.

About two hours in, Amy was more together and had even accepted a cup of coffee from me, albeit terrible stuff from a machine. A doctor had been out to see her several times and had just told her that Rose was alive and even had stabilised some. They had been forced to give her drugs to put her into a coma.

Now we were seated in another hallway near to the ER and the whole place had quietened down. Amy had gone into the bathroom to wash her face and had taken the rest of her makeup off while she was at it. She'd tied her hair back too. Despite everything and the strain on her face, I couldn't help but register yet again how naturally beautiful she was.

"At least they've managed to stabilise her some," I said, taking her hand for a moment.

Amy nodded weakly and stared down into her coffee, hunched over in her plastic chair.

"Who did this?" she asked, running her free hand across her tired eyes.

DEATH NOTICE

"I don't know, Amy." I put a hand to her face and turned her jaw towards me. "But I'm going to find him and I'm going to put him down."

She held my stare, so much there in her eyes. Too much to know exactly what.

Then suddenly they widened. "Brandon!"

"It's okay, it's okay," I said getting to my feet. "I'll go ring him," I said as calmly as I could, and went off in search of a payphone.

As I hurried through the busy triage area, I felt my heart pump erratically. I was in the right place if I was going to have a heart attack. I felt guilty for not considering Brandon earlier. He could be in danger. Or at least, he would be worried about where we were.

When he answered, sounding relaxed and casual, I took in a very deep breath. I told him what had happened. His positive tone immediately dropped away. We decided that there was no point in him trying to come across. I told him to be careful and keep himself safe. We didn't know what we were dealing with here. I'd let him know more as soon as it happened. I reminded him where the guns were and urged him to keep one beside him at all times.

I returned to where I had left Amy. James Samuels was talking to her in the hall along with another officer. His new partner was everything that Lester wasn't. Young, attractive and female. They were all deep in conversation, looking like it was verging on heated. I sidled up to the group, nodded to the two cops, and handed a coffee to Amy. She accepted it absently, then turned back to Samuels.

"So, my auntie was fine when you left?" Amy asked, her voice hard.

Samuel's eyes narrowed, "Yes, of course... I mean." He looked at me, confusion on his face.

"What time did you leave?" Amy snapped.

"I don't know, I guess ten minutes after you," he said.

His colleague looked uncomfortable and a little bemused. I had forgotten that we had left Samuels with Rose and that had been the last we heard from her.

"You didn't see anybody else around?" I asked him evenly.

"No, it was quiet," he said, swallowing hard and holding my stare.

Amy looked fit to pop. "Did you hurt her?" she half shouted, taking a step closer to him.

"What?" He backed away.

I stepped in between them. "Okay, there's been a lot to take in," I said, trying to block Amy with my body.

"Did you?" Amy said, trying to push past me.

"Of course not. Why would you think…?" Samuels started.

"Let's give Amy some space," I said, putting an arm on Samuels and giving him a gentle push. "It's okay," I said raising a palm up to his colleague. "C'mon, let me get you some of this cat piss coffee. Amy, I'll be back in a minute."

I hustled them away down the hall. I glanced back at Amy, still standing there, one fist clenched, the coffee cup in her other hand spilling over her fingers, apparently unaware. I found another quiet corridor, just beyond the soda machines, and stopped.

"What was that about?" Samuels asked, his face pained.

"She doesn't know what she's saying. She's exhausted," I said.

Samuels and his partner exchanged a look. "But why would she…?"

"Like I said, Amy's had a massive shock. She leaves her Auntie's house with you there and when she goes back, she's… well you know what."

Samuels nodded, a faraway look on his face. "Yeah, but still. I'm a cop."

"Lester's a cop." I gave him a look.

His lips straightened into a line.

"Are you here to take statements?" I asked, redirecting the conversation.

"Yeah. The sheriff and a team are at the house now. State Forensics should be there by now as well," he said.

"Good," I said. "Why don't you get yourselves a coffee? I'll go check on Amy and then I'll give you a statement, okay?"

They said it was. I went back to Amy, and she was in a bad way. It took me nearly half an hour to calm her and stop her from having another go at Samuels. A doctor came and said that Amy could sit

DEATH NOTICE

with Auntie Rose for a brief time, and I took the opportunity to go and finish up with Samuels. Forty minutes later and they were on their way, leaving a State Trooper on patrol for Rose's safety.

The rest of the night and the following morning was another blur. Most of the time saw me and Amy sitting on plastic chairs, hour after hour with nothing much happening. We didn't sleep any, though we both let our eyes close for a few seconds at a time. I smoked half a deck out the front between attempts at comforting Amy.

Around six the next morning, a doctor told Amy that Rose was very sick, but not in any immediate danger. He said she should go home and get some rest. She wouldn't. Amy told me I should, but I said no too. At about nine, Amy insisted that I go to the motel and get an hour or two's sleep, get Brandon and we could come back together later.

"I'm really not sure about this," I said.

"What good are you to me if you're a zombie the next few days as well as me?" she said.

I shrugged.

"And besides, I'm worried about Brandon. We don't know who did this and I don't want him over there by himself."

I gave in and promised to be back in a few hours.

I don't remember driving Amy's car back to the motel or much of the conversation with Brandon when I got there. I was running on empty. I do remember having a last smoke and a small measure of Bushmills. I then allocated myself two hours sleep and set my alarm.

It felt like five minutes. I woke up, feeling like I had the worst hangover of all time. I showered and brushed my teeth and Brandon, the legend, had rustled me up some scrambled eggs and toast.

The rest of the day was completely bizarre and felt like three long days in one. Again, most of it was spent waiting on cracked plastic chairs. Only this time, there were three of us. There was no change with Rose. Doctors and nurses occasionally spoke with Amy. She was allowed in with Rose for brief periods. We went through every emotion. We went through every possibility of who could have done this. I smoked a lot. I drank a lot of bad coffee. We convinced Amy to go off for a lie down a few times on a couch in a visitor's room. By evening she insisted again that we should both leave and get a sleep but refused to leave herself. We made her promise that she would let us take over the vigil in the morning for a while. Reluctantly, we drove away in Amy's car. We had no idea that the day's events had barely even begun.

DEATH NOTICE

Part 3: Bowels of Love

Chapter 48

It's fair to say that I was tired. Brandon was pretty beat too. We drove and smoked. Despite the cold night, we kept the windows down. Amy would probably be pissed that we were smoking in her car, but there was little chance we'd drive all the way back without doing so. I found a little blues station and we passed the time with some pretty cool Howlin' Wolf and Johnny Lee Hooker tunes. We didn't talk much. The roads were quiet. A light drizzle had begun to fall. I had the wipers on low. I slowed once we were off the intersect on the edge of Six Mile, approaching the main bridge into town.

Something must have caught my eye as we began to cross over. It may have been the beam of the car picking out something. Whatever it was, I slowed and was alert. That was just as well because all at once a van with no lights on came out of nowhere, trying to shunt us from the side. I managed to skid to a stop, almost ploughing the car into the barrier above the river. The van chunked into reverse, looking to pull back and maybe have another go. I slammed Amy's car into reverse too and ripped back across the bridge. Suddenly Brandon had a Glock in his hands and was winding down the window, then leaning out as we flew backwards. The van had righted itself and was hurtling towards us.

The same van.

Brandon plunged off two rounds, both smashing through the windshield.

The driver ducked down, then grinded the gears into reverse again.

Now we were each reversing away from one another.

The van swerved off the bridge, spun around clumsily, then took off towards Six Mile.

"Bugger it," I said and worked the gears and bolted off forwards again, flying across the bridge in pursuit.

"Let's get the fucker," Brandon said.

I nodded. "Nice shooting by the way."

The van tore through the town. Luckily not much traffic was around to get in the way. We chased after him, keeping close. Brandon ducked out the window a few times, gun in hand. He couldn't get a clear shot.

"Steady on, Sam Jackson," I said. "You don't want to miss and hit someone."

Brandon gave me a look. "Sam Jackson?"

I shrugged.

We carried on at quite the clip. The van did a loop around and took the other bridge out of town. There was no room to pass him. I didn't know if shunting him would do much good and it wasn't my car either. The van clattered off the edge of the bridge and accelerated up to near seventy before we were even on the freeway. When we sped onto it, he immediately got up to ninety and pushed on.

I gave Brandon a wink, "As Sam said in Jurassic Park, 'Hold onto your butts.'"

I floored it, pulling into the left lane to pass him. He saw my move early and swung over to block me. I slammed on the brakes and skidded back into the right lane.

"Bastard," I said.

The next exit was for Westbrooke, and he swung off onto the slipway. I'd lost some ground and tried to keep my speed up as I veered off behind him. He carried on through the outskirts of the town. It was a single lane road and there was a big food lorry up ahead, and a bend beyond that. I made up some ground. Suddenly he pulled out into the oncoming traffic, just before the bend.

"Maybe he'll just get himself killed," Brandon said wryly.

He only just made it and sped up along the empty road ahead. I was struggling to get around the lorry, dipping in and out into the centre of the road.

"Sod it," I said and pulled out into the oncoming lane, just before another bend.

"Shit!" Brandon said, reaching for the handrail. Maybe he was looking for an emergency cord. I put my foot down and was about halfway into passing the big lorry. Then a SUV appeared, coming right at us from around the corner.

We shouted "Fuck!" in unison and I hit the brakes and pulled us in back behind the lorry, just as the now braking SUV whistled past us, its driver hammering down on his horn.

"Yeah, same to you too, dickhead," I said under my breath.

I waited for a straight run, then pulled out and managed to get past the lorry and pulled back in again.

"Where is the bastard?" I said when we were finally ripping along, just outside the town centre. There was no sign of him.

I slammed my fist on the wheel. "Shite!"

We both scanned all around. There were some smart-looking treelined streets, a school closed up for the night, and a doctor's surgery. I slowed as we passed the three or four roads, looking up each one. I couldn't be sure, but I saw no sign of him. I thought our best option was to press on. Next, we passed by a fenced in housing development. I paused at the front gates. It all looked to be in darkness and there was a padlocked chain across it. We went on. Then we passed a little clump of shops, all closed up for the night, then five or six more residential streets. We both cursed. A lot. He could be up any of them. Now we were almost in the town centre. He could have been anywhere.

We'd lost him.

Chapter 49

I didn't phone the cops right away. What was the point? I needed a drink, and a smoke. Brandon did too. I thought smoking weed in Amy's car might be pushing it, despite the fact we'd nearly just got it written off. I walked around with him outside while he had a joint and then we found a bar. It was a trampy looking place, but their drinks were cold, and I wasn't feeling fussy. I took a local beer along with a Jameson's, ice and lemonade. Brandon settled for a bottle of Bud. He was still young.

"You alright?" I asked after taking a sip from both.

"If I wasn't used to this crap by now, there'd be something wrong with me."

"I suppose so," I said.

I felt tired, but the adrenalin was still pumping around me. There was no time to process anything. I felt we were no closer to figuring out who had taken Lisa, despite everything that had happened. My poor brain was crammed with various emotions and questions about Lisa, Auntie Rose, Amy, my father.

"You think it was our guy?" Brandon asked, lighting up a regular smoke.

I ran a clammy hand over my face. "I think it was the same guy who tried it last time. Other than that, I don't know."

"Can't believe he got away again," Brandon said.

"Don't remind me."

"It wasn't the finest attempt by him, was it?" Brandon said.

"Well, I think you scared the shite clean out of him."

Brandon smiled. "How come you say *shite* sometimes and not *shit*?"

"Because it sounds cooler? I don't know."

"I did scare him, though, didn't I?"

"You sure did." I chewed on the end of a cigarette before lighting it. "That's why it's weird. The difference."

"What do you mean?"

"This guy. If he's lifting girls, that's one thing. He's not a professional so to speak. He's some kind of psycho maybe, right?

DEATH NOTICE

But he plans it out, maybe. Gives himself time. Taking us on is a different ball game. If it's him coming at us, he's messed it up each time."

"Sure did."

"It's not his thing."

"People fighting back, not just lifting young girls."

"Yeah, maybe," I said, finally lighting up my cigarette, the anticipation at its peak. "But it doesn't seem to fit with the shooting. I mean, shooting an old lady in the leg and chest?"

Brandon shrugged, "Might not be that different from targeting young girls, targeting someone older. When he tries people our age, I say *our age* loosely you understand," Brandon said and shot me a grin, "when he tries that, he comes out bad."

"That's true," I said. "But why go after Rose at all?"

"Same reason he would go after us, I guess. He thinks we're getting too close."

A long day became a long night.

We drove out to the Sheriff's Department to tell them what had happened. We didn't see anyone we knew there, but they were all well aware of recent events. They were actually pretty nice to us. After we made our statements, we headed back to the motel. I debated whether to ring Amy or not. She had enough on our mind, but I wouldn't forgive myself if something else happened and I hadn't told her. We rang her from the motel, about one in the morning. We were on Brandon's mobile, both smoking, on the sofa, totally done in.

She had answered after the first ring. At least we hadn't woken her. We told her what had gone on.

"God, I can't believe this," she said after listening carefully to us both on speaker. "You're sure you're both okay."

"We're fine, Amy," I said. "I just want you to be extra cautious. We've really no idea who we're dealing with here."

"I will. There's still a trooper out front. And I've got my gun... *guns,* actually."

"Good," I said. "We'll try and get a couple of hours sleep, then be back with you early morning, okay?"

"Don't rush, Walker," she said.
Frigsake. Back to Walker, are we?
"Okay. But we'll be there early enough."
"And we'll bring donuts," Brandon chimed in.
We hung up.
I slumped back against the sofa and exhaled slowly.
"Game of cards before bed?" Brandon asked.
"Yeah, I'll grab the beers."

DEATH NOTICE

Chapter 50

The Killer had found an out of the way garage that wouldn't ask too many questions. He paced in the alleyway outside, wearing an out-of-character hoody, jeans and baseball cap. The mechanic had clearly known what the holes in the windscreen were caused by. There was a look in his eye when an extra couple of bills were pushed into his palm. It probably wasn't the first time he had seen holes like that.

The killer felt exposed.

He didn't like being out in public like this.

He was anonymous when stalking potential prey. He didn't like stepping out in public outside his carefully crafted image. Certainly, he always did his best to avoid a link to anything nefarious. And now here he was. Bullet holes no less. The van had been paid for in cash several years earlier and there was no paper link to him at least. But still. He scolded himself for how they had got the better of him again.

He got into the van and strapped on his belt.

Stupid.

Careless.

He knew he should have had a better plan. He almost wished he hadn't tried to take them out in the first place. They weren't even that close. Clueless imbeciles. Now he had no choice. He had been shamed by them. He had been made to look foolish and for that they would have to pay.

The killer glanced in his rear-view mirror and saw the mechanic looking towards him. He was stood in his oil-stained overalls, his face set. Then he turned on his heel and began tinkering with a head gasket on his workbench.

It wouldn't do.

The killer undid his belt and got out of the van.

"Sorry, do you have a rest room I could use quickly?" he asked, striding back into the garage. He picked up a wrench.

Before the mechanic could answer, the first blows rained down on his head.

Chapter 51

I got maybe five hours sleep. It wasn't enough, but it was something. When we got back to the hospital the next morning, Amy was fast asleep. A side room had become free, and the nurses had insisted that she take it. We had no intention of waking her. Instead, we got coffees and returned to the all-too familiar row of plastic seats. There was not much change with Rose, we were told. About an hour and a half later, Amy emerged, tired eyed and groggy, in the previous day's clothes.

"Morning…" she croaked, "…or evening. I've lost track. What time is it?"

It was difficult to tell at the best of times there, with the burning lights on full, a constant state of brightness.

"I'm sure you don't know which way's up," I said. "It's about ten in the morning. Did you sleep much?"

"I got a bit."

"How 'bout going back for a few hours at the motel? Do you good." Brandon said.

Amy shook her head. "I'll maybe go for a shower and lay low for a couple of hours. They say Auntie Rose is stable for now. I've another meeting with my friend from the FBI. I thought you guys could come too?"

"Of course. Whatever you need," I said.

Shortly afterwards, she let me drive her back to the motel, while she half-dozed on the passenger seat. She had a quick shower and at half past twelve she was looking just shy of a million dollars. Then we were all on the way to meet her ex-colleague, Jed Wilson. We met him for a light lunch in a pizzeria we'd been to once before. Jed was early thirties, tall, well turned out in a nice suit, no tie. He had thick black hair, kept short and a pair of thin, round glasses. He was personable. I liked him. He wouldn't have struck me as typical FBI. More like an affable maître de.

"Jed's been working on a profile for our guy," Amy said, once we were all settled and had talked through the highlights of the last few days. Jed had listened attentively while slicing up his pizza

DEATH NOTICE

with a knife and fork. "I think it's going to really help us," she added.

Brandon and I both nodded, between mouthfuls of breadsticks with garlic butter. Jed put his fork down, smiled uncertainly and dabbed his chin with a napkin.

"Now... this isn't official and is very much just an early sketch."

"I know you, Jed," Amy said. "You'll have been as thorough as you can with what you have."

"But, honestly," he said, lifting up his briefcase and taking out a blue binder. "It really is only a start." He threw up his hands and smiled again. "And these things can be *waaay* off. You know how it sometimes goes, Amy."

"I'm just grateful for what you've done," Amy said. I noticed her place a hand over his, the way she had done with me before. I struggled not to wince.

There was a lull in our chatter while Amy began scanning through the folder. The rest of us quietly chewed on our breadsticks and sipped our Birre Moretti's. After a few moments, Amy passed the folder to me. I leafed through it, picking out a few key details: *probably male, probably white, 18-45, likely criminal record, at least average intelligence, could lead a double life, access or ownership of a van, access to armed weapons, probably lives within a fifty-mile radius of the disappearance, likely even closer...*

I looked up at Jed, gave a half smile and blew out my cheeks.

"It's my best guess," he said, smiling and giving a shrug. "One problem we have is that we cannot be completely certain that it is the same person involved with Lisa's disappearance. The attacks with the van and the masked attack on you three," then turning to Amy and placing a hand on hers, "or on your Auntie Rose."

Amy looked at him widely, tears in her eyes.

"But you think it probably is, Jed?" I asked.

He rubbed an eye, tilting his glasses with his other hand. "It's fairly likely, in my opinion. As I said, if I make certain presumptions. it is reasonable to suppose that in this area it is the same person abducting the girls. I'd say it was him who orchestrated the attacks on you with the van too. I think the guys with the masks were just some locals who wanted to throw their weight around. However, the attack on Rose," he gave a shake of his head, "I can't make it fit either. I mean… I'm not saying it is not the same person definitively."

"I have the same feeling," I said.

"I can't come up with a sensible reason as to why that happened to Amy's Aunt," he went on, glancing at Amy with concern. "Not if the profile is largely correct. Either way, I think we are unfortunately dealing with a person or persons who are very dangerous."

DEATH NOTICE

Chapter 52

"Seems a nice dude," Brandon said as we drove away from the restaurant in Amy's car.

"He is. A real gem," Amy said, turning around in the passenger seat to look back at Brandon.

"Given us something to go on too," I said, resisting the urge to light up a smoke in the car in front of her.

"Yeah, there's a lot there," Amy said with a sigh. "I'll have a proper look through it before I go back to the hospital."

"Nice of him to do it for you," I said.

"Yeah, we always got on well. Most other people in the FBI, not so much." She made a face.

"You two ever…?" I started and wished I hadn't.

Her mouth tipped open. She gave me a strange look. "Me and *Jed*?"

She began to laugh, for the first time in a long time. "Oh my God, no."

I shrugged. "Seems a good guy. People would probably say… pretty handsome too." I felt my cheeks flush.

Jaysus, shut up, Mick.

"A lot of *guys* would," she said, smiling.

"What?"

"Jed's gay, Mick."

"Oh."

Brandon leaned forwards, "Really? But he's not… y'know…"

"Camp?" Amy said. "Not every gay guy is like Jack in *Will and Grace*."

"Yeah, I know," Brandon said.

"Very backwards of you, Brandon," I said with a grin.

"Oh yeah," Amy said. "Because you're such an openminded, modern man."

I raised an eyebrow. "I'd say Jed is more like the Will Truman character in that show."

This time both their mouths dropped open as I threw the car into fifth.

Back at the motel, Brandon and I chugged coffee as Amy took a long shower next door. Afterwards, Amy joined us and took a couple of cups and a cold pancake. Amy said that she was fine just to return to the hospital by herself, but I talked her into letting me come too. Brandon offered as well, but Amy talked him around. He was probably relieved. The kid had already gone above and beyond time and time again. I guessed that he might send off a few texts to Zara as soon as we left.

The afternoon went slowly. So did the evening. Amy was holding up, considering. Some of the time she became upset, some of the time just lost in thought. At other moments, she chatted about regular things, seeming more like herself. At one point she was allowed in again to see Rose and this time she asked if I'd like to go in with her. Inside the little room, Rose was hooked up to all sorts of machines. It was similar to my father's hospital room, though a little newer. A little less bleak, I thought. There was a low light on attached to the mechanisms above the bed. There were two plastic chairs placed beside the bed. Amy led the way, went across and took her auntie's hand. She spoke gently to her as if she was awake and then sat down. Amy ushered me across, and I sat.

I looked down at Rose's slightly shrivelled looking body, her face looking much older than it had done. Her hair looked thin and greasy. The energy was absent, along with her smile, warm voice and quiet elegance. I felt a surge of rage in the pit of my stomach. How bloody dare somebody do this to her.

Amy turned to me and then looked at me strangely. She must have seen something in my face.

"I know," she said nodding. Understanding.

"We're going to get who did this to you, Auntie Rose," she said, turning back and again taking the pale hand, the veins raised and prominent.

"We'll find who did this," Amy said again. "And we'll find Lisa, do you hear me? And you're going to get better, just you see."

Amy's last syllables caught in her throat. She turned to me and cried into my chest.

"It's okay," I said, stroking her hair.

I wondered if Amy believed any of the promises she had just

made.

We stayed that way for some time. The gentle tick of the clock on the wall. The raspy breathing of Rose beside us.

Eventually Amy lifted her head and wiped her face.

She gazed at me, her lips slightly apart, her eyes full. "Tell me about visiting your father. I mean, properly... everything... how you feel about it."

I let out a little sigh. Wilde came to mind again.

"'Men become old, they never become good,'" I said.

Then I told her about it all.

Chapter 53

That night, Amy agreed to come back and sleep at the motel. We left the hospital at about ten, approaching the motel just before eleven. From a distance I could see the office was in darkness, long locked up for the night. There were a few dim lights on in other rooms, though most of the cabins were vacant.

As we approached the gate, Amy jolted, grabbed my arm and said, "Stop!"

"Bugger," I said, pumping the brakes and pulling up on the wasteland on the right.

"Sorry Mick, it's just... I've got a bad feeling."

I swallowed and kept my voice level. "A *bad feeling*?"

"I don't know." She rolled her eyes with embarrassment. "Brandon was texting back and forth earlier, but I just remembered he never replied to my last one. That was hours ago. And look up there," she said, pointing off past my room in the distance. "There's a car tucked in around behind, you see it?"

I squinted through the blackness, and I saw it. I nodded.

"It's probably nothing..." she said, looking unsure.

"Probably just a bad feeling, but it's not like we haven't had a lot of bad things happen lately." I tried an encouraging smile. "Let's go check it out on foot."

I killed the lights and switched off the engine. We each took out our weapons. Amy had her Glock and I had my Colt. To be exact, my 1976 Colt M19. The weapon I had been given as a young IRA recruit. It still felt good in my hands. We checked our guns, then got out and naturally both paused at the side of the car. There was no noise. The rooms, a few hundred yards beyond, had not altered in any way. Nobody had come out. No lights had been switched on and turned off. There was a breeze on the air, the hushed sounds of leaves rolling around, and a lock or chain lightly clinking in the wind someplace. We walked on, keeping low, guns at our sides. Amy led the way. It reminded me of one of our earlier scouting missions, back when we barely knew one another. Even that was

DEATH NOTICE

still less than a year ago. What were we now? Old friends? It certainly felt that way. And I hoped perhaps much more.

We were quiet as we passed by the empty cabins and just as quiet as we passed the remaining two. Television shows could be heard as clearly as if we were inside watching. A ball game was on in one, and an old Clint Eastwood western in the other. As we went by Amy's empty room, the noises faded into the distance, replaced by something else. Men's voices. Indistinct, but somewhere beyond. Amy shot me a look. I had been at somewhere around twenty five percent alertness, now it was closer to ninety. The voices were coming from inside my motel room. We both crept up, stopping just shy of the windows, the curtains shielding those inside. But the voices were now quite clear.

Two men.

Belfast accents.

Bollox.

This wasn't our child stalker. This was something else. This was something from home. It all fell into place instantly. Someone had been on the plane. Somebody *had* been following me. Maybe not the van, maybe yes. That was probably still our other guy. But this was people after me, and me alone.

Amy shot me another look, her eyes wide, as we both listened.

"I'm not going to fucking ask you again, ye wee nigger-boy, do you hear me? Where is he? Where's Mick Walker?"

My Colt felt slippery in my perspiring hand.

"I'd do what he says," said the other one, his voice low and menacing. "You know we ain't messin' about. Just look at your knee."

That gave me an added jolt.

I ducked down beneath the window and came up the other side. I eased my face close to the glass and managed to peer through a crack in the curtains. The two men were standing with silenced guns in their hands. Between them was Brandon. He was tied to a chair, a gag hanging down around his chin. His face was bloodied and pale. Much worse was his knee, bleeding from what I guessed was a bullet hole.

I nearly vomited.

This was all my fault.

Then another piece of the jigsaw slotted into place before the man even spoke again.

"And you know what we did to the old lady. Come on now, lad, this is your last chance."

Amy stared at me, her lips apart.

Everything was there in that look. Everything and nothing.

Helplessly, I stared back at her. Tears filled my eyes.

"I'm sorry," I mouthed across to her.

She shut her eyes and shook her head at me.

What did that mean? She didn't blame me, did she? What would that even matter? Rose and Brandon had both been shot because of me. Whatever she did or didn't think, I would always blame myself. That was immediately clear to me. Another few chains to carry around with me.

"M'on, ye black bastard," shouted the first, shattering my brief reverie. Then there was a sickening thud as he punched Brandon in his stomach. Brandon doubled over as much as he could in the chair.

I ducked back under and over to Amy. There was no time for soul searching. Brandon could still be saved. I only had seconds before any further damage was done. Already, Brandon would maybe never walk properly again. I'd seen dozens of kneecappings in my time. Sometimes just the results. Other times, I had been part of it. *Punishment shootings.* That's what we had called them. Punishment for what? Some act of insubordination or other, whatever the army council thought justified it. I had no time to feel any other mounds of deep dug guilt. That would have to wait too.

Amy moved off with the instructions I whispered, and I crawled back under the window. Then I got on my feet and bolted across the front of the rest of the building. I got around the side of their car, a BMW. The little red light flashed on the dashboard. Thank God for that. I moved around the side of it, braced myself and began rolling back and forth on my heels, pushing the car with every ounce of strength. I managed a tiny piece of momentum going and pushed even harder, following every brace with a push.

DEATH NOTICE

Finally, the car's alarm screeched into life. I ducked down and hid behind the car.

Moments later a slice of light swept across the gravel as the front door opened. Then there was the trudge of footsteps. The car alarm wailed on, undeterred. It was the smaller man, gun in one hand, car key in the other. I leaped up and struck him across the face with the butt of my Colt. He buckled. I hit him again on the top of his head and blood spurted out. He fell to the ground. I leaned over him and finished the job. I reached over to his hand and pressed the key fob. The wailing of the alarm ceased abruptly. I got quietly off my knees and approached the door, my gun raised. I was able to peer around and could see the other man stood beside Brandon's chair, his gun pointed at Brandon's head.

I backed behind the doorway.

No clear shot.

I swivelled the Colt and held it in part by the barrel, my finger still in the guard.

"It's Walker. Your buddy's dead," I shouted.

There was a long pause.

"Come out, Walker, or your wee mate is getting shot in his head. He's already got one in the knee."

I walked in an arc, approaching the door a few feet out, my gun raised, dangling on my finger, but pointed back at me.

I remembered that night in Belfast in 1992.

"Alright, I'm coming," I said. "Nobody else needs to die here tonight." I approached the door very slowly and locked eyes with the man.

He was about forty, dark hair with no greys and still with a few youthful curls. His face was ruddy and his eyes cold.

"Hold it there," he said as I was almost inside.

I stopped.

He licked his lips and gave a brief cough.

"Put your gun down," he said.

I paused, then said loudly, "Chassis."

"What?" he said, with a tilt of his head.

Instantly, the internal door crashed open as Amy burst through it, gun raised. The man turned, swivelling his gun towards her. I spun my Colt around my finger, aimed and pulled the trigger. I caught him in the shoulder.

He yelled as I took a step inside.

Amy's gun boomed in the brief quietness.

Now he had a bullet in his other shoulder too.

He dropped his gun and went down. Amy strode on, scooping the gun away with one foot, before giving him a kick in the head with the other.

DEATH NOTICE

Chapter 54

Amy kept her gun trained on him as I attended to Brandon.

"You're okay, mate. It's going to be grand," I said, ripping off a piece of curtain and using it as a tourniquet.

Brandon was semi-conscious, his eyes lolling in his head. He was very pale. If it wasn't for his bonds, he would have fallen over.

I stood up, eyeballed the man on the floor. He was in a bad way. He expression resembled that of a Halloween pumpkin. He was bleeding, but it looked like the bullets hadn't gone through. He was still conscious, though groaning. There wouldn't be long.

I turned to Amy. "We need to get Brandon to a hospital."

"What about him?" Amy said, gesturing to the man.

I looked at him. "What's your name?"

"Fuck off," he mumbled.

I gave him a kick in the ribs. He wheezed and doubled over.

"James Joyce," he said.

I went to give another kick. "Alright, alright," he said quickly as I pulled the kick.

"McKeegan… Andy McKeegan."

"Right, well, Andy, are there any more of youse?"

He blew out his cheeks. "Does it fuckin' look like it?" he said with a gesture of his hand.

"You shot my Auntie?" Amy hissed.

I looked to her. Her face was set, her gun arm steady like rock.

He didn't say anything.

Amy took a step closer. "I asked you a question," she said.

He glared back.

Amy's gun was now almost against his face.

He flicked his hair away from his eyes, then eyeballed her. "Yeah, I shot the old bitch."

The night shook with the bark of Amy's Glock.

I'd seen enough of bloody hospitals.

Amy and I were yet again seated in the ER. Brandon was in with the surgeons. They had told us that his life was not at risk, but the damage to his knee was bad. Amy had driven us at breakneck speed back to the hospital again. I had sat in the back with Brandon, putting pressure on his wound and comforting him best that I could. He was in and out of consciousness and even managed a weak smile a few times. Through tears in my eyes, I had told him how sorry I was. When he was wheeled away on a gurney, it was all I could do not to sob like a little child.

"It's not your fault, Mick," Amy said again.

I was bent over, cradling a plastic cup of coffee. I looked up at her and tears pricked my eyes. I shook my head and looked back down.

"I mean it. It's not your fault." She put a hand on my shoulder.

I looked up again and a big tear dropped from her own eye.

"I'm so sorry, Amy," I said. "For all of it."

I felt like I had been gut-punched. My heart was sore. Really sore. I pictured Brandon and Auntie Rose in their respective hospital beds because of me. An image of my father in his own bed came into my mind's eye and I pushed it away. There was only so much I could deal with at once.

"Mick, you didn't ask for any of this. You didn't do anything wrong. Men came to kill you. They did these things."

"Ultimately…" I began, trying to find the words. "It *is* my fault. None of this would have happened if I hadn't done the things I did in the past. Everything last year wouldn't have happened either."

"And you, me and Brandon would never have met," she said, her eyes wide.

"You'd both have been better off. Here I am, coming here to try and help you and bring all of this," I said.

"You came here to try and help me. Exactly. You were trying to do *good*. You went to visit your dying father. You didn't do anything wrong. You dropped everything before that and tried to find Lisa."

"And I haven't even done that." I got up. "I'll be back in a minute. I'm going for a smoke."

Amy was being so fair and kind. It was more than I deserved, and I couldn't handle it.

DEATH NOTICE

It was raining outside, but I didn't care. I lit up, filled my lungs and exhaled as I walked around the side of the building. I passed by folk being taken out of ambulances on stretchers and patients in dressing gowns having a sneaky smoke outside. I felt choked. I never cry much. But something had pulled apart my insides and it came out with a sudden rack and a sob. I cried hard. After about half a minute I was done. I felt better for it. I wiped my tears, finished my cigarette, and went inside to phone Kate.

Chapter 55

There was a payphone inside, beside the snack shop. I went through the whole rigmarole of fake business names, passwords, *Cortez* and all of that.

"Hello, Michael," came Kate's measured English voice. "Your calls are like buses. Nothing for ages and then several all at once."

I told her what had happened. She listened and made a few sympathetic noises.

"You need me to sort out the mess at the motel?" she asked evenly.

"Listen Kate, I'm sorry… I didn't…"

"It's alright Michael. This is not your fault. Do you think your cover has been compromised in New York too?"

"I don't think so. I think these two followed me off the plane. I think they've been following me since we landed."

"Okay, I'll make a call. Michael, you don't sound like yourself, are you…?"

"…I'm fine," I said. "If you can help with that, I'll appreciate it. I'm just worried about the kid. I'm worried about Amy's aunt. Hell, I'm worried about Lisa."

"And your father."

"Yeah, him too."

"What will you do now?"

I exhaled slowly and ran a hand through my hair. The phone started to beep. I hoked a few more quarters out.

"I guess I'll stay somewhere further out of town. Somewhere nobody else from back home will find me if they try. I don't think they will though. They'd have nowhere much to start. It's clear that these two were just fumbling their way to try and track me down. They couldn't know anything about where I live now. It's hundreds of miles from here. I'm not going back there until I find Lisa anyway."

"I understand, Michael."

After the call I brought Amy a cup of coffee.

DEATH NOTICE

"Thanks," she said. "You okay?"

"Fine. Any news?"

She shook her head. "I've been thinking… I guess I owe Officer Samuels an apology."

"Don't worry about it. He'll understand. Listen, I rang Kate there."

I filled her in on our conversation. We drank our coffees and talked through everything. The conversation began to drop off as we were distracted by the various comings and goings in the ER. An hour or so later a nurse said we could go in to see Brandon.

I felt sick.

I felt like running away.

Another side-room.

Another person I cared about sick and in a hospital bed.

The smell of bleach, starched sheets, a pain in my gut.

When we went in, I was surprised to see that Brandon was awake. I was further surprised when his face lit up as we entered.

"Brandon, honey," Amy said, hurrying over and giving him a hug.

"You okay, buddy?" I asked and took a seat in a chair beside the bed. Amy sat down alongside me.

"Been better, Mick. Whatever they're pumping into me feels pretty sweet, though."

"It'll save you a few quid on weed," I said.

He nodded, smiling, then winced a little as he adjusted himself. His face was a better colour than before but was battered. He looked very small in that big bed.

"Listen mate, I'm…"

"It wasn't your fault," he said firmly.

"See?" Amy said, looking at me and raising an eyebrow.

"But…"

"No, Mick. Those motherfuckers came looking to kill you. Not your fault. All I want to say is thank you. To both of you. You saved my life."

"You're very welcome," Amy said, and gave me a look.

I sighed. "You're welcome." Then I got up and leaned over. "Give me a bloody hug, mate."

They let us stay with him for almost an hour. He became visibly more and more tired, yawning and red-eyed. We didn't ask him about the prognosis for his knee and he didn't say anything about it. When the nurse led us back out into the waiting area, Trent Peterson was standing with another cop, both with cups of coffee. He tipped his hat to us.

"Sheriff," I said.

"We need to talk," he said.

DEATH NOTICE

Chapter 56

"That sure is some goddamned mess up at the motel," he said.

I nodded. Amy nodded.

We were seated in a quiet area near to the payphones, out of earshot of anyone. Peterson squinted at me from behind his bushy eyebrows.

"You don't wanna tell me about it, I suppose?" he said.

"Do I have to?" I asked.

"Well… no, you don't. You seem to have some pretty high up friends. I've had some interesting calls this evening. I can't make you do shit. You know a fella called McGoohan?"

Amy and I shared a look. "Yeah, I know him."

"He used to be my boss," Amy volunteered.

Peterson seemed to reflect on this, twisting at his moustache with finger and thumb, "Uh-huh."

"So, what happens now, Sheriff?" I asked.

"Well, I've been told to give you folks the VIP treatment. Strict orders. I'm used to Staties trying to order me around, but this here's Federal."

"And what is the VIP treatment going to be exactly?" Amy asked.

"Well, now. First off, when you're ready, I'm to take you two to get your things. I'll leave a guard on your buddy's door too. Then I'm to make sure y'all get to wherever it is you want to go."

"Great, thanks," I said.

"Uh-huh. And another thing… I was told to get your car finished ASAP. There's two mechanics working on it through the night. Both of them on triple time."

My Hornet. I hoped she was okay. Kate had really come through.

The Sheriff cleared his throat, leaned back and finished his coffee. He sloshed the last of it around his mouth, then set the cup down and leaned back in the chair. He fixed his eyes on me.

"So, I guess you really ain't gonna tell me what all this here's about?"

"I guess not," I said.

His eyes went to the ceiling, settled on the fluorescent lights, then came back to me.

"Okay, I guess. If that's the way it needs to be." He sighed and got up heavily. "Let me know when you want to go."

Amy checked on Auntie Rose, and I checked in on Brandon. Half an hour later and we were in the Sheriff's SUV. We didn't spend long at the motel. There were various teams working at it and a cordon with a guard was in place at the edge of the car park. We gathered our things and got the hell out of there. We didn't particularly want him to know where we would be staying, so we got him to bring us back to the hospital afterwards and left our things in Amy's trunk. He agreed to keep in touch with us through Amy's cell phone and said he hoped that my car would be ready in the morning. By the time we got back to the waiting area, we were both beat. We didn't want to leave for a while, so we found a quiet corner, albeit doused in harsh light, and lay down across a few seats screwed to the floor. Against the odds, we both soon drifted off to sleep.

DEATH NOTICE

Chapter 57

At about six, we stumbled down to the café and got ourselves some cooked breakfast and coffee. We spent some time with Brandon, checked on Rose, and then Peterson phoned. True to his word, my baby was ready for collection. We picked her up from a garage nearby and I tried not to show how excited I was. It seemed misplaced. I checked her over. She looked even better than when I'd bought her. Even better than after my former boss had worked on it in the garage he ran. We went off in search of a hotel. We found a little place about twenty miles away, off the beaten track. It was a quaint joint, with a small bar and only a few dozen rooms. We agreed to put our heads down for a couple of hours. Four hours later and we were on our way back to the hospital once again.

Serious Groundhog Day.

Brandon was asleep when we arrived. We were allowed to see Rose and I sat with her beside Amy for an hour or so.

"I'm glad you told me about your dad," Amy said suddenly at one point, breaking the peaceful reverie.

I nodded. "It helped talking about it."

"I'm glad." She blew out her cheeks. "It's been a tough few weeks. For all of us."

"Last year would have taken some beating, but I think we can safely say we're there."

"Yeah. For sure."

I let the quiet seep back in for a few moments. Watched Rose's laboured breaths.

"You know, getting to see him, it gave me a sense of, I don't know... peace?"

"Yeah, closure maybe."

"That's too American for me," I said and gave her a wink. "It's true, though. I've had a lot of mixed feelings about my da for all kinds of reasons. A lot of guilt too. Seeing him so vulnerable, getting to have a conversation with him, everything kind of just fell away."

"I know. Sometimes, you can just let it all go."

I gave a snort. "You know, I still remember the first time I really stood up to him. Was really annoyed at him as a kid."

Amy let go of Rose's hand and sat back in her chair, her kind eyes searching my face.

"What happened?"

"I had a cat called Roxy. I frigging loved that animal. One day I came back from school, I guess I was about seven. My da sat me down and told me that he had to ask the vet to put the cat to sleep. I actually couldn't believe it. I searched the house. Thought it was some kind of cruel joke. Then I cried. Cried and screamed at him. Far as I was concerned- he'd killed my cat. I couldn't understand it." I shook my head. "All I can think about now is how hard it must have been for him. He was probably sad about the cat too, just tried to do the right thing. Then he has his kid giving him shit. I don't know."

Amy got up and hugged me. We stayed like that for a time. Then she stood, wiped her eyes and sat back down. She smiled at me.

"Michael Walker, you're nothing but a big softie. You're not the tough guy you seem to be."

I shrugged. "I never said that I was."

We spent the day at the hospital, going between the two patients. At about seven we decided to head back to the hotel. We were both starved and found a McDonalds and got some food to sit in with on route.

"Nice?" Amy asked after she finished her quarter pounder meal.

"Yep," I said, as I picked at my last few chips following my Big Mac. "It always is. Just that I'm also usually hungry again half an hour later.

"True," she said.

We chatted, then I brought us over a couple of coffees before we hit the road.

"Amy, I've been thinking."

"Dangerous."

"Thanks. So, I'm of course worried about Brandon and Auntie Rose and that's all been some unexpected madness the last few days but…"

DEATH NOTICE

"You want to get back to looking for Lisa too."

"Yeah."

"I get it. Of course I get it. And I appreciate you thinking like that too."

"It's just that time is still of the essence. I already felt guilty about going back to Ireland and…"

"We've talked about that, Mick," she said and frowned.

"I know, I know. Seeing as we both still seem pretty awake, and those two are safe, how about we take a detour and have a quick look at something?"

"Okay, sure. What did you have in mind?"

"Well, we know that the guy with the van was probably nothing to do with the IRA guys. He showed up first before all of that. He's got to be our guy."

"Probably."

"He's our best shot, anyway. So, I was thinking that the closest we came to him was when me and Brandon chased him the second time and he disappeared."

"You think we should go have a look around there?"

"Yeah, I mean, we've got nothing to lose. The local cops have been busy, and I doubt they've done much investigating. They never did much to start with."

"That's true. Yeah, of course, let's go take a look."

"Good." I took a tentative sip from my paper cup. "God, I'd kill for a drink out of crockery for a change.

"Me too. So, if we're doing some investigating, I guess you think you're Holmes and I'm Watson?" A smile played at her lips.

"No, that's not going to work. I've already settled on that partnership with Brandon. Let me see, we have to find another two. I always liked Columbo."

"So, what? I play his dog that's always sitting in his car?"

"Aww, no. Come on now. You can at least be one of his underlings. That annoying detective guy who turns up sometimes."

"Gee, thanks. That's sexist, anyhow. It doesn't have to be two men. Let's make it Cagney and Lacey."

"Alright then, if I can be Cagney."

Chapter 58

The Hornet purred quietly as we swept along, listening to Neil Young. I'd put on *Harvest* and Amy had even hummed quietly along with *Heart of Gold*. We passed over the bridge where the chase had begun those few nights before, already a lifetime ago. As we approached Westbrooke, I slowed.

"This is where we lost the van man," I said.

"Do you want to pull over and we'll take a walk?" Amy asked.

"Sure."

It was cold out, but dry. We both zipped up our coats and began along the pavement. I still can't call it a sidewalk.

"He could have gone up any of these streets," I said.

"Yeah, maybe. You lost him further back there?"

"Yeah. He just frigging disappeared."

We both slowed, then stopped and looked around. I fished out my deck and lit up a smoke, breathing out away from Amy's face.

"You think he just went home? Maybe up one of these streets?" she asked.

"I don't know. I'm not sure he'd want to do that."

"Me neither." Amy chewed on that, then started walking on. I followed on beside.

"What're you thinking, Amy?"

"I'm not sure. Maybe he has somewhere nearby. Some place that he uses. Jed's profile mooted the idea."

I swallowed. "You mean somewhere that he takes them?"

Amy nodded.

We walked on in silence. Our way was lit by streetlamps every hundred yards or so. A few cars passed by, but nobody was walking the streets. We came upon the school. Amy stopped and peered through the black painted fence. There were dim security lights on inside.

"Still seems to be in use," I said.

"Yeah. But all locked up for the night."

She walked on; her eyes fixed ahead.

DEATH NOTICE

Next, we came upon the row of shops. Again, they were all closed. Amy sighed, spun around on her heel. She shook her head, looking up and down the road.

"He could've gone any goddamned place."

Then her eyes narrowed.

"What's that up there?"

I followed her gaze.

"It's some kind of half-finished development," I said.

"Will we check it out?"

"Yeah, sure. We drove past it that night and it had a big padlock on the front. We didn't think he'd have had enough time to get in and get locked up again. But yeah, let's take a look."

We crossed the road and quickened our pace towards it. Amy stared ahead with intensity.

We first went over to the front gates. The big padlock was there and didn't look like it had been touched for a long time. We looked through the railings. Inside was almost pitch dark, but we could make out five or six houses, some with windows, some only with empty square holes. Beyond that were mounds of dirt, almost as big as the houses. It was a development halted early on. The site was surrounded by a six- or seven-foot fence.

"Let's have a walk around," Amy said.

The fencing at the right side of the gate faced a row of trees a few metres in front of the adjoining street. About three quarters of the way down was another gate. We looked at each other. Amy hurried off, with me close behind. This gate had a deadbolt as well, but there was no padlock attached. Amy went over, pulled it free and opened it up.

We looked at one another.

"Take a look inside?" She pulled out a small Maglite.

"Yep." I grabbed the Colt from inside my jacket.

We made our way slowly across marshland, squelching as we did so. Amy turned the torch on the ground.

"Fresh tyre marks," she said.

I nodded.

She kept the torch angled down and we followed the trail. We passed by a couple of half-built houses with no windows or doors.

The muddy ground was all churned up, but there was a clear path where some kind of vehicle had gone through recently. Towards the rear of the development, just a row before the huge mountains of dirt, the tracks came to an end.

"Looks like it ends here." Amy pointed to where a driveway was meant to be.

It was beside a house with a number six on the door. This building was one of the few that had doors and windows, though it was still unpainted and presently being attacked by moss. We carefully tramped across where a small lawn might be in the future, up to the front door. I tried the lock. It was a solid double lock, brass, though dulled by the elements. No give in it. The door looked thick, with a few inches of double-glazed glass three quarters of the way up.

"Let's look out the back," I said.

Amy went first, she now had her own gun out and moved forwards, hand over hand with the torch. Her stance made me think of Clarice Starling. I followed a few steps behind, glancing at the windows, all covered inside with ragged grey newspapers. The back door was wooden with a brass handle. Much of the door was glass.

"I could try kicking it in," I said.

"It didn't work too well the last time you tried breaking down a door."

She had me there.

"Here, keep this on the door, would you?"

Amy handed me the torch. she took her gun by the barrel and turned her face away. Amy cracked the pistol grip down on the pane, a few inches from the handle. It took two forceful blows and then the glass gave way and left a shattered six-inch hole. Amy eased down her sleeve, then brushed away loose shards before reaching in and turning the lock. She carefully brought her hand back out and took her torch from me.

"Easy peasy," I said.

She tried a smile, but it didn't quite come. Her face had a sickliness about it.

DEATH NOTICE

I pushed opened the door and we moved to each side. Amy went ahead and I followed behind. The torch picked out bare walls, a plaster-stained floor and empty spaces for units in what was once going to be a kitchen. We moved on through. I was struck by the coldness inside, but also the smell. It was horrible. It was pungent and sickening, and there was something that told me it would get worse. I figured Amy had the same thought; she seemed to stiffen.

We moved into a dark hallway. Again, there was only dusty concrete for a floor and roughly plastered walls. We approached the door to the room on the left. The foul smell grew in strength. I put a hand on Amy's shoulder. She turned and gave me a sad nod.

She pushed the door open.

The beam of Amy's torch picked out a snippet of the macabre scene.

There was a flash of limbs in various stages of decay.

I gagged. The stench was truly dreadful.

Amy moved the beam back and forth, a shake in her wrist. There were several bodies, some clearly quite old, some recent. They had been posed in a grotesque seated position. Some were still upright; some had crumbled in on themselves. There was nothing in the room but death. Five bodies in all.

Then Amy gasped and stepped forwards. I followed, the bile from my stomach desperate to escape through my mouth. It was all so overpowering: the smell, the horror. The freshest corpse sat there lifeless, eyes staring.

There was something approaching a smile on her face.

Lisa.

Chapter 59

I do not remember a worse time in my life.

And there have been plenty of bad times.

Watching what Amy had to go through was its own horror. Two hours later we embraced in a small room at the Sheriff's Department. The sobbing I thought may have finally ceased. She had cried for much of those two hours. She pulled her head up from my wet shirt and looked me in the eyes.

"At least we found her," she croaked. Then she slipped her head back onto my chest. Her body was racked, but no further tears flowed for now.

The police had been swift to arrive, Sheriff Peterson himself leading the pack. They had been kind too, going the extra mile, allowing us our space when they could. They treated Amy with kid gloves, but respectfully. The sheriff had been especially compassionate with her, going up a level in my estimations. Yes, he was probably a redneck who cooked the books and cut some corners, but he still had a heart. It would have been a traumatic enough scene for them all to deal with too. It wasn't the norm in these parts. It wasn't the norm in any parts.

After they let us go, I drove with the windows down. The stench seemed to cling to us, the horrifying scenes burned into my mind's eye. Guilt weighed on my chest. What if I hadn't returned to Belfast? Both Lisa and Rose could still have been alive. Amy had cried in fits, at times almost screaming. It was awful to see. I did my best to comfort her, feeling totally out of my depth. In the silent moments my thoughts returned to the terrible images. What kind of sicko poses them like that? And just leaves them rotting there? I'd seem some things in my time, but nothing approaching someone who could do that. I had tried focusing on the road, but the images of the rotting corpses flicked through my mind, like passing traffic.

The sheriff had stayed at the scene. James Samuels was there too and had taken our provisional statements. We had been allowed a few moments of quiet time in the dreadful room, if Amy was up

DEATH NOTICE

for it. Almost immediately, Amy got overwhelmed and ran from the room. She hadn't gone back in again.

I came back to the present and held Amy tighter. Now we were at the station. Samuels had said he would meet us there shortly. Amy wouldn't yet have the luxury of going back to the hotel and being allowed simply to mourn. We sat on more uncomfortable, plastic chairs. We were brought coffee, and it was actually pretty good. Shortly afterwards, we were brought to an empty interview. After a few more minutes, there was a knock at the door and Sheriff Peterson stepped in, hat held respectfully at his side.

"Michael, could you step outside with me for a moment?" he asked.

I looked at Amy. She raised herself up and nodded.

"I'll be back in a few minutes." I followed Peterson outside and down the hall.

"Terrible business," Peterson said when he shut the door to his office. I sat at the other side of his big desk. Samuels arrived and sat with us too. "Never seen the like of it in my county."

"How's Amy doing?" Samuels asked, turning to me.

I rubbed a hand through my hair. "I don't know. She's crushed. She's had a lot to deal with."

He nodded.

I blew out my cheeks. "In time... I guess she might get over it. But it's more likely she never will."

"It'll help when we catch this son-of-a-bitch," Peterson said fervently, puffing on the end of a new cigar, just getting it going.

"We will," Samuels agreed.

"I hope so," I said, fishing out a cigarette. "What've you got so far?"

Peterson blew out a thick plume of smoke, set the smouldering cigar in his ashtray and leaned back. "Troopers are there now. They'll push hard to handle the case. Wouldn't be surprised if the FBI want it too."

"But for now it's yours?" I asked.

"Yeah, for now."

"We've our own team there too, co-handling the scene, taking pictures, talking to neighbours," added Samuels.

I nodded.

"What we've got for sure is a serial killer," Peterson said, retrieving his cigar and chomping down on it. He offered a mirthless laugh. "Never expected to say those words in this town. He doesn't seem to have killed any of them at the building site. It seems like this house was the sick bastard's gallery."

"Looks that way," I said, before taking a long inhale. "How did they die?"

"That's the thing. There are no obvious signs. I stayed until the doctor and the Trooper team checked all the bodies. There are no outward signs. No bullet holes, no wounds, not even bruising on their necks... The ones that still had enough flesh to see anyway," he said with a shudder. "And they all had those crooked smiles on their faces." He shook his head again.

"When do you think you'll know more?" I asked.

"I suppose we'll have an idea in the next couple days. Poisoning or something would be my guess."

"What about IDs?" I asked. "Obviously there's Lisa for a start. What about the others?"

"We don't have much. Some of those bodies are pretty old. One thing is for sure... none of them is Stacy Vanucci."

DEATH NOTICE

Chapter 60

After my chat with Peterson and Samuels, they said I could get Amy and we could go for now. We didn't say much to each other in the car. Amy looked shattered. I turned up the heat. The car was cold, and I hoped that Amy could catch a wee nap. She was still wide awake. She wanted to go back the hospital, saying she wanted to be near Auntie Rose. She made it clear she wanted me to go to the hotel. She gave me a look. I didn't argue. I dropped her there and took off again. I stopped at the hotel bar for a brace of whiskeys and then went up to bed. Despite everything, I managed to get over to sleep quick enough.

I was woken at nine by a call on the hotel room phone from the sheriff.

"Michael, were you awake?"

"Aye, yeah... Just dozing," I said, sitting up and rubbing my eyes.

"There's been a development," he said.

Now I was *really* awake. "Go on."

"We've been looking into the housing development. We've got the deeds on who owns it. It went bust about six years ago. A name came up."

I waited.

"One of the owners is Marcus Crawford."

"Fuck."

"Yup, that's what I said," he said with one of his throaty chuckles.

"You think he's our guy?"

"It's a good lead anyway. I'm outside his office right now."

"You not been to bed yet?"

"That's what coffee's for, son. His receptionist says he's not due in today. We're going to hit his house now."

I scrambled out of the bed. "Sheriff, can I come with you?"

"That's why I'm calling. Your friends in high up places told me to give you whatever you wanted. I guessed you'd want to join us on this. You must do as I say though. No heroics."

"Yeah, of course, whatever you say. Give me the address."

He gave me it and I scribbled it down. He hung up and I hurriedly picked up some clothes and headed for the bathroom. Six minutes later I was back in the Hornet. On the highway I drove with my knees on the steering wheel while I checked the chamber of my Colt. Things were moving fast. I considered ringing Amy but dismissed the idea. She could be pissed at me if she wanted to be. She didn't need this right now and I didn't want her getting hurt. I fished a smoke out of my jacket pocket and stomped down hard on the accelerator.

DEATH NOTICE

Chapter 61

"This is still my show. For now," Peterson said. "The Staties are helping out, but I'm in charge."

Peterson was joined by Samuels and two other cops that I didn't know. We were outside Crawford's home; a red brick detached in a nice part of town. I had my Colt out and the sheriff didn't object. He had a revolver and the rest of the team brandished shotguns. We advanced towards the house.

"Michael, you stay in the middle, alright? Consider yourself deputised. This is an arrest. Don't go firing any goddamned rounds 'les I tell you, okay?"

"Okay."

Peterson gave a nod to the bigger of the two cops and the man set his shotgun down against the porch window. He rolled his shoulders, took a step back and then launched himself at the door, leg raised, kicking beside the lock. The door flew open with a crack and he grabbed up his gun again. The three of us advanced inside while the last men stood guard at the door.

"Law enforcement," Peterson hollered as we went inside.

There were no lights on, but it wasn't dark yet. We moved as one through the hallway. Our guns barrels swept the surroundings with our eyes. The big man led the way into a living room. We followed.

"Clear," he said when he found it empty. Everywhere was brightly furnished and smelled fresh and clean. We moved out and along the rest of the hall towards a large kitchen. We moved cautiously together. Peterson breathed heavily. There were sweat stains visible on his tanned shirt, under his armpits. The kitchen was a bust too.

"Upstairs," Peterson said, pointing back down the hall with his revolver. "Take it easy, now."

We made our way up the staircase. The house smelled even better up there. Like lavender and rose petals. I was just glad it was nothing like the stench of the abandoned development. About halfway up, there was a creak from somewhere above us. Then a soft thud. Peterson paused and raised a thick eyebrow.

"Let's go get the bastard," he said.

He pushed on ahead of us. We quickened to stay close, our own feet now loud on the stairs.

Another creak from above.

It was from the room on our left.

"C'mon out, Crawford," Peterson shouted. "Hands above your head."

We waited.

The smaller cop chewed his gum like it was his dinner. Samuels's face was set. His head flitted left and right. Sheriff Peterson lifted his hat for a moment and ran the back of his gun arm over his sweaty brow. He nodded to the big guy.

"Alright, Crawford. We're coming in."

The big cop reached for the handle. He turned it sharply and pushed the bedroom door back.

We raised our guns.

The curtains were drawn on the large bedroom. It was dark inside and smelled of the morning that had passed: deodorant, soap and coffee.

All at once there was a screech and movement.

A rush towards us.

A black and white cat with huge yellow eyes flew past us and sprinted down the stairs. I thought the big guy was close to blowing a hole in it. And the sheriff was close to having a heart attack.

The house was empty.

No Crawford.

No missing girl.

Chapter 62

"He's in the goddamned wind," Sheriff Peterson said grimly.

"It would appear so." I blew into my coffee cup.

We had gone off to a diner together to get a cup of coffee. The others had stayed and waited for the Troopers to arrive.

"Son-of-a-bitch skipped out before we could get there." He rubbed at his temple, then leaned back to pull out his cigars. At this cramped table I noticed again how tall he was. It was like he had to be folded into the booth.

"What now, Sheriff?" I asked.

He puff-puffed, starting up his cigar. He blew out towards the ceiling. "I have hand it over to them now... the Troopers."

"Just like that?"

"Just like that." He put his elbows on the table and tilted his head. "You got me wrong, fella. Maybe you think I'm just some hick sheriff. Maybe you think I'm some redneck with his own agenda." Then his bushy moustache parted in an open smile. "Maybe I'm all those things, but I ain't a fool. I ain't too proud to mess around with something like this. I gave it a shot and we missed him." He shook his head. "But we don't have the resources to chase this guy from here to kingdom come."

"The Staties do," I agreed, sparking up a Marlboro.

"Yup. Might need them FBI guys too."

"Yeah?"

"And any other goddamned agency available. I'll take whatever help we can get. We need to nail this bastard."

I nodded. I ran it all through my mind. Marcus Crawford. Where was that slimy scumbag? Not just slimy. A killer. A *serial* killer.

"Where does that leave me?" I asked. "What can I do to help?"

He blew out a cloud of smoke and broke out the smile again.

"If I'm on the sidelines, son, you're nowhere."

Afterwards, I went to the hospital to be with Amy. But I looked in on Brandon first. He'd been in plenty of pain. The nurses told me on the way in that this could be one of the worst periods. The adrenalin was gone, surgery was done, and the body was starting to think about trying to heal. They'd given him a decent dose of morphine. He was pretty out of it. I sat with him for a while, but I wasn't certain if he even knew that I was there.

I went on and found Amy. She was just about holding it together, despite her bloodshot eyes and the strain on her face. I sat with her and Auntie Rose for a while, mostly in silence. We were quiet, each of trying to process all that had come to pass. The peacefulness was welcome. After a time, I convinced Amy to come with me to get a cup of coffee in the canteen.

While we were down there, Rose died.

DEATH NOTICE

Chapter 63

The killer's eyes were everywhere. He was very agitated. He caught himself on, realising how it might be showing. He slapped a half smile on his face and walked down the next aisle. Thankfully nobody was in it. Fluorescent bulbs shone down on the rows of saws, chisels, nails and screws. He couldn't focus on the task at hand.

They had found his lair.

He shivered like someone had just walked over his grave.

Damn them.

He looked down at his clenched fists. His knuckles were red. He slipped his hands into his pockets and went along the rest of the aisle, inspecting the various tools, yet taking nothing in.

What to do.

He was shaken. Almost shaken right from his foundations. His beautiful crypt was no more. His collection was gone. All his work, *taken* from him.

A young mother with a pram started up the aisle.

He cast his eyes away and shuffled along the way he had come. He reached for a clear, perforated bag of nails and held it as if assessing the contents. He bounced the bag in his palm until the woman was gone. When he set the bag back down, he found small grazes on his hand from gripping the nails too tightly before letting go. He shook his head and moved off to another aisle.

This wouldn't do. None of this would do.

He must carry on with his work. What else was there?

Chapter 64

It was hell.

If Amy had been hanging together by a few threads, they were now all gone. They had been dissolved by her tears and burned in the fire of her fury. I didn't know what to do with myself, where to place myself, nor what to say.

I did my best. I'm not sure that was good enough. I can't remember a harder week. Yes, I'd had bad times. I'd had dangerous times. I'd had painful times. But seeing someone I cared that much about, in that kind of suffering... it was something else.

Somehow, we managed to go about making the arrangements. One Death Notice, then another. I didn't know the names of many of the other victims, but there would be notices for them too. Lisa's disappearance in one way or another had led to them all.

Five days later and we had a funeral for Auntie Rose and her only child. Brandon was too poorly to make it, and so was Amy's mum. Her mother was completely distraught, and Amy was torn. She went to stay with her for a night while I carried on with some of the funeral organisation and the back and forth with the police investigations. Despite the couple of absences, it was a huge funeral. As if the entire town had turned out along with the town beside. The funeral service was nice. Isn't that what people always say? But it was. Amy managed to withstand it all, like a solid oak. Yes, she cried, she faltered, but she did it all while emanating dignity and grace. I was so proud of her. More than that, I was awestruck.

It was a relief to make it to the hotel reception afterwards. This was a much smaller affair. By invitation only. I found a moment to sneak off into the grounds, loosening my tie and collar, before releasing my Marlboros and Zippo. I stood in the mild breeze, surrounded by a clump of trees, and took in a long drag.

"Finding a minute's peace, Michael?"

I turned.

It was Dustin McKeith, one of the forty invited to the reception.

DEATH NOTICE

I raised the cigarette. "I don't know about peace, but I'm having a cheeky smoke anyways. You want one?"

His eyes narrowed, then his brows parted. "I don't... usually. But, yes, go on then. Thank you."

I passed him one and we took a seat on the adjoining bench, smoking together. His thick, black hair was parted neatly as usual, and he was wearing a fine black suit with the standard black mourning tie.

"A terrible business," he said absently, before taking a drag and considering the cigarette as if it were a strange object.

"It is. Though which part do you mean specifically?" I asked wryly.

"True enough. All of it, I suppose. Amy appears to be doing well... As far as can be expected."

"She is. She's a tough cookie, that one."

"How's young Brandon? An awful thing to have intruders twice like that."

"It was. He's doing alright. Healing, slowly. It'll take time."

McKeith nodded and flicked away some ash.

"It was unconnected, then? To Lisa, I mean."

"Yeah, nothing to do with it," I said, a little guilt pang going through me.

"Terrible," he said again, shaking his head. "And it seems there is no sign of that Marcus Crawford fellow."

I gave him a look.

"It's okay, the police told me about him," he continued. "I know that he's their primary suspect. More than that. I think there's no doubt. He's our guy."

"Yep. And we missed him." I crushed out my cigarette. "Just missed the little bastard."

McKeith carefully stubbed out his cigarette on an overhanging branch before setting it down on the arm of the bench. He stood.

"Hopefully we'll get him, Michael," he said, his furtive eyes settling on my own.

"I hope so."

"A clever man, to pull the wool over everyone's eyes. To get so close to people."

"That's the truth," I said. "Back home, we've a lot of mythologies: fairies, giants, all that shite. There's a creature called the pooka. It's a changeling. It can take on any animal or human form. If you meet him, you've got trouble, and you don't even know it. I think we've got a pooka here."

McKeith blinked a few times, then nodded his head.

"I think you're right, Michael. God, help us."

DEATH NOTICE

Chapter 65

I was only a few minutes behind Dustin McKeith, heading back towards the function room. I bumped into Sheriff Peterson on his way out. He looked strange to me, all dressed in black. It was the missing Stetson that really did it.

"Michael, you got a minute?"

"Yeah, sure, Sheriff," I said. "I could be convinced to have another cigarette."

We ended up back at the same spot. The bench was still warm.

"We've made progress on a few things. I thought you'd want to know," he said, getting right to it. "I didn't want to speak to Amy yet. She has enough on her plate. If you could…"

"Yeah, of course. I'll fill her in when the time's right. What have you got?"

He frowned. I wasn't sure if it was due to his news or from trying to get his cigar end to catch in the breeze.

"Well, there's no news on Crawford. He's vanished. His family have no idea where he is. I believe his wife. She's distraught and she seems an honest lady."

I nodded. "The Troopers widening out the search?"

"Sure. Notices at airports and harbours and all of that. I don't think he's stupid enough to try to fly, though. Not under his own name anyways. Of course, it could be he already had a fake ID and has already flown."

I blew out my cheeks. "Not great."

"No." Peterson knitted his bushy eyebrows and gave me a look. "The forensic people have some preliminary fundings."

"Okay."

"Some of the bodies were in a worse state than others… But you already know that."

"Yeah, I still see them when I shut my eyes."

"As do I. Some were more *recently* deceased. They've started tests on them. You remember there were no obvious signs of death?"

I nodded again and chomped down on my cigarette, wishing I'd brought my whiskey outside with me.

"Well, it looks like they were all injected with a sedative to start with."

"Something to make them easier to handle."

"Sure. But that's not what killed them."

"What was it then?"

"Do you know what nitrous oxide is?"

I thought about it. "Don't think so."

"Laughing gas. Kind of stuff your dentist might give you."

"Oh yeah, that rings a bell. Jesus. And it can kill you?"

"In enough quantity, yeah. And with enough exposure. It deprives the body of oxygen. They tell me the body just eventually starts shutting down."

"Jesus, some sick bastard."

"Yep. Seems he kept them alive for long periods too. He probably had a mask strapped onto their faces, pumping it into them for long spells each day."

I shook my head. Then I had a thought. "So, the last missing girl might still be alive?" I asked quickly.

"Could be. God willing, we can get to her in time."

I finished my cigarette and lit up another. The sheriff crossed his long legs and sat back on the bench. We sat in a reverie of tobacco smoke.

I looked over at him. "That's why they had their faces all contorted up like that."

Peterson nodded. "They died laughing."

DEATH NOTICE

Chapter 66

I had been feeling all kinds of depressed before my garden powwows, but afterwards I was critically miserable. I tried covering it up from Amy, which I think I managed. After the funeral was all over with, she was exhausted and a little drunk.

"There's so much I want to say to you, Michael," she slurred as I left her to her the door of her hotel room. "It's not enough... but it all comes down to *thank you*." She clung arms around me in a hug, tears in her eyes.

I felt an uncomfortable electrical current race through me. The cause was all different feelings jumbled into one mess. I felt good that I had been some kind of help, but as far as I was concerned, I'd caused much more harm than good. If it wasn't for me, Rose would still be alive, and Brandon would still have both his knee caps intact.

All I said was. "You did great today, Amy. Go get some rest."

I unlocked the door for her.

I needed a few nightcaps from the mini bar, but afterwards I slept okay. The next day was a Tuesday. I remember it because I discovered on Teletext that The Glens played Bangor in The League, and they won three-nil. I remember more so because it was the day that everything changed.

I left the hotel early, determined to do something. Anything. I retraced our steps over the last few weeks. I walked the streets and I went to the cop shop and talked things over again with Peterson and Samuels. I went to see Zara. The kid tried to be helpful. She didn't tell me anything new but tried her best. I caught her just as she was going to visit Brandon. She had bought him a basketball magazine, a pack of sweets, and perhaps most thoughtful of all, a small baggy of weed.

My mind felt clear but at the same time nothing made sense in my mind. It was all registering, but nothing was fitting together. After a sandwich in the car, I went to visit Dustin McKeith around three in the afternoon. He buzzed me into his office himself. When I went inside, there was nobody else there but him.

"Nice to see you, Michael. How are you doing?" he asked, striding into the outer office and shaking my hand.

"Yeah, alright, I guess. Have you got a couple of minutes?"

"Certainly," he said. He smiled, but his eyes didn't. Maybe I had caught him in the middle of something.

"Don't worry if you're busy…"

"No, no, not at all. C=Can I get you a coffee?"

"I'm fine, thanks," I said.

He was dressed in a grey polo shirt and brown trousers. He looked tired, but his voice had the usual lilt and confidence within it.

"Has there been… any progress?" he asked, meeting my eye.

"No, sadly not. I've just been walking around, trying to make sense of it all. I feel pretty useless, to be honest."

"Nonsense," he said warmly, pouring himself a coffee out of a jug from a hot plate in the corner. "You've been there for Amy all this time… and for Rose. You can't perform miracles."

"I guess not," I said.

"It's like what I used to say to my patients when I was a dentist. 'I'll try my best, but I might have to pull it out.'"

He turned to set the jug back down.

I felt myself glaze over slightly.

That's right, he had been a dentist before.

A dentist.

Laughing gas.

Don't be stupid.

"Come on into my office," he said, leading the way.

"Yeah, thanks," I said absently.

Then a second bolt hit me even harder than the first.

As he opened the door, my eyes fell on the picture.

The girl, crouching, with her head to one side. The Schiele print.

That's what the posed corpses had reminded me of.

"Are you alright, Michael?" he asked, looking at me with concern.

DEATH NOTICE

I looked away, took a step backwards. "Yeah... yeah. No, actually... I'm not. I haven't eaten all day. Now I'm feeling a little nauseous."

My eyes returned to his face. I did my best to hide my turmoil.

"I'd better go eat something. Can we take a rain check?"

"Of course. Are you sure I can't get you anything?" He looked at me strangely.

He took a step forward and put a hand on my shoulder. His eyes seemed to bore into mine. He still wore a half-smile, but I couldn't tell if it was real.

"No but thank you. I'd better go. I'll be in touch."

I offered him the sincerest smile I could muster and left.

I burst out the front door and took in a huge lungful of air. I panted and hurried off along the footpath. Then I quickly replaced oxygen with nicotine and tar.

It all clicked, it fit.

It was him.

McKeith was the killer.

Chapter 67

"I'm glad you're both here," I said.

I'd composed myself somewhat on the drive to the hospital. I'd gone straight to Brandon's room and found Amy there with him.

"You rushed off early this morning," Amy said, looking a little pissed off.

"Yeah, sorry. I wanted to take some time and go over everything."

"And you found something," Brandon said, sitting up in his bed. He looked the most animated I'd seen him in days.

I nodded.

"What is it, Michael?" Amy asked urgently.

I sat down on a plastic chair beside her.

"I went to see McKeith."

"Okay," Amy said slowly.

"I think it's him," I said simply.

"What's him?" Brandon said.

I took a deep breath and reminded myself that Brandon couldn't read my mind. Rather than snap or give him a sarcastic response, I opted for straight information.

"He's the killer."

"But we know who the killer is," he said.

"I think maybe we were wrong."

Amy looked at me closely, her eyes narrow. "Tell us."

I told them about the dentist thing and the Schiele painting.

Brandon didn't look convinced. "You're basing this on a picture on his wall and that he used to be a dentist?"

"I know it sounds a stretch. But come on, I've always said there's something off about him. Seems a big coincidence that somebody close to all of this has a history of using laughing gas. It was like a double whammy. Bam-bam, when I saw that picture. I realised that was the image I had in my head that I couldn't place when I saw the bodies."

"Why would he pose them like that?" Brandon asked.

DEATH NOTICE

"I don't know. Because he's a psycho?"

"Didn't he have an alibi for when Lisa went missing?" Amy asked.

"Yeah, but we can look into that. I doubt the sheriff's guys did their due diligence. Plus, remember he told us his son went missing and died? Maybe that messed him up. Maybe there was more to it than that. Who knows?"

Brandon shrugged, adjusted his leg with a grimace, and lay back a little. "I don't know, Mick. Maybe, I suppose."

Amy was watching us both silently. I turned to her. "What do you think, Amy?"

"How about Marcus Crawford, then?" Her voice was almost inaudible.

"I guess it was just a coincidence that he was a part owner in that land. It was a big group of investors. Anybody could have been using the place. There was no security."

"True," she said. "But where is he then?"

"If the killer is McKeith, or somebody else, I suppose they made him disappear. To make him take the fall."

She nodded thoughtfully.

"I'm going to ring my friend Jed. Get him to do some more digging on McKeith," she said, hoking her cell phone from her bag.

She stood and went outside to make the call.

"You're pretty sure about this?" Brandon asked.

I blew out my cheeks. "Well... yeah. There's something about him, there really is. It *feels* right. I think he clocked me staring at the picture too. There was something in his face. It wasn't exactly that his mask had slipped. But I think it was about to."

Chapter 68

"He's going to ring me back in a little bit," Amy said when she returned a few minutes later.

"Good," I said. "Will we check on the alibi now?"

"Sure. What way do you want to play it?"

"Can I have your phone?" I put out my hand and she gave it to me. "I've got an idea."

I cleared my throat. "Hello, is that FAM? Uh-huh."

Amy and Brandon smirked at my generic American accent. I thought it was pretty good.

"And who am I speaking with? Yes... uh-huh."

I told the receptionist that I was ringing from the IRS under the terms of the increased inspections regarding the charity. I asked for some random information first. Without too much trouble she also gave the name, phone number and address of the retreat that McKeith was meant to be at when Amy disappeared. I hung up and rang the retreat. They said that McKeith had paid for the week, but they did not keep records of when residents came and went. Most people didn't stay there all the time and there were no records kept of who went in and out of the spa, or who attended the various classes.

I told Amy and Brandon this.

"So, it doesn't rule him out," Brandon said.

"No, it doesn't," I said. "What do you think, Amy?"

Her eyes looked like they were bubbling with something, but her mouth was expressionless.

"I like him for it," she said.

"More than Crawford?" I asked.

"Yeah, a lot more."

"Me too," I said.

A few minutes later, the doctor came to do his rounds and I took Amy to the cafeteria for a coffee and a slice of pie.

"Good cheesecake for a hospital," I said.

Amy nodded absently.

DEATH NOTICE

"You're as convinced as I am, aren't you?" I asked.

She nodded. "It makes sense. Because he was making Auntie Rose feel better, I ignored the way he was. I can see how everything would fit if it's him now. Y'know, he has a bad experience, loses it. He sets up a charity dealing with vulnerable people. Some of whom he has taken from their loved ones."

"A sick power trip," I said.

"Really screwed up." She raised her mug of coffee and blew over it. "A twisted psychotic trying to control everything around him, pulling their strings, getting off on it... if it *is* him."

"He even gets them to donate to the cause. If it's McKeith, how twisted is that?"

Just then her cell phone rang. We were in a quiet corner, so she accepted the call from Jed Wilson. She spoke for about five minutes, making a few notes and taking sips from her mug here and there. I watched her, drinking my own coffee, the caffeine and adrenalin combining to make me wired. I was surprised that Amy had been in agreement with me. She was in control, but I could see that she too was a bundle of nervous energy. I half wished now I'd confronted him earlier. I was a bundle of nervous energy too. One that needed an outlet.

"Well," she said after hanging up. "Some more interesting facts about McKeith."

"Go on," I said.

"There was a lot more to the death of his son. He had apparently been missing for a few days. At first McKeith didn't report it to the police."

"That's pretty weird," I said.

"Yeah, but that's not the weirdest part. The son's girlfriend went missing at the same time."

"Shit."

"Uh-huh. She's never turned up."

"What? Damn." I had a think about that for a second. "How did the son die?"

"A few days after he had gone missing, McKeith said he came home and found him in their garage. He had hung himself."

"Jaysus." I reached for my smokes, then remembered we were in a hospital cafeteria. "So, what do you think? You think McKeith had something to do with it? His son? The missing girl?"

"I don't know. I think there's something messed up there," she said. "Enough to put him around the bend maybe."

"But the cops had nothing on him?"

"No, nothing. The boy's death was ruled as a suicide and the girl is still listed as a missing person. McKeith was questioned a bunch of times, but no charges were ever brought."

"So now with no family; son dead, wife dead, McKeith ups sticks and moves across the country. Then he sets up this charity working for missing people and a whole lot of girls start going missing here."

"Yep. I really think it's him, Mick."

I nodded. "Let's go pay him another visit. Let's go to his house."

DEATH NOTICE

Chapter 69

We went back up to the ward and found Brandon by himself, drinking from his plastic cup of juice. We told him the latest and he seemed more convinced too.

"Okay, but be careful, guys," he said earnestly.

"We will." Amy gave his arm a little squeeze.

"I guess I can't go with you this time."

"You always slow us down anyway, mate," I said with a wink.

Brandon gave me his eye roll.

"We'll just call there and sit him down. We'll see if we can pressure him into giving something away. But we need to go armed," Amy said, her tone now low. "We don't know what's going to happen when we get there."

"Yeah, I've been thinking about that," I said, slipping my jacket on. "I think we should tell Sheriff Peterson too."

"Really?"

"Yeah, he's turned out to be pretty sound. I think he'll be interested in what we have to say. He really wants to catch the killer and three is better than two."

Amy shrugged. "Okay."

We hugged Brandon goodbye and told him everything would be fine. Then I drove us over to the Sheriff's Department. We were let in by the now familiar cop on the desk, led past the conference room filled with Troopers, and then taken on into Peterson's office. He was in there looking tired and pissed off, chewing down hard on his cigar. When we told him all that we knew, he actually brightened.

"I'll buy it. I was having trouble making Crawford work for it. There's enough to take a swing at it anyway," he said.

"And we can keep this between just us?" Amy said.

"Yeah, we'll do like you say. Go and have a chat with someone on the margins of the case. We're simply visiting somebody who's been helping with the search." He pointed a thumb in the direction of the conference room. "Those sons of bitches in there don't need to know nothing."

My now fully restored AMX Hornet swept us out of town and towards McKeith's place. There were three of us again, out trying to catch the bad guy. This time instead of a young black kid, we had an old white dude.

"I assume you're both carrying," Peterson said from the back seat, loading shells into his shotgun.

"Yeah, we're good," I said.

"Alright, then. So we're clear, I'm in charge here. But I trust you both. Some time you should tell me about your past, Michael. I reckon it to be a good story."

"Nah, there's not much to tell," I said, glancing towards Amy.

McKeith lived alone on the outskirts of town. It was an old farmhouse on a plot of three acres. Apparently, the charity business paid the bills alright. We drove up the driveway, past a few barns and an empty overgrown field. I pulled the car up beside McKeith's Honda and parked in front of the house.

"Looks like he's in," I said.

The house was large; two storeys, covered in wood cladding. It looked in good enough shape but could have done with a lick of paint or two.

"Are you bringing that with you?" Amy asked, checking her side arm, nodding to Peterson's shotgun.

"Well honey, it ain't just for show," Peterson drawled.

"We're not going for the subtle approach, then," I said, checking over my Colt M19 before slipping it back inside my pocket.

"I've changed my mind about the cosy chat. No point. Whatever happens, I'm bringing him in," Peterson said.

"Fair enough, big man."

We got out and took in the surroundings. There was a breeze blowing across the field. A few pieces of metal somewhere were clinking in the wind. There were lights on in the house, but the barns were in darkness.

"Let's go have that quiet word." Peterson headed off purposely towards the porch.

We followed close behind him and climbed up the four wooden steps to the veranda and front door. There was no bell, so Peterson

DEATH NOTICE

made a fist with his free hand and hammered on the door. The sound echoed across the silence.

Nothing.

He knocked again.

I thought I might have heard movement from inside but couldn't be sure. I tried the handle. The door was locked, but it didn't look like it would give us too much trouble.

"Take a look around back?" Amy asked.

Peterson nodded.

We moved around the side of the house. On the right was a detached garage. We moved between it and the side of the house. There was frosted glass on the windows at the back. I could make out curtains inside. It was maybe a bathroom. Along the wall were a few bins and a stack of firewood. Amy tried the handle on a side door to the house. It was locked and looked solid. I moved across to the garage. I tried to pull up the front shutter, but it was locked. I tried the door on the left side. It was locked too. I put my eye to the crack in the door frame. I squinted and could make out a white van. I blinked and then squinted, took another look. Then I stood back up and walked over to Amy and Peterson.

"I think we've found our van," I said, nodding to the garage. "It's white and a little beaten up. Windows are all there now, though. But it looks like the one that took a run at us."

"Well, heck," Peterson said, with a slanty grin. He cocked the shotgun. "We're on then."

I slipped out my Colt. Amy had her Glock already in her hand.

"Easy," I said, touching her hand. "You're no good to anyone if you get hurt."

"It's too late to help Lisa or Auntie Rose now," she said. Her face eased. "But there's one thing I *can* do. None of this would have happened, if it wasn't for him."

We set off towards the rear.

Another door, another solid lock.

"Damn," Peterson said under his breath.

We stepped away from the wall and considered our options.

"Guess we need to go in the front, and pretty hard," I said.

"Looks that way," Amy said.

Peterson took his hat off with his free hand and used his thumb to mat down his hair.

Suddenly there was a creak from above.

Then a blast from a gun.

"Ahhh," Peterson cried, falling to the ground.

I looked up to catch a glimpse of McKeith, with a rifle pointed out from an upstairs window. I swung my arm around and plunged off a couple of rounds. Amy did the same. The window shattered and McKeith ducked back inside. We grabbed the Sheriff by his shoulders and collar and pulled him in towards the wall, and away from any more fire.

"Goddamn it," he wheezed.

We got him propped up against the wall. He was bleeding from his left shoulder. Amy ripped open his shirt and I bent down to take a look before she pressed her hands on the wound.

"You'll be alright," I said. "It's a through and through."

Peterson nodded his now sweaty brow. "I've had worse... now go and get that sicko."

"We need to call you a doctor..." Amy started.

"No time. I'll be alright. That girl could still be alive, but now the bastard might kill her. Go on."

"He's right," I said, making a makeshift gauze from the ripped shirt and pressing Peterson's hand on it. "Keep that on it, hard as you can."

I stood. "Let's go get him."

Amy got up too, looking at Peterson uncertainly. "We won't be long."

"Keep the pressure on, Sheriff," I said. I put his Stetson back on his head and led the way, carefully back around front. We were there in seconds, panting slightly, guns raised.

"You ready?" I asked.

"Yep."

I kicked in the door and hurried inside. We went side by side along the corridor. It was dim, illuminated only by a streak of light from upstairs. A door off the hallway to the right also had a rim of light around it. The hall was old fashioned *country*, with lots of old pine furniture and woodwork. But the walls were lined with

DEATH NOTICE

modern art prints. There was more Schiele from what I guessed, and I thought I recognised a Klimt or two.

"Split up?" Amy asked.

"Okay... but be careful."

She moved to the stairs and glided up them, her gun rotating around with ease. I watched her for a moment, then pushed open the door. I went inside, shuffling in a crouch.

I waited, poised on my hunkers.

No sound. No faint breathing.

I got up and scrambled for a switch on the wall. The room was suddenly flooded by light as I found it. It was a large, traditional dining room; salmon-coloured walls with an eight-seater oak table, sideboards and cabinets. I took in a deep breath and went back out to the hall. I kicked the other door open, taking it half off its hinges in the process. It was a formal living room. I could train my Colt on most of it from the doorway. Fairly satisfied, I went in cautiously.

It was empty too.

I crossed through it and on into a kitchen. The light there was already on. It was fairly large inside and recently decorated. It was originally roomier. There was an annex built off to the side, jutting into the room a few metres in a block shape. It was some kind of small, windowless extension. I immediately focused in on it. It had a green wooden door. The structure was built from concrete painted white. I tried the handle. It was locked.

That's when I heard it.

There was a faint moaning sound from inside. It almost sounded like somebody laughing.

"Hello, is anyone in there?" I shouted towards the lock.

There was a muffled response.

I took a step back and launched a kick at the lock. It rattled and the wood pulsed for a millisecond, but I didn't do much to it. I hopped on my heels, put the Colt in my back pocket, then rushed around the kitchen, opening drawers and cupboards. The best I could come up with was a small hammer, the business end smaller than my fist.

It would have to do.

I went straight to work, whacking it around the lock as hard as I could. After six or seven swings, I caught my breath and had another go with my foot. This time the door gave way, and I was straight inside.

What lay before me, struck like a bullet. The strange smell hit the back of my throat, making me gag. Inside was a small annex; maybe fifteen feet by eight. It was lit by one bare bulb, hung from the ceiling, lighting up the bare plasterboard. At one end was a chair and some kind of medical machine plugged in beside it.

In the chair, slumped, with a mask over her face, was a teenage girl.

DEATH NOTICE

Chapter 70

It was Stacy Vanucci. Her eyes rolled in her head. Stacy was in dirty clothes and making a weird noise, somewhere between a groan and a twisted cackle. I hurried across to her and ripped the mask from her face.

"Stacy, are you okay? I'm here to help you."

Her eyes had trouble focusing on me. A drip of saliva hung from her mouth. She couldn't do anything about it. Her hands and legs were cable-tied to the chair. I moved behind her to see if I could undo them, half facing the door.

"Just leave her where she is, please, Michael."

I looked up. McKeith was standing in the doorway, his rifle pointed at my head. His voice was even, his arm steady. I straightened up and raised my hands, moving alongside the chair. Stacy's eyes widened and she gave a whimper.

"McKeith, you aren't getting out of this…"

He laughed. "I was never getting out of this. None of us are getting out alive anyway. Have you never heard that before, Michael?"

"Some sooner than others," I said. "Come on. Just let her go and we can talk."

McKeith glanced over his shoulder, then moved fully into the room.

"Over there," he commanded me, gesturing with the rifle. His face was mottled and contained something approaching a snarl.

I stepped across to the right side of the room, up against the wall. McKeith took up position behind the girl, now resting the business end of his gun on the top of her head. She made another pitiful noise.

"Miss Amy will surely be here any moment," McKeith said, glancing towards the door. He knew Amy wouldn't open fire if he stood like that.

My eyes darted about the room, my brain thinking rapidly, but no ideas were coming to mind. I looked back at McKeith. His Adam's apple bobbed once in his throat as he stared back at me, dead-eyed. He was dressed in a black polo shirt and beige trousers. His face was set now, his eyes small, a few droplets of sweat on his forehead.

"It was the painting, wasn't it?" he asked softly.

"Yeah, that was one thing," I said. "Plus, I thought you were a dick from the moment I met you. I just didn't know you were a full-blown nut."

He smiled.

"No matter. As I said, everything must come to an end eventually."

There was a very small noise from somewhere beyond the annex.

"Ahh, Amy. Do come in," McKeith called brightly. "Slow and easy, please."

A few moments later, Amy appeared in the doorway, her gun immediately trained on McKeith. She took a few steps inside.

"I think that's far enough, thank you," McKeith said, making a small circle through Stacy's hair with the rifle.

"Just let her leave," Amy said through gritted teeth, her eyes blazing. "You shoot her, I'll put one in your skull before you breathe back out."

"I was just discussing this very thing with Michael," McKeith said conversationally. "Nothing lasts forever. For me, it is of little consequence."

"I doubt that's completely true," I said. "I don't think you really want to go out with a bullet in the face, in the middle of a scene from a horror movie."

He laughed again. "You'd be surprised."

"You tried hiding your tracks hard enough," I said. "I think you still want to get away with it all."

He sighed. "I really don't care that much either way."

"So, this is some kind of twisted revenge because your son died?" Amy asked, her voice hard.

McKeith squirmed a little and his voice raised in pitch. "You know nothing about it."

"We know it probably made you do all of this sick shit," I said. "Taking girls and doing *this* to them." I waved a hand towards

Stacy. She was slumped in her chair. Looked to have lost consciousness.

"These girls that I have taken. That I have, *removed* from society. They can be dangerous too. Oh, yes. Not always as sweet as they look." There was anger in his voice now.

"Is that what happened back home?" Amy asked. "You son's girlfriend messed him around? Made him off himself?"

"Quiet!" McKeith screamed. His face was purple.

"Maybe he hurt women too. Is that it?" I said in a quiet voice. McKeith turned and his eyes bore into mine. He licked his lips. Said nothing.

"Or maybe it was you?" I pointed at him, an idea shaking loose. "Maybe it was *you* that hurt her. *Killed* her even? Yeah, maybe just an accident… at first. So, your kid can't cope, kills himself over it all. Am I close?"

"Careful, Michael," he said, danger in his voice.

"Whatever it is, it doesn't excuse all that you've done. Done to their families. Even getting close to them. Pretending you're something that you're not."

He looked at me smugly. "Like the pooka? Those naughty little imps."

"Yeah, exactly like that."

I wanted to push his buttons. There was no easy way out of this. He was desperate, he had nothing much left to lose. I had to drive him into making an error.

"You're a twisted fuck is what you are," Amy said suddenly.

McKeith turned his head towards her. Maybe she was thinking the same as me. Or maybe she just didn't have her rage under control.

"Whatever messed up thing happened with your son," Amy continued, "what you've been doing is unforgivable."

"It's just as well I really couldn't care less what you think, Amy," he replied evenly.

"What about Marcus Crawford?" I asked. "Was he just a convenient scapegoat? You killed him too, I suppose?"

"Oh, him. Yes, he's out in the barn," McKeith said absently. Then a smile played on his mouth, "That reminds me that I still have some cleaning up to do out there. Not my tidiest work."

"Somewhere inside you, surely there's something left of a man, no?" I tapped my finger against my temple. "You must know what you've been doing isn't right."

"I think that we must view the world in very different ways, you and I. 'Bodies have their own light which they consume to live: they burn, they are not lit from the outside.' Do you know who said?" McKeith asked.

"Enlighten us," I said.

"Our friend, Egon Schiele."

I shrugged.

"I think I'll just shoot you in your goddamned head," Amy shouted suddenly. "Take my chances with the girl."

She was definitely goading him now.

That got McKeith's attention. He tilted the rifle up to point at Amy. "This might blow yours in two first," he yelled back. He was sweating more now and there was a shake in his voice.

I readied myself.

Amy and McKeith seemed to fire their weapons simultaneously. Everything slowed. As the first swirls of cordite appeared, I whipped my hand back and pulled my Colt from the back of my jeans. I pointed and fired, aiming for centre mass. Two of my bullets took McKeith in the chest. One of Amy's had already hit him. My face fell as I turned towards Amy to see McKeith's round had glanced her cheek, blood seeping from it. My first thought was relief that it hadn't been her skull. McKeith crumpled to the ground behind Stacy with a cry. His rifle spilled across the floor.

All at once there was a noise in the doorway. We both swivelled our weapons as Sheriff Peterson stumbled into the room. His shirt was drenched in blood, and he was using his shotgun like a crutch. He took in the scene and shook his head. The sheriff's face was pale, and he had a grave expression. He shuffled in a few steps and looked down at the barely alive McKeith. Peterson looked up at the ceiling. He breathed out heavily, weighing down on his gun.

"It would be a mercy all round."

Amy strode across the room, aimed, then sent McKeith into the next world.

DEATH NOTICE

Epilogue: Crooked Timber

"Out of the crooked timber of humanity, no straight thing was ever made."
Immanuel Kant

I stopped at the corner shop and picked up a packet of smokes. Maybe I would cut down tomorrow. It was two months later, and we were all back in New York. The city was heating up and I'd had a good night's sleep.

"So, you're really not going to tell me what this is all about?" I asked.

Brandon was starting on a small one-skinner as we walked away from our local shop and towards the old Meatpacking District.

"Nope," he said.

We carried on. Brandon was still walking with quite a limp and had been issued with a crutch, which he rarely used. The doctors said the knee would improve, but it would never fully heal. I tried not to wince when I noticed a step giving him a shooting pain. He had kept in touch with Zara, and they had even visited one another a few times, making the long trip by Greyhound bus.

"I reckon you're going to like it," Brandon said, looking pleased with himself.

"Like what?" I made a face.

"You'll see."

Over the proceeding weeks, we had all done our best to heal. We were getting there. One week to the day after McKeith was killed, I got word that my father had passed. I didn't attempt to go to the funeral. But I did write a letter to my mother. Within it, I tried to explain everything that had happened those nine years earlier. I didn't know if she would read it, let alone try and understand my actions, but the writing of it did me some good.

We walked on slowly for another twenty minutes before I spotted Amy up ahead on the corner of a row of shops. The street was an up and coming one, but it wasn't the worst part of the neighbourhood. We passed a new deli and crossed the street. Amy was stood looking at me, with a goofy smile on her face. She looked beautiful. She always did. But after a couple of months of recouperation, she was more like herself. As we grew nearer, she moved her head and the sun's rays glanced off her cheek. The stitching had been done well, and her makeup too, but I could still make out the scar from McKeith's bullet.

"So, what is this? *This Is Your Life?*" I asked.

"Maybe," she said, giving me one of her full-beam smiles.

This woman amazed me. She was that rare someone with so much goodness inside, so much love for her family, and she still had the strength to put her life back together despite everything.

Brandon threw down his joint roach and stamped on it, before grinning at me excitedly.

"Come on, for frigsake. Tell me," I said to them.

"Look beside you," Amy said.

I turned and looked at the building. It was a corner store, or it had been. A grocer's originally, I think. The windows were all covered in newspaper and the once green paint on the walls had almost chipped away.

My eyes narrowed and I looked back at them. "What am I looking at here? A boarded-up shop?"

"It's what it could be, Mick," Brandon said.

Amy nodded. Her face was serious.

I looked back at them blankly.

Amy gave me one of her eye rolls. "The rent's cheap. This area has loads of potential. It's going to be a real hive in a few years. I spoke with the owner yesterday, and it could be yours from the first of the month."

"Mine?"

"Yeah," Brandon said simply.

"For what?"

"Whatever you want it to be," Amy said, putting a hand on my arm. "I was thinking maybe a bookshop."

I felt my eyes widen. I put a hand through my hair and looked back at the building.

DEATH NOTICE

"Jaysus," I said. "I wasn't expecting that."

Amy shrugged.

"What do you think, *Walker*?" she asked, accenting my name, her eyes playful.

I blew out my cheeks. I looked at the building, then back at them.

"I think it'd be nice to paint it green again."

Author's Note

Firstly, thank you for buying my book, I hope you enjoyed it. If you didn't; to hell with you. Just kidding. But if you didn't, I'll try even harder with the next one. I always love to hear from readers. Feel free to get in touch. I'm on all the usual social media, dear help me, even Tok-Tok.

All the best,

Simon.

Printed in Great Britain
by Amazon